Hidden Enemies

Hidden Enemies

Trish Kocialski

P.D. Publishing, Inc.
Clayton, North Carolina

ISBN-13: 978-1-933720-60-9
ISBN-10: 1-933720-60-3

9 8 7 6 5 4 3 2 1

Cover art: Arlington, Virginia (Sept. 11, 2001) — Smoke and flames rose over the Pentagon late into the night, following a suspected terrorist crash of a commercial airliner into the southwest corner of the Pentagon. Part of the building has collapsed meanwhile firefighters continue to battle the flames and look for survivors. An exact number of casualties is unknown. The building was evacuated, as were the federal buildings in the Capitol area, including the White House. U.S. Navy Photo by Photographer's Mate 2nd Class Bob Houlihan.

Edited by: Day Petersen

Published by:

P.D. Publishing, Inc.
P.O. Box 70
Clayton, NC 27528

http://www.pdpublishing.com

Acknowledgements

All stories need the gentle hand and guidance of a good editor and I'm very lucky to have had Daylene Petersen as my editor on all my stories. Day has helped me hone my craft to make my stories not only grammatically correct through her editing skills (and gentle prodding!) but also by being a true fan of my characters. Thank you Day, for all you do!

Along with a good editor, a writer needs the support and assurance of her publisher. In this respect, I am equally lucky to have Barb and Linda of PD Publishing backing me all the way.

Barb and Linda were the first to convince me to publish my stories and I'm thankful that they are still in my court and willing to publish my stories. By the way, they too are fans of my characters!

Putting together a novel is not an easy chore and it consumes a good deal of time. If one writes in addition to a full time job it means hours of time at home are spent away from family and loved one's. To this end, I'm very blessed to have a supportive partner who encourages me to continue writing my stories. Thank you Carol, for sharing the time we have together and for your endless support of my writing.

Finally, a writer relies on readers to perpetuate the call for more stories. I'm thankful for all the readers who are fans of Colonel Peterson and Agent O'Malley! I hope you enjoy this story as much as the previous four. Thank you for your emails asking for more!

Dedication

This story is dedicated to the 184 men, women, and children who lost their lives in the attack on the Pentagon on September 11, 2001. May they rest in eternal peace and never be forgotten.

Colonel Deanna Peterson concentrated on the words displayed on her computer monitor. Her jaw muscles flexed as she re-read each line, word by word. The sorrow visible on her face was evidence of the fact that it was the most difficult letter she had written during her entire Army career. She scrolled through the letter one final time and then hit the print function.

"Well," she said to herself as she sat back in her leather chair, "the fat lady is singing."

A tall woman, Dean was nearly six feet with the build of an athlete. Her long dark hair was fashioned up, per military regulation. Her tan, the result of a week of leave from which she had just returned, accentuated her eyes. They were a magnificent blue, almost sapphire. Even the crow's-feet that radiated from the corners of her eyes could not diminish their magnetism.

Dean looked around her spartan office, taking in the few keepsakes she permitted herself to display. She stood and walked to the credenza where a triangular case held a tattered American flag, partially burned but folded officially, that she had salvaged from one of her first undercover operations. She had recovered it from a dead terrorist who had put his lighter to it, just prior to departing this plane of existence. A neat hole in the middle of his forehead evidenced the lethal accuracy of her aim. Her next three shots took out his team who were about to blow up three captive soldiers.

There were also a few photos, mostly of her in her early Army years. There were snapshots with her buddies as they finished an obstacle course, outside the barracks, and of her in jungle camouflage, grinning into the camera. Another photo was of her pinning silver first lieutenant bars on Bill Jarvis. She sighed at the thought of leaving her protégé. She had met with Bill earlier in the day to tell him of her decision. Though he knew she was taking the right course of action, he hated her decision and had tried to talk her out of it.

Bill, what am I leaving you with? Have I taught you enough to deal with the enemies that seek to destroy us?

She picked up a photo taken in the Oval Office as the President pinned a Purple Heart on retired Major Tracy Kidd for the wound she received while pursuing a terrorist in the Bahamas. Dean remembered every detail of that operation, including Tracy's remark as she pulled her out of the sinking helicopter: "You really know how to show a girl a good time." Dean laughed, as she always did when she remembered that moment.

And there was Katie, the woman with whom she had fallen totally and irrevocably in love, the woman with whom she would spend the rest of her life. What a team they had been on that operation. Katie received the Department of Defense Medal for Distinguished Public Service for her role, and Bill was awarded an Army Distinguished Service Medal with a promotion to the rank of captain. Dean grinned. She had gotten her own kudos, too: a promotion to full colonel and the Silver Oak Leaf Cluster for her Distinguished Service Medal. She wasn't the youngest person ever to become a full colonel, but she was close.

Dean walked to the window and looked out into the courtyard of the Pentagon. Sighing, she thought about all the things she would miss about the military...and then some of the things she wouldn't miss. Moving over to the printer, she removed the letter. In a mere whisper, she said, "Well, Dean, it's hard to believe that you've survived in this life for twenty years. It's a good time to be proud of what you accomplished and walk away."

Back at her desk, she was putting the letter into a file folder when her door slammed open so hard and fast that it banged against the doorstop with a loud thwack. A staff sergeant snapped to attention and shouted, "Colonel, you're needed in the IOC immediately!"

She didn't challenge his having opened the door without knocking; the terrified look on his face was enough to convince her to follow him without the slightest delay. Dean dropped the folder on her desk and followed the sergeant out the door. Knowing they could reach IOC faster by the stairs than by using the elevator, they ran to the stairwell. As they rounded the first landing, Dean's thought was that something had happened to Bill. He and his partner, Dirk, had been there all night, working hard to make it unnecessary for her to write the letter of resignation. As they took the stairs down two at a time, she asked, "What's happened?"

"An airliner has crashed into one of the World Trade towers," the sergeant said in a breathless voice as he skidded to a stop at the landing door and held it open for her. "Smoke and flames are blanketing the impact area."

Dean was fully aware that there were annual training exercises being operated by Stratcom, the US Space Command, and NORAD, but only the planners were privy to the various scenarios. "Is this part of a *Guardian* scenario?"

"No, ma'am. It appears to be a genuine incident. We could see the damage on the big screen as we did our satellite scan of the East Coast...and the civilian news agencies are starting to broadcast it."

"Was it a military or civilian plane?" she asked as they ran through the unusually deserted corridor.

"They think it was a commercial jet," the sergeant supplied.

"Where's Major Russell?"

"Not sure, ma'am. Captain Jarvis asked me to get you ASAP."

At the Intelligence Operations Center, the sergeant held the door open for the colonel to precede him. As she entered, the hairs on the back of her neck began to prickle, definitely not a good sign. The activity level was in high gear as personnel rushed to and fro, answered ringing phones and typing furiously on their keyboards. The big screen on the back wall flashed off, then a snowy screen appeared, and finally a satellite feed provided them with a real time view of New York City. Smoke was billowing from the site of the World Trade Center.

Watching intently as the scene unfolded before her, Dean strode to the console that controlled the big screen. "Sergeant, get in tighter on the tower." She looked at the clock above the screen. It was 0858 hours. "When did the impact take place?"

"Right around 0845 hours, ma'am. We were doing our scheduled scan of the East Coast as part of the *Guardian* exercise and detected the smoke trail."

As the sergeant scanned closer, Captain Bill Jarvis appeared at Dean's side. The view on the screen focused in on the city blocks occupied by the World Trade Center. The upper third of the north tower was obliterated by smoke.

"This is it, ma'am," Jarvis said softly. "This is what those bastards were planning."

"We should have been able to stop this," Dean snapped as they surveyed the carnage depicted on the screen. "You were right on target with your take of the situation, Bill. Everything pointed to this type of action, but without hard evidence, all we were able to get the authorities to do was for the FAA to send out toothless warnings to the airlines. No one planned for an attack on our turf. All that time spent on exercise scenarios and worthless warnings, when we should have had people running down all the intel and looking for chinks in our security."

The sergeant at the console punched a few keys and then looked up in panic. "Colonel, there's another plane entering the area." His fingers flew as he quickly typed in some codes and the view on the screen focused on another commercial airliner. They could just make out the United Airline designation on the fuselage.

"It's headed for the other—" Everyone in the IOC watched in horror as a second airplane crashed into the south tower and exploded.

"God damn it!" Dean growled. She placed her hands on her hips and turned to face Captain Jarvis. "Where's Russell?"

"He said he was going to be in around 0900. He was stopping at Fort Belvoir to check on the garrison control exercise before coming in, and then he has a meeting with the general at 0930."

"Russell and his damn games," she muttered. "This isn't just random...it's a coordinated attack. Has the Air Force scrambled their fighters?" Bill nodded affirmatively. "All right...get in touch with the FAA and find out what they know. See if there are any other surprises out there. I'll be in Russell's office, talking on the phone with General Carlton."

At 0920 Captain Jarvis entered Major Russell's office. "Colonel, the FAA is going to shut down all New York City area airports. They're also reporting that eleven aircraft are not communicating with FAA facilities or are flying unexpected routes."

"Christ! Do they know where the hell they are?"

"Ma'am, it sounded like pure chaos at the FAA," Jarvis answered.

"Are the planes still sending their transponder signals?"

"American Airlines Flight 77 is not sending their transponder signal. It stopped around 0856 hours, and they lost radar contact shortly thereafter."

"Where did it depart from?"

Bill looked her in the eye. "Dulles."

The colonel and the captain stared at one another for a brief moment, and then both looked at the clock above the large screen. The time was 0922 hours.

"It's headed back to D.C.," Dean barked. "Have Sergeant Gaines get the satellite image switched to the D.C. area." Jarvis nodded and left at a dead run for the IOC.

Dean snatched up the phone and dialed General Carlton's office. As soon as the line was picked up, she said, "Give me the general, Tibbitts."

"Yes, ma'am."

The call was transferred and the general immediately came on the line. "Colonel, what did the FAA have to say?"

"There's at least one other plane out there and I believe it's headed to D.C."

There was a hesitation on the line. "The President is in Sarasota, so I doubt if they're headed to the White House," General Carlton said softly. "Where do you think they'll hit?"

"Impossible to know at this point. There are a number of strategic targets here, ma'am. I'm pulling up the satellite of D.C. now."

"Right. Major Russell is here with me; we'll call it in to the emergency response center. Call me when you get the feed up."

"Yes, ma'am." Dean slammed the phone back in the cradle and rushed to the ops center.

At 0935 hours, Sergeant Gaines was entering code into the computer as fast as he could, zooming the view down to the D.C. area in big chunks at a time, each time looking for commercial aircraft. Each view change seemed to occur in slow motion as the pixels appeared on the screen and then slowly sharpened into focus. They located the plane just in time to watch in horror as its flight path curved sharply and headed directly toward the Pentagon.

Dean hit the speed dial to the general's phone and pressed the receiver to her ear. When the general picked up, she calmly said, "Target's the Pentagon, ma'am. God help us." The room was silent for a brief moment, then all hell broke loose as evacuation procedures were implemented. Potential safety was several long corridors away.

The Pentagon was composed of five rings, with five main corridors connecting each ring. The A ring, or inner ring, looked into the inner courtyard, and the E ring was the outer ring. The IOC was in the C ring, near corridor 5. At 0938, American Airlines Flight 77 hit the west side of the Pentagon at an angle between corridors 4 and 5. As soon as the IOC, on the outer edge of the impact area, stopped shaking and the pieces of debris stopped falling, Colonel Peterson slowly got up off the floor and looked around the room in the faint emergency lighting. Many of the personnel were injured and bleeding, but most seemed to be mobile. Smoke was filtering through the ceiling and there was a definite rise in temperature.

"Let's get everyone out of here, Bill, then we'll do a search and rescue."

Those who were able helped the injured out of the IOC. In the hallway, they could see that the primary impact area was at the edge of the Army section and slicing into the Navy area beyond. Smoke was billowing from the west side, so they sped toward corridor 6. As they rounded the corner toward the Mall side of the Pentagon, they met another group of staffers who were helping the injured exit the building.

"Get everyone out of the building, fire drill procedures; form up outside the main entrance!" Colonel Peterson ordered. She turned to Captain Jarvis. "C'mon, Bill, let's see if we can get to General Carlton's office."

The two officers raced toward the west side of the building, taking corridor 5 back toward the A ring at a run. Staffers, both military and civilian, all of whom were injured or shaken, were picking their way through debris toward them.

"Anyone see General Carlton?" Dean asked as she passed by the officers in the group.

"No, too much smoke," one coughed.

A civilian employee put a restraining hand on Dean's arm. "There's heavy smoke and fire and the debris is still falling as you go past the C and B rings. I don't know if you can make it to A."

Dean tersely nodded an acknowledgement, but she and Bill proceeded toward the A ring. At a restroom, she said, "In here," as she pushed open the door. The water lines had ruptured and the faucets didn't work, but there was still water in the toilets. She pulled down several paper towels and soaked them in a toilet bowl. Wringing out the towels, she and Bill flattened the sheets and put them over their noses and mouths to filter the smoke. By the time they reached the intersection for the A ring, they could barely see and their eyes were stinging from the smoke and acrid fumes. They were crawling on the floor trying to stay below the smoke, but it seemed to be everywhere. Thick and black, it rolled over them as they crawled. The debris smelled of burning jet fuel, PVC, and electrical cables. Turning a corner, they touched two bodies. They rolled them over and recognized the general and Major Russell.

Dean checked the major's carotid, while Bill sought a pulse on General Carlton. "He's alive," she said, yanking his arms over her shoulders and maneuvering him back the way they had come.

"General's alive, too." Bill took the general's wrists and pulled her onto his back. Grasping both of her wrists with his one hand, he replaced the damp towels over his nose and mouth with the other and he too started back toward safety. Given the weight and awkwardness of their loads, they weren't able to crawl, but picked their way as quickly as they could through the debris and the dense smoke.

The route was slow and treacherous, and as they passed the C ring intersection, they could hear voices from the other side calling for help. "Hang on. We'll be back for you," Dean shouted, and they redoubled their efforts to get the major and general to safety.

As they turned the corner toward the C ring corridor, heading back to the Mall side of the building, they spotted a fire rescue squad moving toward them. Dean stopped and propped the major against the wall.

"You guys got here fast," she commented as she straightened and stretched out weary muscles.

"We were doing a crash simulation on the helipad when the plane hit," the first fireman explained.

"Score one for Russell," she said under her breath. "Get these two out of here," she commanded, and then turned and ran back toward where they had heard the cries for help.

Two rescuers took the general off Bill's back, and two others grabbed Bill by the shoulders and started to haul him away.

"No!" He pulled free of the man's grasp. "I need to go with her! I promised to watch out for her."

"Sir, you need to get out of here. We'll get the rest of them out...and the colonel." The men reclaimed the captain and handed him off to other firemen that were coming down the corridor. As he was forcibly maneuvered toward safety by the rescuers, Bill craned his neck to look behind him. He watched in desperation as Colonel Peterson's form was enveloped by the heavy smoke, then he broke free and ran past the fire crew, following the colonel into the smoke filled corridor. "I've got to go with the colonel," he shouted over his shoulder. The firemen nodded in acceptance and followed after him.

Still holding the towels over her nose and mouth, Colonel Peterson shouted, "Where are you?"

"Over here," came the gasping reply.

Dean turned toward the sound and felt rather than saw her way toward the rasping voice. The heat was becoming unbearable and the smell of burning jet fuel and charred flesh was stronger as she went into the room where the voice was coming from.

"Okay, I'm coming to get you," she said as she clawed through the debris of fallen ceilings and pipes, over barriers of concrete and smashed furniture. The heat coming from the floor below was oppressive, but the flames were providing some light. The smoke was still thick but seemed to be thinning just a bit as the fire spread. Dean had a fleeting thought that it was similar to walking through a battlefield at night, with only one's senses of touch and hearing to guide the way. She reached a doorframe where the door was torn from its hinges and lying on a pile of desks and chairs that had been blown across the room. She could hear coughing and ragged breathing.

"Hold on, I'm almost there," she said by way of encouragement as she started to tear at the rubble.

"Let me help you with that, Colonel," Bill said as he grabbed the corner of the desk she was trying to move.

"What are you doing here?" she shot quickly and then shook her head, a crooked smile appearing on her face. "Glad to have you at my side, Bill. C'mon, let's get the rest of this rubble cleared."

It took a couple of minutes, but they managed to remove the heaviest of the debris that was on top of the fallen soldier. Lifting the final collapsed piece of wallboard, she saw that it was a young private; she recognized her face. "Hawadi. What are you doing here?"

"I just transferred here this morning, ma'am."

"Damn bad luck, Hawadi." Dean did a quick check of the young woman, who appeared to be in fairly stable condition, considering she'd had half the office furniture thrown at her. Her severely broken leg was going to make extrication not only difficult, but painful. "Is anyone else in here?"

Private Hawadi shook her head. "Most had just left on a break. There was another soldier waiting over there." Hawadi pointed out a section of the room where the wall and ceiling had fallen in. A bloodied hand was protruding from the pile of rubble.

"Bill, go check on him," Dean commanded as she finished her quick exam of Hawadi.

The captain moved cautiously over the wreckage and checked for a pulse. "He's dead."

"Do you see anything we can use for a splint?" Dean coughed hard as the smoke got thicker.

As Bill looked around for something to use as a splint for Hawadi's injured leg, the building was rocked by a series of small explosions, and chunks of steel and concrete fell all around them. "Nothing useable." He removed his belt and went back over to Hawadi. He tied both of her legs together with the belt. "This will have to do."

"Look, this place is getting ready to go. Your leg is badly broken and this splint won't help much but it's better than nothing. We need to get out now. I'm going to have to grab you and go."

The young woman nodded her understanding and Dean slid her hands under Hawadi's arms. "Okay, are you ready? This is going to hurt."

"I am ready; please hurry." Another chunk of concrete thudded to the floor between them and Bill.

Dean grabbed the private firmly under the arms and Bill supported her legs. As gently as possible, they lifted her quickly. To her credit, Private Hawadi muffled her scream.

"You're a good soldier, Hawadi. Just a bit further and we'll have you clear." As soon as they were clear of the last of the debris, they backtracked carefully to the doorway. Hawadi was a lot lighter than Dean had expected and they were able to get her out of the office without much difficulty. By the time they exited the doorway, two firemen appeared, holding powerful flashlights. They took the woman from Dean and Bill.

"You men are a welcome sight," Dean said as they reached her. She leaned against the doorway, gratefully relinquishing Hawadi to the fireman. "Get her out of here."

"You too, ma'am. Follow us out."

"Right behind you." Dean turned to find Bill; he was about to go back inside. "Captain," she called, "let's get out of here before this place falls apart completely." She coughed violently as another wave of dark smoke rippled through the area.

"I'll be right with you. I just want to get that soldier's tags," Bill rasped as he disappeared into the office.

The first fireman took the private in his arms and the other stepped forward to assist the colonel. As the coughing wracked her body, Dean staggered away from the doorframe. She walked unsteadily into the hallway, the rescuer's flashlight playing on her soot smeared form. From the floors below, a rumble started its way up the devastated building, causing the floor to shift and buckle. There was a loud crack, and the walls and ceiling began to crumble. The exterior wall of Hawadi's office collapsed inward, blocking the doorway completely. A large chunk of crossbeam came down from the ceiling, clipping Dean across the back of the head, neck, and back. It dropped to the floor, trapping her legs as she fell forward into the outstretched arms of a fireman. Dazed, she blinked as the beam of the flashlight hit her eyes. For a brief moment, she thought she saw Katie rushing toward her and she reached out... Then everything went black.

Chapter Two
May 25 — Four Months Earlier

It was a mild day in May, and summer had definitely arrived. Thanks to the string of miniature roses Katie had planted alongside the path, the air had a sweet smell. The heady aroma was enhanced by a chorus of cardinals twittering happily at the bird feeder Dean had built and installed near the front windows to entertain the three felines inside. Katie stopped at the mailbox and extracted the contents, absently flipping through the mail as she walked up the path to the house. "Well, it's about time," she growled when she saw the envelope from Dean's insurance company. Tucking the mail under her arm, she pulled out her keys, unlocked the front door, and entered. After punching in the security code to keep the alarm from sounding, she placed the mail on the bench by the door, along with her backpack, then took off her light jacket and hung it on the coat rack. Three calico cats came romping through the house to meet her with loud meows of greeting.

"Hello, girls. Are you hungry?"

The cats wove between her legs as they waited until their owner greeted each one with a scratch behind the ears before they scampered off to the kitchen, tails erect, in anticipation of the evening meal. The days were definitely getting longer, and Katie was pleased to see the flowers blooming outside the kitchen window. "Life is good," she proclaimed as she prepared the cats' meal. Placing three bowls down on their individual placemats, Katie watched her charges eagerly devour the proffered food.

Watching Sugar consume her portion with relish, Katie puzzled over what had caused the cat's complete turnaround. The bad news at a veterinary visit the previous fall was that Sugar's brain tumor was beginning to grow again...but now, well, now she was the picture of perfect health. Right after the New Year, the tumor had just disappeared, and every check-up since showed no sign of the tumor returning. No one could explain it, but Katie really didn't care how or why it happened; she was just glad to have Sugar healthy.

"Okay, kids, I'm going to jump into the shower before Dean gets home." The cats looked up as she spoke. "Now, no begging Dean for another meal," she threatened, shaking a finger at them. "You girls are just ounces away from having to go on a diet!"

Spice meowed loudly in defiance, knowing that she was svelte in comparison to her mates. "Yeah, you too, Miss Princess!" Spice winked at Katie, then went back to finishing her meal. The other two looked up and seemed to nod at their mistress before turning back to their evening repast.

Before heading to the shower, Katie went back to the front door to get her backpack and the mail. She dropped the mail on the kitchen table. Knowing that Dean had been expecting a reply from the insurance company, she placed that envelope on top of the pile. In the bathroom, Katie turned on the shower taps and then stripped off her clothes. When she stepped into the shower stall, the water was nice and hot, just the way she liked it. Standing under the powerful massage spray, she let it soothe her tired muscles as the stress of the day washed down the drain. Just as she reached for the nylon buff, a faint sound alerted her to another presence in the room. She closed her eyes and listened intently, concentrating on the sounds around her. She heard the click of the shower door opening and closing. A smile formed on her face as two hands reached around her waist and she felt the strong abs and supple breasts of her lover as she was pulled back against Dean's body.

"Hey," Dean cooed in her ear as her hands drifted upward. "I see that my insurance company finally decided I didn't lie about my SUV being stolen."

"Mmm. Hey to you, too." Katie purred as she placed her hands over her lover's and tilted her head back to receive a kiss. "It's about time. They've been dragging their feet on paying you since January. Guess the personal note from Lieutenant Green helped."

"Yeah, that helped...and my threat to file a complaint with the state attorney general didn't hurt, either." Dean nibbled on Katie's body from her shoulder up to her earlobe and received a satisfying moan for her efforts. "Sure is a nice night," Dean whispered into Katie's ear, "and it's supposed to be a beautiful weekend. What say we take a road trip tomorrow? Maybe pack a little picnic lunch?"

"Oh, that sounds like a great idea. Where do you want to go?"

"Hmm." Dean thought for a bit. "Wherever the roads are empty and the car wants to go. Work for you?"

"Hon, anywhere with you works for me." Katie turned to face Dean. The love she saw in the brilliant sapphire eyes filled her with a profound sense of peace. She gently cupped Dean's face in her hands. "I'll follow you anywhere," Katie whispered, then stood on her tiptoes so she could place a kiss on her lover's lips. They held each other, enjoying the sensual stimulation of their intimate contact, heightened by the hot water that cascaded over them. Katie pulled away slightly, licking the water from Dean's lips as she moved. "What a nice way to end a hectic week." She nestled her head under Dean's chin.

Dean closed her eyes and sighed as Katie picked up the nylon buff and poured on some body wash. "Yeah, it sure is. How was the graduation ceremony?"

"Very nice." Katie turned Dean around and applied the soapy puff to Dean's back. "Ruby Black Hawk was selected as the top cop in the class."

Dean nodded, turning around for Katie to continue the cleansing. "That's the young woman from the Oneida Nation in New York, right?"

"Yes. She had the highest scores all around...and more importantly, the respect of the whole class."

"What assignment did she pull?"

"She's been assigned to the Native American unit here in D.C."

Dean smiled in approval. "Not bad for a rookie, but then, she was the top cop and deserves the posting." Dean took the nylon buff from Katie and rinsed it out before applying more body wash and assuming her turn at their shower ritual. "So, you have some time off before the next class starts, right?" She got a brilliant smile in answer. "What are you planning to do with the break?"

"Well," Katie began in a low voice, "I thought I'd spend some quality time with my special someone." She moved closer and wrapped her arms around Dean. "A nice road trip tomorrow sounds like a good start." Katie moved closer and placed a soft kiss on Dean's lips, then began trailing kisses down her neck, stopping every so often to lick a trail through the water coursing down Dean's chest. Soon the soapy nylon buff had completed its tour of Katie's body and found its way to the rack below the showerhead. Dean placed her soapy hands around Katie's back and pulled her in for a deep, enduring kiss. When they eventually parted, the water wasn't the only thing in the shower stall that was hot.

"Thanks for picking up dinner. It was nice of Ming Soo to add the extra fortune cookies."

"I figured it was better to get the take-out than try to fight the crowds at the Golden Swan. That place has really become popular," Dean remarked as she picked up the empty cartons. "I know Ming Soo would take us without a reservation, but," she looked over at Katie, "I like the intimate atmosphere here much better." With that, she took Katie's hand and kissed it. Dean tilted her head up and gazed at Katie, a crooked smile appearing as she kissed her hand again.

The kisses, and the look, made Katie's temperature rise, and her face flushed at the sensuality of the simple contact. They gazed lovingly at each other, their dinner momentarily forgotten. Spice's insistent meow startled them out of the sexual haze that had them entranced, and they laughed and shook their heads.

"Think she's trying to tell us something?" Katie asked, still smiling.

"Yeah. Your dinner's getting cold."

Katie reached for one of the fortune cookies, tearing the cellophane wrapper and then snapping the cookie in half. She popped half into her mouth and pulled the fortune from the other half. "Your destiny lies before you. Choose wisely." She set the slip of paper down. "Well, that's profound." Katie watched as Dean went through the same procedure to reveal her fortune. "What does yours say?"

"Your destiny lies before you. Choose wisely." Dean looked up and smiled at her lover.

"You're kidding, right?"

"Nope. That's what it says." Dean tossed the slip over to Katie.

Katie chuckled as she tore open the next wrapping and broke open the cookie. "Well, let's see what this one says." She set the cookie aside and read the fortune. "Your destiny lies before you. Choose wisely." Katie dropped the paper strip on the table and watched as Dean read her second fortune.

"Ditto." Dean looked up at her lover, who was shaking her head in disbelief. "Really," Dean affirmed as she reached for the last one. Opening the cookie and pulling out the paper, she chuckled. "Yep, looks like our destiny lies before us," she drawled as she wadded up the slip of paper.

Katie chuckled as she crunched on a piece of cookie. "Guess we'd better choose wisely."

"Yeah, looks that way. I wonder if the whole batch held the same fortune." Their laughter grew louder, drawing the other two cats in from the living room. The felines looked up at their mistresses and then at each other before returning to their previous positions in the living room.

Laughter subsiding, Dean changed the subject. "How about if we take a walk down to the river? It's still early and it's nice out."

"I'd like that," Katie agreed as she helped dispose of the plates and containers from dinner.

Out back of the house, they followed the stone path that led to the water. Dean placed her arm around Katie's shoulders, pulling her in close; Katie reciprocated with an arm around Dean's waist. The night was warm, and the light from the moon illuminated their way to the river. As the path opened on to the water, Dean led Katie to the teakwood bench on the flagstone patio near the river's edge. They sat in comfortable silence, watching the moonlight dance on the ripples of the Occoquan River. In the distance they could hear the call of a dove cooing to its mate.

"Mmm, this is nice." Katie sighed as she leaned into her partner. "We should come down here more often."

Dean nodded. "Hopefully, we'll have more time to enjoy it this summer."

"It seems like a lifetime ago that we came here when I when I returned from El Paso," Katie said as she thought about that first night. "I was so nervous. I was sure of my feelings for you, but I didn't know if you felt the same way about me."

"Really?" Dean turned to face Katie.

"Yeah, really." Katie sighed. "We had been apart for quite a while, and well...I was afraid you were having second thoughts about us moving in together. And then there was my decision to leave field operations and transfer to the DEA training center in Quantico."

"But you did that so we could be together more."

"Yes, that was my intention. But I hadn't talked to you about it, and on the flight back from Texas, I was beginning to doubt the wisdom of that unilateral decision. My insecurities were rearing their ugly heads." Katie shook her head and sighed. "I wasn't sure you were ready for me on a full-time basis. I mean, I barely got my memory back from the Catskills caper, and then I had to take that assignment in El Paso. We hardly knew each other—" Her words were abruptly impeded by two lips descending onto hers. When Dean pulled away, Katie smiled up at her. "Guess it was silly of me, but I *was* nervous."

"Hmm, well, if it will make you feel any better, I'm the one that's nervous tonight," Dean offered shyly.

"You are? Why?"

"Well, you just reminded me that we really haven't known each other that long. I guess...it's just been, what...seventeen months, thirteen days..." she looked at her watch, "...fourteen hours and fifteen...sixteen minutes since we met. I mean..." Dean faltered, "it's just that, well...I knew um, from that first kiss...that..."

Katie placed her hands on Dean's cheeks and peered into the beautiful blue eyes she knew so well. "So did I," she offered, softly placing a kiss on her flustered partner. "So, what's your point?"

"Ah, my point...well...that would be this." Dean reached into a pocket and pulled out a channel set sapphire and diamond ring and held it out to Katie. "I was hoping that maybe, well, that maybe, you and I...might want to..."

"Colonel Peterson, are you proposing to me?" Katie asked a blushing Dean. "Because if you are...the answer is..." she reached out and pulled Dean to her, whispering a breathy "yes" just before their lips made contact. As lips parted, Katie finished her sentence, "I would love to spend the rest of my life with you."

Dean released a happy sigh of relief. "You know, I've been in a lot of very tight spots in my lifetime, but this one gave me such knots in my stomach, you wouldn't believe!"

Katie chuckled as she laid her head on Dean's shoulder. "Oh, sweetheart, I didn't know I was so intimidating!" That comment earned her a raised eyebrow.

"Seriously," Dean began, "I know you love me as much as I love you. I just wasn't sure you would want to make a commitment like this, especially knowing how risky our careers are."

Dean turned away from Katie and stared at the river. "When I was making my way across that rock face under Niagara Falls, I made up my mind that if I didn't get to you in time to save you, I was going to untie myself from the lifeline and follow you in. My life would have been empty without you in it."

"Oh, Dean...I couldn't live without you, either."

Tears fell as the women embraced each other tightly. They held on for a very long time, allowing their emotions free rein. Releasing Katie, Dean took the ring and prepared to slip it on Katie's finger. "Will you marry me?"

"Yes." The word came out without hesitation, and was followed by a fierce embrace and a long-lasting kiss.

Chapter Three
May 26

"I have the lunch packed. Are you ready to go?" Katie yelled from the kitchen.

"You bet I am," Dean replied from where she stood directly behind her lover.

Katie grabbed her chest. "Arrgh! How do you do that?" she croaked.

"I have—"

"Yeah, yeah...many talents. I just wish you'd make some noise once in a while so I'd know you're really a human and not some alien that can pop in at will." They both chuckled as they gathered the picnic basket, blanket, portable CD player, and cooler.

Katie stood looking at the three felines lined up at the door. Bending over to be nearer her charges, she tilted her head. "Okay, girls: no hairballs, no fighting, no tearing through the house and getting into trouble."

The three cats looked at each other and then back up at Katie. Spice, obviously the elected spokescat for the trio, issued a thunderous, reverberating meow before turning her sleek body and sauntering over to a patch of sunlight on the floor. The other two followed Spice's lead and joined her, sprawling out to absorb the warm rays.

Marveling at the way they seemed to understand every word, Katie shook her head. "You know, sometimes I wonder if they actually understand what we say."

"Wouldn't surprise me a bit," Dean agreed as she held open the door for Katie. "Your car or mine?"

"Yours. I don't feel like driving, and besides, this was your idea."

They packed their items in the front boot of the sleek black Boxster, put down the top, and secured the touring cover for the drive. Dean escorted Katie to the passenger door and held it open, taking the blonde's left hand in hers and giving it a kiss. "Your wish is my command."

"Ooo, I think I'm going to like this engagement thing," Katie cooed as she slipped into the passenger seat.

Within a half hour they were driving down the back roads on their way to a destination only the car seemed to know. Not being in any hurry, they decided to take roads they had not traveled before. Right turns were followed by left turns, with the road winding over gently rolling hills. Their general heading was toward the southwest. The sun was brilliant where it hung in a clear blue sky; the countryside was blooming with wild flowers, and fruit trees were beginning to show miniature versions of their anticipated final product. They took the scenic route, snaking through the Virginia countryside and passing through small towns with names like Catlett and Calverton, and larger towns like Culpepper. They made several stops along the way to check out some of the local crafts stores, and even an antique shop or two. On the southwest side of Charlottesville, they followed State Road 20 through Keene, then swung west on 626 to 647 and found themselves at the entrance to James River State Park. Paying the three dollar weekend fee and picking up a park map and brochure, they pulled through the entrance. It was just about noon.

"It says here," Katie pointed at the brochure, "that this park just opened in 1999 and is still under development." She looked over at Dean. "That's pretty cool — a newbie park." She continued reading from the brochure. "There are primitive camping sites here, too. Maybe we could come camping some weekend?" Katie opened the park map and scanned it quickly as Dean drove the Boxster at the ten mile per hour speed limit. "Let's head to Green Hill Pond and park there. Then we can find a place to enjoy our picnic."

They followed the signs to Green Hill Pond and found that the parking lot was empty, save for two other vehicles. Assuming that the newness of the park accounted for the low attendance, Dean and Katie were thrilled to have the place almost completely to themselves. Dean popped the boot hood to retrieve their refreshments then she put the top up and locked the car, knowing that a good pocketknife would make her efforts moot, but figuring she'd at least made an attempt at securing the vehicle. She wasn't about to have another battle with her insurance company over a second claim involving an "unsecured" vehicle.

"Lead on, McDuff," Dean directed as Katie grabbed the backpack with the blanket and the portable CD player. Dean slung the collapsible cooler over her right shoulder and carried the picnic basket in her left hand to balance the load. "What did you pack in here? It must weigh twenty pounds."

Knowing that it would be much lighter after lunch, Katie chuckled.

The walk to the pond area was short, and when they got there they were surprised by the views before them. They took the boardwalk across the end of the pond and followed it around to a set of stairs that led to a scenic lookout where they had a terrific unobstructed view of the James River.

Katie pulled out the map she had stuffed into her back pocket and selected a site to set up their picnic lunch. Dean followed her, groaning comically and quizzing her at regular intervals as to whether they were there yet. When Katie finally stopped under a large oak tree with a view of the river, Dean nodded in approval, then set down her load to help spread the blanket. Within five minutes, their blanket was neatly arranged and they were sitting down to enjoy their lunch, listening to Chip Davis' *Romance* on the CD player.

"Wow," Dean exclaimed as she opened the picnic basket. "This is quite a spread you have here: cheese, crackers, apples...mmm, grapes too. Let's see, chicken salad sandwiches and two splits of wine... Nice touch. Where'd you dig these up?"

"I found them at that warehouse wine store we stopped at a while back. They're just the right size for picnics." Katie pulled out the brochure again to check the park rules. "Hmm, this brochure says alcohol is prohibited. Maybe we should put them back in the cooler."

"Nah, look around ya. Nobody is going to notice. It's not like we have a case of booze here. We'll just be discreet."

"Whoa... This is coming from my by-the-book Army colonel?"

Dean grabbed the brochure. "Hey, it says here 'public use or display of alcoholic beverages is prohibited'...so, we won't give any to the public and we'll keep it under wraps."

Katie shook her head at her partner's creativity. "You are incorrigible!"

"Yep. That's me. Now, can we eat? I'm starved."

They broke out the rest of the food, along with plates and utensils, and in short order polished off the contents of the picnic basket. The load would definitely be lighter on the way back.

After a lengthy and tiring trip down, and then back up, the James River, Boy Scout Troop 758 paddled their canoes up to the dock. Their scoutmaster stepped onto the dock and began barking orders to his weary troops. "Okay, men, tie off your canoes, grab your gear, and line up on the dock." He blew his whistle three times. "C'mon, let's hustle now. Go, go, go!" he shouted.

At the shriek of the whistle, two of the younger scouts jerked into action and both attempted to leave their canoe at the same time, causing it to tip violently and dump the boys into the river with a splash. Relieved of their weight, the unsecured canoe slipped away from the dock and was caught in the current.

When he heard the splash, the scout leader looked down the dock and immediately spotted the canoe floating off. "Terrance!" he shouted at the Eagle Scout of the troop. "Go get that canoe!" He charged down the dock, stopping in front of the two boys who were spitting water and wiping their faces. "You two are absolutely worthless! Why don't you go join the Girl Scouts?" He paused, letting the intended shame of his remarks sink in. "C'mon, c'mon...get out of the water and get in line!" he ordered gruffly, then turned and stomped off the dock.

The boys bowed their heads, fearing further repercussions from their scoutmaster if he should see the tears of pain that welled up in their eyes. There were bloody scrapes on their knees and elbows from where they'd grazed the dock before hitting the water.

"Jeepers," the smaller one whispered, "this is supposed to be fun?"

"Be quiet, Jay. He might hear you."

"Maybe he should hear us, Billy. Maybe the other guys are fed up with him, too." Jay looked at the faces of the rest of the troop and his suspicions were confirmed. "It looks to me like everyone else has pretty well had it, too." Jay looked over his shoulder at the Eagle Scout paddling after the canoe. "Except for Terrance, but then, it would be hard to vote your own father off the island."

"Yeah, well, there was no one else willing to take our troop, so it's either him or nobody."

"At this rate, I'd rather have nobody." Jay sloshed out of the river, limping as he joined the rest of the kids on the dock.

When the leader got to the front of the troop, he blew his whistle three times to get their attention. "All right, men, pick up that gear and let's get moving." Waiting only a few seconds for them to comply, he started them off jogging up the path.

Dean was propped up against the trunk of the oak tree, her hands slipping affectionately through Katie's blond hair as she stared off into the distance. The peace and solitude she felt surrounding her had eased away the tensions of the week, and now she was lost in blissful thoughts of the future with Katie at her side. Katie was dozing lightly, her head pillowed in her partner's lap. Dean's gaze returned to Katie's face, taking in the soft features and lines of her lover's countenance. She loved to watch Katie sleep. The CD player was playing *Fresh Aire III*, and "The Cricket" was just starting.

Dean looked around, imagining the little critters out there pausing to listen to their brothers on the CD.

"Hi," Dean whispered as she watched Katie's eyes blink open.

"Mmm. Sorry I dropped off there. I'm just so relaxed." She stretched a bit.

"I know what you mean. We'll have to come here more often. It's very peaceful. Maybe a camping trip would be fun."

Katie drew herself up into a sitting position and peered around the area before scooting up and perching herself in Dean's lap. She placed her hands on Dean's chest and moved forward, capturing Dean's lips with a teasing kiss. Pulling away, she could see that she had elicited the desired effect, as a longing for more intimacy shone in her lover's eyes. The response, however, was not what she anticipated. First, Dean rotated her baseball cap, moving the bill out of the way, and then she wrapped her arms around Katie and rolled over on top of her, allowing her right leg to rest in a very strategic spot between Katie's legs. The move startled Katie and the firm pressure of Dean's right knee elicited a moan.

"Mmm, Dean," Katie moaned, "we're kinda in the open here."

"You should've thought of that before you teased me with that kiss," Dean growled, then placed her lips purposefully on Katie's, feeling the heat of passion rising between them. Dean was not the kind of person that went in for public displays of affection, but since she had not seen a single person pass by their spot in two full hours, she felt relatively safe. However, she kept her senses on the alert as she planted a few teasing kisses of her own. As they continued the pleasurable taunting, the crickets on the CD player burst forth with their loud playful tune, masking the Boy Scout troop as they came running full speed up the path and caught the two women by surprise. Dean barely heard them just before they burst into the open as they ran up the hill with their scoutmaster in the lead. As they got closer, she heard him calling out a familiar cadence and a shiver went down her spine, causing her to freeze in place.

"Don't move," she instructed. Her outstretched body hid Katie as she kept her head down low and rolled onto her side so her back was to the boys. Her hair was tied back in a ponytail and had slid down along the side of her neck. The black Army ball cap, which she was wearing backwards, stood out to the passing troop. With any luck, she might just look like some guy making out with his girlfriend. At least she hoped that would be the case. "Just stay out of their line of sight and we'll be okay," Dean whispered.

"What's wrong? Is it someone you know?" Katie inquired in a low voice.

"I'm not sure, but I recognized the cadence. It's one my class created for PT during our Intelligence training at Fort Huachuca." She listened as the cadence faded, along with the huffing of the youngsters as they trekked past. Dean waited a bit longer until she was certain they had disappeared into the forest before she slowly turned and stole a glance in the direction they had gone. "Okay, they've moved out of sight." Dean pushed up into a sitting position, continuing to display her back toward the path.

"Do you have any idea who it might have been?" Katie asked as she sat to face Dean.

Dean shook her head and frowned. "There were thirty of us in that class, so it could be any one of twenty-nine people. I have no idea if it's someone who is still in the Army and posted to this area, or if it's someone from that class just living in this area."

"Let's hope you don't find out." Katie stood and offered Dean her hand. "C'mon, let's pack up this stuff and go home."

Terrance caught up to the wayward canoe and tied it onto his, then paddled back to the dock where he secured them both. He gathered up his backpack from the canoe and strapped it on. The Eagle Scout gazed over his shoulder at the string of canoes, making sure they were all properly secured. Satisfied, he nodded in approval and headed up the path to the campsite. He wasn't in a hurry; he knew that his father would have the rest of the troop busy with a lesson of some sort before preparation of the evening meal. He loved his father, but found it harder and harder to please him, and really hoped that a new scout leader could be found for their troop. His dad was too demanding of the scouts, and of him in particular. He wanted to tell his father to lighten up on the boys, but knew he would be chastised if he did, so he kept silent and tried to help the younger boys as best as he could. Terrance realized that things with his dad had changed when his father had been passed over for promotion to lieutenant colonel nearly a year earlier. Since then, he'd been impossible to live with, and things were getting worse. His second and last chance for promotion was coming up in September, and Terrance could feel the pressure building already. Secretly, the young man hoped that his dad would be passed over again and as a result, would retire from the Army. He had enough time in, and Terrance knew his dad could easily find a civilian job. Maybe then he would be able to relax and spend more time with his mom, and things would get better at home.

Terrance was lost in his thoughts as he cleared the woods and entered the picnic area. The first thing he noticed was a tall, dark-haired woman in jeans, flannel shirt, and a black baseball cap. To the seventeen year-old male, she looked like a goddess. Her radiant smile seemed to light up the area brighter than the sun in a room full of mirrors. He was awestruck, and his forward progress slowed to slow motion as he watched her gathering up picnic supplies with her blonde companion. "Wow," he whispered to himself, "I think I'm in love."

Terrance watched as discretely as he could while he continued up the path. He took in all of the woman's features, memorizing every detail. Then he noticed the gold Army lettering on her ball cap. "Army?" he questioned, and wondered whether his father knew who she was. He continued watching as the two women walked down the opposite trail, heading toward the parking area. The young scout checked his watch and decided to change direction and follow the women to their car...from a distance. He stopped when he saw them load their items into a black Boxster and drive off, and then he jogged off toward the campsite, his teenage heart throbbing wildly.

"Dean?"

"Hmm?"

"Did you see that scout following us to the car?"

"Yes."

"Do you think he recognized us?"

"Doubt it. I don't know many kids." Dean looked over at her partner with a questioning look. "Did you recognize him?"

"No. I just thought it was strange that he followed us to the parking area instead of taking the path that the rest of the troop took."

"Yeah, I caught that too. He wasn't with the first group, so maybe he's with another troop, besides he couldn't have seen us—"

"Kissing," Katie interjected. "So, we don't have to worry about it, right?"

"Right." But in her mind, Dean wasn't quite so sure, and reprimanded herself for the lapse in caution she normally observed while in public places.

Nearly twenty years in the military had taught her to hide her orientation well. The Army, no matter what accomplishments female soldiers had achieved, was still a "good ole boys club", and many soldiers were still homophobic in the extreme. The "don't ask, don't tell" ruling was a pathetic, ineffectual policy to protect gays in the military, and virtually useless, forcing soldiers to serve in silence. Soldiers perceived to be gay were still singled out by their comrades and dealt with harshly, occasionally being subjected to beatings or even death. The fact that she had reached the rank of colonel attested to how well she was able to keep her personal life safely tucked away where homophobic and jealous eyes couldn't pry. But there were those that were envious of her rise and covetous of her position and rank, and they would do anything to discredit her to her superiors. One never knew who her enemies were, and the fact that her immediate superior was also a female would not insure her safety. If push came to shove, General Mary Carlton, for all her wisdom and compassion, would not sacrifice her own career. Dean was certain that the general would do everything in her power to thwart an attack on her, but knew that eventually the proverbial line in the sand would be drawn and the general wouldn't cross it. In two months, Dean could safely retire with twenty years of service, however she wanted to stay in for a full thirty. She was too young to retire, and she was afraid that the lack of the daily challenge of intelligence work would take its toll.

Katie looked over at Dean and noted the furrowed eyebrows and the tense posture as Dean drove the back roads toward home. "Hey, love, you okay? You look tense."

"Nah," Dean covered as she forced a smile. "It's just the glare of the sun." She twisted the bill of her ball cap around to the front, affording more shade for her eyes. "That's better," she muttered, and concentrated on relaxing her posture. "We should be home around six. Supposing I grill a couple of steaks for dinner?" she suggested cheerily. "We have that bottle of Shiraz that would go nicely with those filets we bought."

Distracted for the moment, Katie's mind turned to the suggestion and began planning the vegetables to go with the meal. "I could whip up a nice salad, and maybe some steamed broccoli. I can take care of those while you do the grilling."

Dean gave Katie a broad smile. "Don't forget the spuds," she said, laughing as she reached over to give Katie's thigh a gentle squeeze. She left her hand there, finding comfort and security in the simple gesture. *Your destiny lies before you. Choose wisely,* she reflected. *Guess I blew it today.* She sighed as she considered her options. *Whatever the future brings, I'll always have Katie at my side.*

Chapter Four
June 4

"Morning, Colonel," the sergeant greeted as he recognized the tall woman coming through the security gate.

"That it is, Sergeant Rowland." Colonel Peterson provided her customary smile for the Marine on duty. "How's Ginny doing? She must be close to nine months now."

"Yes, ma'am!" He beamed back. "Just about any time now and we'll have another recruit in the family."

"Let's see, this one's number four, right?"

Surprised that the colonel would remember, the sergeant grinned. "Yes, ma'am."

"Are you hoping for a boy or girl this time?"

"We're hoping for a girl, ma'am. With the three boys, Ginny's really set on getting her little girl." He blushed before adding, "And me, too. It'll be nice to have a little girl to spoil."

"Well, let me know when she arrives, Sergeant." Dean grinned and waved as she headed toward the bank of elevators and stepped into the first empty car.

"Will do, ma'am, and thanks for asking." He smiled as he turned to face the next group approaching the security gate. As he watched the five officers coming in the door, he wished that everyone could be as considerate as Colonel Peterson. "Good morning, Major Russell," the sergeant called to the lead officer, still smiling brightly.

Major Russell was not in a good mood. As he approached the security gate, he looked sternly at the smiling Marine. "I don't recall your duty SOP to be verbally greeting personnel, Sergeant. I suggest you wipe that smile off your face and get serious about your job!"

"Sir, yes, sir!" Sergeant Rowland snapped as he changed his expression to a somber one, staring straight ahead and past the major.

"Who's your commanding officer?" Major Russell inquired brusquely.

"Captain Hansol, sir!" the Marine barked.

"Well, keep to your SOP or Captain Hansol will be hearing from me," he grunted before moving toward the bank of elevators.

"Sir, yes, sir!" the Marine replied quickly, holding his breath as his peripheral vision watched the officers reach the elevators.

When they were out of earshot, he slowly let out his breath in a hiss.

The five officers entered the next available elevator. As the door shut, another major in the group whispered to Russell, "Have a rough weekend, Len?"

"What makes you think that?" the major replied with a sneer.

"You were a little hard on the sergeant, don't you think? There's nothing in the books that says he can't be pleasant while performing his job."

Major Russell looked over at his colleague and gave him a cold stare. "Just cap it, Rod."

Major Rodney Lowell shook his head and dropped the subject. He wished he knew what was bothering Len, but decided that the major wasn't going to open up about it. He assumed it was probably related to some family difficulties. Military life was not easy, even if you had a great posting like the Pentagon. You just never knew from one moment to the next when you'd be sent somewhere else...and...you never knew when the politicians would back the U.S. into a corner, then turn to the military to get the country out of it. Before you knew it, you could be in the middle of another conflict, trying to keep your butt from being blown off. *Well,* Rodney thought, *at least I'm single and don't have a family to worry about.*

Dean deposited her cap on the hall tree just inside the door of her office and placed her briefcase on the desk. She walked past her leather chair to the window that looked out into the Pentagon's courtyard. Being an aide to the general had its perks; one of them was this coveted interior office on the A Ring with a view of the courtyard. As Dean looked out, she was heartened by the sight of a cardinal flitting from tree to tree. "Why is it that the male birds have all the bright colors?" she murmured as she watched the red bird come to rest on one of the tree branches. She studied the surrounding trees intently until she finally found the bird's mate, its green feathering allowing it to blend into the background with ease. "Well, Mrs. Cardinal," she whispered to the bird, "at least you're not such an easy target, eh?" Dean watched the birds a bit longer and then turned to face the stack of intelligence reports on her desk. With a sigh, she pulled out her leather chair, unbuttoned her jacket, and sat down to begin tackling the paperwork in preparation for an afternoon staff meeting. They were picking up some new staff to replace personnel who had been transferred, and the general wanted her to bring everyone up to speed.

By 1100 hours, Colonel Peterson had waded through the majority of the reports and decided she needed a stretch break before finishing the pile and writing up her remarks. Getting up from the chair, she raised her hands overhead and stretched, then buttoned up her jacket and headed to the cafeteria. Deciding to swing by and see how Captain Jarvis was doing, she changed directions in the corridor.

Bill Jarvis had been the target of a hit-and-run attack by Dean's nemesis, Natasha, back in December. The injuries he suffered at her hands resulted in the removal of his kidney and orthopedic surgery to pin his femur and pelvis back together. A severe bout of pneumonia also hampered his recuperation. All in all, it had been a long, arduous regimen of physical therapy and recovery before Bill was able to return to duty. While his fitness levels were back to acceptable standards for full duty assignments in the Army, they were still below normal for a fitness junkie like Bill. And his dedication showed. He was as tall as Dean, with dusty blond hair and a physique that body builders would envy. He had been on half duty for the last month, having only returned to full duty status as of that morning.

The hardest thing for Bill to cope with was the loss of his kidney. He would have to be especially vigilant about urinary infections to protect the one remaining kidney. The loss would not affect his ability to be assigned field duty, but the Army would probably relegate him to desk duty for the next few months of his career until he was back at full capacity. Lately he had been thinking of leaving the service. Walking the fine line of "don't ask, don't tell" is very difficult and the fact that he was under the wing of Colonel Peterson made him a target by her enemies. The first problem would be to find a civilian job that could satisfy his need for mental and physical stimulation. The second would be his partner Dirk, who also worked at the Pentagon, but as a civilian. Their current work situation was ideal. With both of them in the same building, it was easy to pass off their relationship as being work-related.

Dean rounded the corner and entered the Intelligence Operations Center. This was the heart of Army Intelligence at the Pentagon; banks of computers and digital maps covered entire walls. There were also audio and visual surveillance sections and an interpretation area, where specialists in many dialogues worked interpreting papers, film, and audio collections of intelligence. Then there were the individual work cubicles where analysts took the raw data from the interpreters and map and surveillance experts, and worked up reports that included data from Fort Belvoir. In fact, much of the real collection work took place at Fort Belvoir in Virginia, and reports of any significance came to this room in the Pentagon for further review and recommended action, including collaboration with the other arms of the military intelligence community. What came out of this room usually ended up on Dean's desk for final review and summary before going to General Carlton, then up the line to the Joint Chiefs.

Dean loved the feel of this room — the inherent electricity of intelligence gathering and the analysis processes. She loved fieldwork even more, with its hands-on, down and dirty work of chasing after clues and the ever-present tang of danger. Just walking into this room got Dean's nerve endings tingling and longing for days past. Looking around the room at the younger faces of the field agents going through briefings and debriefings, she sighed. It wasn't that she was too old for field duty. In fact, at thirty-eight, she was probably in the best physical shape she'd ever been in. Her problem was that she had managed to get herself promoted right out of fieldwork. Looking back, her career was stellar, one that any officer would be proud of. She just missed doing the part of her job she loved the best; the drawback of her fast track promotions was loss of field assignments. Then she thought of Katie and the benefit of those same promotions being the chance to spend her off-hours with her lover, and she decided she wouldn't want to lose that. Nope. No way. No how.

Dean spotted Bill sitting at his new desk in a corner office. It was partially enclosed in glass to afford him some protection from the organized chaos of the large room and still allow him to keep an eye on the big maps that were constantly changing as satellites moved in their orbits around the Earth. The captain was reading a stack of intercepted radio transmissions from various parts of the world.

Dean folded her arms across her chest and leaned lazily against the doorframe watching her protégé as he worked diligently on the project before him. She cleared her throat to get his attention. "Care to join me for a cup of high test?"

"Colonel," Bill exclaimed as he stood quickly and assumed attention.

"At ease, Captain." Dean grinned. Pushing off the doorframe, she entered and took a seat in his visitor's chair. "What's got such a lock on your attention?"

"Radio chatter, cell phone chatter, internet chatter." He resumed his seat. "Lots of chatter...too much chatter," he conceded as he flipped though the papers with his thumb. "I'm just trying to get a handle on what might be in the background. I got this stuff on my desk this morning, and I've been working on a matrix to organize it to see if there's anything here that needs our immediate attention. The reports are coming in from all different points, but it's all about the chatter over the airwaves."

"Common threads?" Dean asked.

"At this point, the only common thread is that they're all Mid-Eastern in language," Bill replied.

"Did you tell Major Russell of your concern?"

"Yes. He felt it was a waste of time since this stuff has been around for quite a while." Captain Jarvis looked at his mentor and friend. "I don't know, Colonel. I just have this gut feeling that something's in the works that we need to know about."

"Okay, Bill. I trust your instincts any day. How about a break to clear your head, then we'll look at it together," Dean suggested. "Let's hit the cafeteria. I think I need something decadent."

"Decadent?" Bill repeated with a grin. "Just what were you two up to this weekend?"

Dean pursed her lips, blowing out a little air, and then gave him one of her lopsided smiles, capped with a wink. "C'mon. I'll tell you all about it."

They stood and left the small office, Bill in the lead. As he stepped out of the doorway, Major Russell came out of his office next door with his head down, looking at a paper in his hand. He never looked up. Failing to see Bill step into the main room, he collided with him head-on.

"Good grief, Captain," he barked as he bounced off Bill's chest, "watch where you're going!"

"Excuse me, Major," the junior officer conceded, stepping aside and exposing Colonel Peterson behind him.

When the major recognized the woman behind Captain Jarvis, he faltered for a brief second before recovering. "Colonel, what can I do for you?" he asked in a false tone of respect.

Dean raised an eyebrow as she read through to the major's true feelings. "Major Russell." She paused for effect, pinning him with a commanding stare, "I want a matrix of all the latest communications our field ops have picked up: times, dates, locations, common phrases, and origin of communicants." Dean heard the major gasp at the request as he shot an angry look in the direction of Captain Jarvis. Major Len Russell had been a pain in her butt since their stint together in intelligence training at Fort Huachuca, and this was one time she was glad she had the upper hand. Dean did not make a habit of using her rank as a personal whip, but in this instance, it felt pretty good.

"Captain Jarvis," the major said, "you heard the Colonel. Get on it!"

Dean turned to the major, "No, Major. I need Captain Jarvis for another project right now. He's coming with me. I suggest you handle my request personally. Please have it to my office in," she looked at her watch, "an hour," then she turned to walk away. Bill followed after her, maintaining a serious face as they walked out of the center, too professional to show any sign of puzzlement over the colonel's obvious dislike of Major Russell.

Dean selected a glass of 1% milk and a large piece of devils food chocolate cake that was thickly coated with sugary icing. She looked at her tray and nodded in satisfaction that the contents would surely satisfy her craving for something decadent. She would have preferred whole milk, but Katie was slowly getting her to cut back on fat, aiming at skim milk as the final step down. *Besides,* she thought, grinning at the milk carton, *you can't get chocolate milk in the fat free version yet.*

"Colonel?" the captain queried as they sat down at a corner table in the voluminous cafeteria. He stirred his coffee as his mind assembled the proper words.

Dean took a big bite of cake and looked up at the serious look on the face of her tablemate. "Hmm?"

"Two things." He raised two fingers for illustration. "First, what's got you in this mood? And, second, what's with you and Major Russell? Begging your pardon, Colonel, I know you. It's not like you to do what you just did with the major."

Dean wasn't surprised at the first question, having already alluded to it in Jarvis' office, but the second seemed a bit too insubordinate for a junior officer to be asking his superior, even if it was obvious to him that she had acted out of pique. Reflecting on the latter, Dean nodded and sighed, knowing that she probably shouldn't have put the captain in the middle of her feud with Major Russell. The major had been a prick since their training in Fort Huachuca, and she hadn't been happy about his assignment to fill in for the recuperating Captain Jarvis. Now that he was there, it would be harder to reassign him back to Fort Belvoir, where at least he would be physically out of her sight.

When General Carlson told her she was bringing in a seasoned officer to temporarily fill Bill's spot, Dean had been relieved. But when she was handed the replacement's file, she just about choked.

The past was the past, and she wasn't going to bring it up. As Dean stood in front of the general, she quickly flipped through his military jacket, looking for the letter of reprimand. It was there, but as she read it, it was worded so innocuously, no one would have known the reason for its inclusion. She hissed inwardly at the lack of conviction she'd had at the time. The rest of his record was mostly average, nothing exemplary, passed over for promotions but making the grades on the second go. His Command and General Staff College scores were just average, but somehow, he had managed to pull some plum assignments. The general caught her hesitation, asking if there was a problem, and she responded with a "no". She should have spoken up then, but the letter of reprimand was not enough to make her case, so she decided to just keep a close eye on him. Since Major Russell arrived, he'd been worming his way in and around the general, and Dean could see why he got the plum assignments. He certainly talked a good game, but in the last four months, he hadn't proved his worth to her. He was abusive to his staff, inefficient, took credit for the work of others, belittled the females he worked with, and generally was an apple-polishing toady. To say she thought little of him was an understatement.

Dean looked up at the concern in Bill's face. "I apologize for putting you in the middle. I'll take care of that when we go back."

"No, Colonel, don't bother. It's about time he had to do some work up there," Bill ventured tentatively, and received a raised eyebrow in response. "I'm sorry, ma'am, but the guy is a jerk."

"That's a superior officer you're talking about, Captain," Dean corrected sharply, but just a bit of a turn in the corner of her mouth indicated agreement.

"Yes, ma'am. I apologize for the observation."

Dean nodded and grinned, deciding to drop the subject of Major Russell. "In reference to your first question, I'm in a good mood because Katie and I are planning a little party that we would like you and Dirk to attend."

"A party?" he questioned. "What's the occasion?"

Dean looked around the nearly empty room and blushed uncharacteristically. "A ceremony of sorts. That is, if we can find someone to do it."

Bill looked at his mentor and smiled knowingly. "Ah, so, you bit the big one, huh?"

"You could say that."

"Well, just tell us where and when, and we'll be there. It's about time, you know." Captain Jarvis was truly pleased with the news and his face beamed with delight. "Is Katie excited?"

Dean laughed heartily, remembering how she had caught Katie going through a variety of poses while checking her reflection in the mirror, each pose struck to accentuate the sparkling diamond and sapphire ring. "That's an understatement."

"Hey, how about asking Reverend Martha? I bet she'd go for it."

Dean thought about that for a moment. Martha hadn't taken long to acknowledge her relationship with Katie. She knew within minutes of meeting them, and over the past months her relationship with them had grown. Dean often talked to the reverend when she called her father to check on his condition. The last call hadn't been very heartening. Her dad had already surpassed the doctor's expectations for longevity with his brain cancer, but Martha had been honest about his downturn. Dean knew it wouldn't be long before they got the call to come to Kansas City.

"That's a good idea, Bill, but we're not planning anything soon. My father has taken a turn for the worse, and that's our main concern right now." They chatted a while longer before Dean changed the subject back to the communications surveillance. "So, what's got your gut in a twist over these communications?"

"I'm not sure yet, Colonel. Maybe the matrix will help. There's just a lot of chatter out there and, as I said, most is coming from Middle Eastern parties."

"You think Saddam is planning another move?"

"No, not Saddam directly, it's too widely scattered for that, but there's talk of a 'great day'. Stuff like that. It seems like more of the same rhetoric that's been coming from that area for quite a while now — threats, but nothing concrete. I know it sounds innocuous, and they're just bits and pieces...but it just seems...more intense, you know?"

Dean nodded, knowing that when the hairs on her neck started to prickle...something evil was usually on its way.

"I need to know more," Bill concluded.

"When we get back up to my office, we'll take a look at the matrix. Two heads are always better than one." Dean polished off the last crumbs of her cake while they talked about Bill's therapy routine and set a date to start some light sparring workouts. Looking at her watch, Dean nodded. "Okay, that should be enough time for Russell. Let's see how well he did."

"I'll say this...he managed to get this matrix together in pretty good shape." Dean picked up the sheets of paper and went to work looking for commonalities, clues, any thread that could lead somewhere specific. She went through the matrix once, then three more times before she set it down and leaned back in her chair, resting her head against the high back. Folding her hands together, she began twiddling her thumbs as she closed her eyes in thought.

Having worked with Colonel Peterson for five years, Bill knew every nuance of the colonel's analytic routine, so he sat quietly and patiently while she digested the information.

When she opened her eyes, she looked at Bill and smiled. "You're absolutely right, Bill. There's something there, but there's just not enough information."

Bill was relieved that his mentor agreed with him. He had begun to feel a bit like Don Quixote sparring with windmills, and was glad to have his instincts validated. "I know, and I'm afraid it may be something big."

Leaning forward, Dean rested her elbows on the desk. "Make copies of the matrix and check with the other branches...the civilian agencies, too. Let's flesh this matrix out a bit. And bring me back a copy of this one."

"FBI, CIA, NSA," he ticked off. "Anyone else?"

"That should do for now. Also, see if you can dig into the money trail." She picked up the sheets and handed them to him. "Keep me informed."

Bill took the papers and stood. "Yes, ma'am."

"Bill?" Dean called, "I'm sorry I put you in the middle. I'll take care of Major Russell. I have to go to a staff meeting now, but I'll send for him when I'm done."

Captain Jarvis nodded. "Yes, ma'am."

The staff meeting lasted longer than expected, as many of the new staffers were eager to show off in front of the general and offered a lot of comments. In Colonel Peterson's opinion, there were too many comments, none of which was impressive. On her way back to her office, she remembered that she had promised to talk to Major Russell. Changing direction, she took the elevator and then entered the Intelligence Operations Center and stood before Major Russell's door, pausing and knocking before entering. When she opened the door and stepped in, she found it dark and empty. Checking her watch, she noted that he had probably left for the day. *Well, that's not a bad idea.* She shut the door and walked to Captain Jarvis' cubicle.

Poking her head into the open doorway, she asked, "Major Russell around?"

Bill looked up, but remained sitting at the wave of Dean's hand. "No, ma'am. You just missed him."

"Right. Well, I'll catch him tomorrow. Have a good night, Bill...and go home. That's an order." Dean winked at her protégé.

"Yes, ma'am. Just as soon as I finish looking over these new reports."

Dean waved a good-bye and left for her office, eager to pack up and go home.

Chapter Five
June 7

Dean folded the newspaper and set it in the wooden recycling bin next to their couch. Her fingers trailed lightly across the wood, relishing the smooth feel of her latest project. It was stained a golden oak to match the rest of the furniture in the room. She had just completed the project on Sunday, with a final sanding before adding the Deft finish. Dean had expanded on the arts and crafts table design, personalizing it with her touches. The result was a beautiful mission style end table with a unique storage option for her newspapers. It was totally functional and minus the ugliness of typical recycling bins. Her fingers lingered on the finished surface, enjoying the satisfaction of a job well done before picking up the remote and turning on the television for the evening news.

Katie entered the living room, removed a coaster from its nest on the new table, and set a glass of iced tea on it. "It's raspberry mint. Hope you like it."

Dean looked up with a smile. "Sounds good." She patted the cushion next to her. "Have time to sit a spell and watch the news?"

Katie's face scrunched in disgust. "News? Yuck! Isn't there anything better on?" She sat down in the spot indicated, plucking the remote from Dean's hand. Katie began flipping through the channels before Dean could protest, finally stopping on a rerun of *Charlie's Angels*. "Ah! Now that's more like it." Katie tossed the remote back to Dean. "A bit of escapism for a change."

They settled back and watched the old show, making fun of the way the actors' hair never got messed up in the action scenes. This episode had all the original "angels" and was a lot of fun to watch.

"You ever wonder about those girls?" Katie asked as the show finished.

"In regards to?"

"Their personal relationships. They're always so...chummy. You know, hanging on each other and the like."

"Well, considering the time frame these were made, I'm sure there was no 'sub-script' in the series."

"You mean like in *Xena*?"

"Exactly. Times have changed; writers can get away with a lot more now."

"You have a point." Katie turned to look at her partner. "Guess the world is getting a bit more tolerant, huh?"

"Well, not all of it...and definitely not the military. We're still a long way from being accepted by everyone."

Katie turned back and stared at the television as the next show started. It was a re-run of *I Love Lucy,* the one where she was pregnant.

"Now that was a groundbreaking show," Dean commented. "It was the first show to have the star pregnant in the story line. It broke the taboo of even saying the word, let alone dealing with the issue. The studio caught a bit of flak over it, but it all worked out in the end."

Thinking back to Dean's previous comment, Katie asked, "Do you think the military will ever move beyond the 'don't ask, don't tell' directive?"

Dean's eyebrows furrowed in thought as she turned to look at Katie. "Not in our lifetime. What makes you ask?"

"Just wondering."

"Are you worried about Saturday...or..." She looked down at the sapphire and diamond ring.

Seeing Dean's gaze shift to her ring, Katie quickly reached up and touched Dean's cheek. "No, love, I'm not worried about this." She waggled her ring hand. "But Saturday has crossed my mind a time or two," Katie confessed. "You aren't worried?"

"No. And you shouldn't be either." Dean leaned toward her partner, seeking her lips. Though the kiss was soft, it relayed all the love she felt.

"Honest?" Katie breathed softly.

"Honest."

"But what if—"

"No 'what ifs', Katie. I'm not worried." Dean effectively ended any further conversation with another kiss, followed by another as she slowly and deliberately changed the focus to love and desire. Dean could feel Katie's body begin to submit as her tongue slipped past parted teeth and began a sensual dance with Katie's, teasing at first but then becoming more urgent as each woman responded to the growing need building within, a hunger that brought out a more primal urge to satisfy the lust each was craving. Their hands joined in, unbuttoning shirts and slipping past waistbands as eager bodies moved accordingly to provide easier access to their common goals. Words of love were muffled as mouths moved from lips to naked skin to breasts, each woman exploring the other as though it were their first time making love; as though time was going to end and they had to fill themselves completely or die.

Terrance Russell was doubly excited. Tomorrow was his eighteenth birthday *and* he could take the family's new Dodge Caravan to school as long as he picked up his father at the Pentagon at 1700 hours. Things were looking up for the high school senior. Just one more week of high school, then graduation, and soon he'd be on his way to West Point. Maybe then his dad would be proud of him. He was a bit worried for his brother and sister, though, and often thought that maybe he should opt to go to George Washington University instead of the Point. That way he could stay home and intercede for them when their dad was having one of his bad days. It was going to be a rough summer, too. His dad's promotion board was meeting in late September, and the fall would be really rough if the promotion didn't come through. If that happened...well, he might reconsider staying at the Point.

"Hey, Dad," Terrance said, "what time do I need to drop you off at the Pentagon?"

"Zero seven hundred."

"Great! That gives me plenty of time to get back to school."

"It better. I don't want you getting a speeding ticket," his father replied sternly. "And, remember, no joyriding after school with your buddies. Just get your physical finished and pick me up on time."

"Yes, sir. I should be finished in plenty of time. My appointment is at two o'clock—"

"At fourteen hundred, Terrance! Get used to using military time!"

"Yes, sir...fourteen hundred." Terrance nodded solemnly. "Do you think I could come up to your office?" he added timidly. "It would sure be cool to see the IOC."

"You can meet me inside at the security gate, Terrance. You know I can't get you into the IOC. It's a highly restricted area."

"Yes, sir," he said, obviously disappointed. "I was just hoping."

"Some day, son. General Carlton has a lot of confidence in me, so maybe one day I'll ask for special permission."

Terrance perked up at the possibility and the hope that this boded well for his dad's promotion prospects. "That'd be really cool, Dad. So, you're really tight with the general, huh?" His dad nodded faintly. "That's great!"

"Just be on time, Terrance. Seventeen hundred hours sharp!"

"Yes, sir!" Terrance bounded up the stairs to his room, thinking that maybe the summer wouldn't be so bad after all if his dad and the general were on such good terms.

Dean followed Katie to the Porsche dealership and pulled into the slot next to the service door. Katie pulled her car up to the garage door, got out and locked the car before stepping over to the early bird box. She filled out the information on the envelope and slipped the keys inside. After sealing the envelope, she slipped it into the slot in the service door. Katie's Boxster was due for a routine maintenance visit and a detailing job. Since they no longer had the third vehicle and she had the day off, she'd opted to drive Dean to work and use Dean's car to run errands. The dealership would have given her a loaner for the day, but this way they could spend a little extra time together. And also, she'd rather drive Dean's car than a loaner. A loaner was likely to be a trade-in vehicle that wasn't as well appointed or as comfortable.

"Okay," Katie said as she slipped into the passenger seat, "let's get you to work."

Dean pulled out of the lot and headed to the interstate. Traffic was already picking up and Dean expertly wove her way through the congestion, arriving at the Pentagon in an amazing thirty minutes. It was another beautiful day, already warming up. During the nice weather, the top was always up on the convertible on the way to work, but down on the way back. Dean was meticulous about her appearance in uniform and having the top down with the wind blowing would definitely have an ill effect so — top up on the way in, down on the way home.

"Think I'll put the top down," Katie commented as they entered the Pentagon drop-off lane. "It's warm enough already and the day's going to be a beauty."

"I'll give you a hand with it," Dean replied as she pulled into a drop-off slot near the entrance. The two women turned their attention to that chore, heedless of the military and civilian Pentagon employees who were arriving around them. Katie had just slipped behind the wheel and Dean picked up her briefcase from behind the seat when a dark blue Caravan slowed down as it passed them, having just dropped off its passenger at the entrance.

Thinking he recognized the Boxster, Terrance slowed to get a good look at the tall female as she pulled out her briefcase. His eyes zeroed in on her nameplate as she turned to wave at her companion before walking toward the entrance.

"Wow," he whispered as he recognized the woman from the park. "She's a colonel. Wonder if dad knows her." He looked up at the rearview mirror and caught a glimpse of the colonel as she entered the building. Then he noticed the line of vehicles behind him and moved forward before car horns started blowing.

"How's the monitoring going?" Colonel Peterson asked as she entered Captain Jarvis' office and waved the captain to remain seated.

"More of the same, I'm afraid. Nothing concrete to point a finger at, but still gets my gut in a knot."

"Anything on the money aspect?" She sat in the visitor's chair across from Bill.

He reached for a folder on the top of a pile to his right. He opened it and scanned the pages before handing it over to the colonel. "Lots of big transactions. The money's flowing, but we haven't yet identified the origins. It seems to be routed through numerous cover groups and companies. A lot is flowing out of the Middle East into Europe and Asia." He looked expectantly at Dean as she reviewed the paperwork.

"Not enough to put together a picture, but I agree with your instincts. Something's afoot." She handed back the folder. "Have you checked with the other agencies?"

"I've made my inquiries, but haven't yet received any confirmations or information from them."

Dean nodded, knowing how intelligence gathering was usually kept close to the chest, so to speak. Unfortunately, there were still a lot of fences up between agencies, and turf issues were always problematic. She made a mental note to contact her friends at the CIA and FBI to see if she could loosen some lips. "Well, keep at it, Bill. I hate surprises."

Bill nodded in agreement. "I know what you mean."

"You know what the real problem is, Bill?"

He lifted an eyebrow in response. "You mean, besides turf issues?"

Dean pursed her lips and blew out a short breath. "Yeah, besides the turf issues." Captain Jarvis leaned back in his chair, folding his hands across his abdomen as he watched his superior. "As much as I love the new technology and the gadgets, we're working with a handicap. We've lost the human element." She looked out at the IOC and all the screens depicting live satellite views, and pointed at the room. "Ever since satellite technology was developed, we've relied too heavily on it. We can see the nose hairs on a suspected enemy if he's out in the open, but that doesn't help us gather intelligence on what happens behind closed doors...or tell us whose nose hairs need inspecting."

Bill looked out into the room as he weighed the colonel's words. "I see where you're going, Colonel. We've relied on machines to do our intelligence gathering. We've physically distanced ourselves from our potential enemies in order to protect the human factor." He thought a bit longer. "But, we've also reduced the chance of having our intelligence compromised through capture. And, we still get tips from other operatives."

"Yes, the politicians were convinced we needed to eliminate the human component for safety, and they made us comply. And, yes, we still get some human intelligence...but not like we should." She sighed and leaned forward in her chair, resting her elbows on her knees and clasping her hands together. "Think of it this way." She sat upright and spread her hands. "A human functions at full capacity when all of their senses are in use — sight, smell, hearing, taste, touch. Add to these senses the instinctive capabilities of a good field agent — the ability to see through an action or an idle comment, to feel the hair prickle on their necks, to smell something rotten in a plan — and you have more than the whole functioning. Eliminate one or more of the senses, and the capability becomes limited. We can still function, but not like we can when everything is engaged. Eliminate instinct, and we're further compromised." She looked out into the room and sighed. "We can see a lot and hear most of the time, but we've lost the rest. We're not working at full capacity anymore, and one day, I'm afraid it is going to come back and bite us in the butt."

"I see what you mean, Colonel. So...what do we do about it?"

Dean shook her head. "Not much we can do until the politicians up on the Hill realize what a mistake it was to eliminate the human factor...and until we get better interagency cooperation. We've got to tear down the fences between the civilian agencies and the military ones."

"Hell, the civilian agencies need to tear down fences between themselves," Bill scoffed.

"Well, the military communities cooperate fairly well, but we have a few of our own fences, too." Bill nodded resolutely. "I don't know what the answer is, Bill." She stood to leave. "But someone needs to be thinking about one. Let me know if you get anything concrete."

"Hey," came the familiar voice as Dean answered the ringing phone. "How's work?"

"Same old, same old," Dean answered with a smile. "Data to analyze, reports to write, meetings to attend. How about you?"

"I just got finished with my massage appointment and thought I'd ride up to Old Alexandria and do some shopping. Tracy's birthday is coming up soon and I know how she loves antiques. There's a really neat shop in the old part of town that I thought I might browse through before I pick you up."

"It sounds like you're having a better day than I am." Dean leaned back in her chair and swiveled around to look out the window into the courtyard. "At least you have a beautiful day for shopping."

"Yeah, it's a beauty all right!" The engine of the Boxster started up. "So, I'll see you around five?"

"That's the plan. Come on up to the office if you're early."

"Will do."

The call disconnected and Dean swiveled back to replace the receiver in the cradle, images of her lover filling her mind. As her thoughts returned to her conversation with Captain Jarvis and the human connection, Dean turned back to the window and started to rock. Rocking always seemed to stimulate her thought processes, but today she just didn't have enough information...at least, for the time being. She'd see if she could milk some from her friends at the FBI and CIA. She turned to face her desk and grabbed the phone, punching in the number for the CIA.

"Walter? Colonel Peterson here."

"Hey, Colonel. This a work call or a personal one?" the agent asked with a chuckle.

"Ah, Walter, I'm afraid it's business."

"Figures that'd be my luck. So, what can I do for you?"

"Walt, we've been picking up a lot of chatter over the air and it's got my neck hairs up. I'm guessing someone in the Middle East is planning another terrorist attack...maybe another incident like the U.S.S. Cole. Have you heard anything?"

"Chatter, eh? About a 'great day to come'?"

"Exactly. Got anything specific?"

"Nah. Sounds like a lot of wishful thinking. You guys have really tightened up the military end, haven't you?"

"Yes."

"And your military folk at the embassies have been on alert since the Cole incident."

"Yes."

"Well, things should be secure on your end."

"What about the civilian end? Any guesses on what's afoot?"

"Our analysts are betting it's just a lot of hot air. We've been hearing this kind of talk for a long time and nothing's come of it. The FAA is getting ready to issue another hijack alert, but that's about all for now."

"What about the money trail? You guys looking into that?"

"Not really. Most of what we've seen is going into Europe. The counter-terrorism units there are looking into possibilities, figuring there will be another car bombing somewhere in Germany or maybe England or France."

"What about the other agencies, Walt. Anyone sharing anything?" Dean could hear a chuckle echoing through the receiver.

"Right! And I bet you believe in Santa Claus, too. Most everyone is reporting the same information. I can tell you the CIA is aware of the chatter, and that's about it right now."

"Well, give me a call if you hear anything more solid, okay?"

"Just for you, Colonel. And, you'll do the same if you pick up anything?"

"Yes, count on it. Thanks, Walter."

"You're welcome, Colonel. Tell Katie hello."

"I will. Say hi to Emma from us."

Dean disconnected, then dialed up her contact at the FBI, where she received basically the same information. Since 1995, the intelligence community had been monitoring terrorist threats from every conceivable network, including bin Laden's al Qaeda network, and this seemed to be more of the same. Contacting the FBI, NSA, and the Department of Defense, she found that most everyone attributed the chatter to more of these threats, and the concern was for U.S. interests and personnel overseas.

Dean blew out a whispered breath. "Well, at least folks are hearing the same things." She headed to the IOC to let Captain Jarvis in on the results of her conversations. On her way back, she stopped by the security station to alert them to Katie's potential arrival.

"Have you heard the good news, ma'am?" the young Marine corporal at the station asked.

"What news would that be, Corporal?"

"Sergeant Rowland just got a call from his wife. He took off for Bethesda."

"Well, that is good news, Corporal. Thanks for filling me in."

"You're welcome, ma'am."

Dean headed back to the elevators and her office, smiling at the joy a new baby brought to a family. She'd often wondered what kind of a mother she might have been, but the danger and uncertainty of her career kept any thoughts of adoption at bay. Well, now, things might be different. She and Katie never talked about the prospect of raising a family, whether through adoption or insemination. Dean tried to visualize herself pregnant, and started chuckling. Katie, on the other hand, would look adorable if she was in the family way. She was still chuckling to herself when she stepped off the elevator and was nearly tackled by a body rushing into the elevator.

"Urff! Watch where you're—" Major Russell raised his head and looked into the deadly sapphires staring at him. "Colonel, pardon me. I..."

"Wasn't watching where you were going?"

He paused and seemed to consider his answer. "Um, yes, Colonel. Pardon me." He hurried into the elevator as the doors began to close.

Dean continued to eye the man as he stood in the elevator, his eyes fixed on the papers in his hand. Just as the door closed, she thought she saw a smirk appear on his lips, and she felt the blood in her veins begin to warm. *Some day, Major, you and I will have a come-to-Jesus talk,* Dean thought as she turned and headed to her office.

There was a gentle knock on Dean's door and she issued a command to enter without raising her eyes from the papers on her desk. Katie walked in and stood at attention in front of Dean's desk.

"Special Agent Katherine O'Malley, reporting as requested!"

Dean looked up and beamed a warm smile at her lover. "At ease, Special Agent." She looked at her watch and sighed. "Where does the time go?"

"Well, you must be having fun," Katie chimed in.

"Fun?"

"Yeah. You know, that 'time flies when you're having fun' thing?"

"Ah, well, if you can call analyzing intelligence and putting the highlights into a meaningful ten minute report for the Joint Chiefs fun, then, yeah...I'm having fun!"

"Oops. Bad timing?"

Dean looked down at her papers. "No, not really. I was just re-reading the final version. Let me finish up and then we can drop this off to Sergeant Major Tibbitts as we head out."

Katie took a seat and watched as Dean studied her report. She never ceased to marvel at the strong lines of her lover's face. Her sapphire eyes could express every nuance of emotion and pierce right through you. The firm jaw, high cheekbones, and the lips...oh, how she loved those lips. Dean could convey complete messages with her expressions alone. And her lips...well, they could give you chapters of information with just a simple caress. A smile etched its way across her face as she watched Dean's jaw clench and unclench, and then the head nodded subtly and the papers were laid flat on the desktop.

Dean looked up and raised an eyebrow in question at the sultry look on Katie's face.

"Umm, just letting my mind wander a bit, Colonel."

"Just don't let it wander too far. We have to walk out of here with our clothes on." Dean waggled her eyebrows in true Groucho fashion that raised a full blush from Katie. "We better head out before you melt."

Dean placed the report in a file folder and inserted a few files into her briefcase before snapping it shut. Katie went and retrieved Dean's hat from the coat rack and opened the door as Dean came around her desk. As she held the door open, Katie motioned with a wave. "After you, Colonel."

The walk to General Carlton's office was shorter now that the renovations had been completed. The Pentagon had just undergone some extensive remodeling, and their offices had moved into the new area this past spring. Dean silently opened the door to the general's outer office and was greeted by Sergeant Major Tibbits. As Katie stepped out from behind Dean, the sergeant major's smile broadened.

"Special Agent O'Malley," he said warmly, "it's good to see you."

Katie reached the man and wrapped him in a warm hug. "Hey, what happened to just plain old Katie?" she said as she embraced him. "I'm not one of your Army cronies."

"Yes, ma'am," he said automatically, then corrected, "Katie." They released one another and he turned his attention to Colonel Peterson. "Ma'am."

"Here's the Joint Chiefs report for the general. If there are any questions or corrections, I'll take care of them in the morning."

"Yes, ma'am. The general said she wouldn't be back from the Hill and to leave the report in her safe." Tibbits accepted the report and took it into the general's office, slipping the report into the open safe, then closing the door and spinning the dial. "All tucked away, ma'am. Anything else you need tonight?"

"No, thank you, Tibbits. We're just heading home." They turned and headed toward the door, Katie waving at the sergeant major and giving him a wink.

When they were out in the hall, Dean looked at Katie and shook her head. "You are such a flirt."

Emerald eyes sparkled mischievously as Katie donned an innocent look. "Who, me?" She batted her eyelashes. "I was merely trying to inject a little humanity into his day."

"You are so bad," Dean said softly, shaking her head.

"That's why you..." Katie left the sentence unfinished, knowing Dean understood the rest.

Heaving a sigh, Dean said, "Yes, so come on, let's go home."

At the elevators, they stepped inside with several other personnel on their way home. Stopping at the security station to ask if there was any news from Sergeant Rowland, Dean noticed a young teen waiting by the door. As she looked his way, their eyes met and she felt her neck hairs start to prickle. She concluded her conversation with the corporal on duty, and then she and Katie exited the building.

A minute later, Major Russell came down the hallway and met his son at the door. "Glad to see you're on time, Terrance."

"Yes, sir," the excited teen responded as they exited the building and walked the short distance to where their vehicle was parked. After they got in the vehicle, Terrance turned to his dad and asked, "Dad, do you know a Colonel Peterson?"

Just the name sent anger spiking through the major's body. He turned and looked at his son, answering with a nod, fearing his voice would show the anger that was just under the surface.

"Yeah?" Terrance confirmed excitedly. "Do you work with her? What does she do? Wow, she's really beautiful." The teen sighed. "I've been wondering who she was since that day I saw her and that blonde at the park. Man, what I wouldn't give to be older right now."

Major Russell turned slowly and looked over at his son. "You saw her and a blonde at James River Park?" His son nodded eagerly. "When was this?"

"Last weekend."

"Just when last weekend?" he added.

"I was coming back to camp after securing the canoe that got loose. I saw them under that big oak tree on the trail from the river. They were packing up their picnic things and I watched them go to her car. Man, what a cool car she drives...a black Porsche Boxster!"

Russell's mind raced back to the previous weekend and the timeframe to which his son referred. He remembered double-timing the troop up the hill from the river and passing a couple lying together under a tree. Could they be the same two people Terrance had seen? He searched his mind, trying to recall what the couple had been wearing. He didn't remember much about the other person because the taller one was pretty much blocking his view. He did remember seeing a black Army ball cap on that taller person, and maybe a plaid flannel shirt. A big grin appeared on his face as he remembered they were lying on the ground...lying closely together on the ground...almost like lovers. "Terrance, do you remember what they were wearing?"

His son didn't even have to think twice about it. "The colonel had on jeans, a blue plaid flannel shirt, and a black Army ball cap. Her hair was pulled back in a ponytail. The blonde also had on jeans and a blue tank top under a denim shirt. She was pretty cute, too, but the colonel was the one that got my attention."

"I'm impressed, Terrance. Your recall is very good."

His son blushed at the compliment. "It wasn't hard to remember, Dad. They're both totally bodacious looking babes." The look his father gave him made him realize he had slipped into speech that his dad hated and he was talking about a superior officer. "Umm, I mean, they were...very attractive and easy to remember."

"Son," Russell began as a grin broadened on his face, "would you like to take the van to the movies tonight?"

"Wow! That would be great. Thanks, Dad!"

The father and son rode the rest of the way home in silence, both making plans for the evening.

Chapter Seven
June 8

Dean removed her jacket and tucked it neatly behind the driver's seat before slipping behind the wheel of the Boxster. Katie got into the passenger seat and looked at her silent partner. Dean hadn't said much on the way out to the car, and Katie knew something was bothering her. She wondered what had brought on the sudden change.

"What's wrong?" Katie asked as Dean turned the key in the ignition. The low rumble of the engine's purring nearly overshadowed Katie's question.

Dean readjusted the rearview mirror for her height and just caught a glimpse of the teen she had seen at the entrance. He was slipping into the passenger seat of a dark blue Caravan, but she could not clearly see who the driver was.

"Dean?"

"Hmm?" Dean acknowledged as she looked over her shoulder, slowly backing out of the parking space.

"What's wrong, hon?"

"Wrong?"

Katie sighed heavily and turned to face her. "Yeah, wrong. And, don't pull that 'nothing's wrong' bullshit on me. Something's gnawing at you."

Dean glanced at Katie and gave in, knowing that Katie would keep at her until she'd have to spill the beans anyway. "Did you see the kid waiting in the security area?"

Katie thought for few seconds, playing back their exit from the building. She remembered the conversation with the corporal, a few other military folks leaving at the same time, but didn't recall seeing any kid. "No. I guess I was focused on the conversation you had with the corporal on duty."

"Well, off to the left of the entrance, I saw a young man waiting. I didn't think much of it until our eyes met. He's the scout from the park."

"Uh, oh. That means that someone who works here saw us."

"Yeah, that's a possibility, but it doesn't mean that whoever he was waiting for was with him at the park."

"But it's got your neck hairs twitching, huh?"

"Yep." Dean reached up and scratched the nape of her neck while she kept the Caravan in her rearview mirror. It turned onto

Washington Boulevard, heading toward Arlington Heights. When the van turned the corner, she did manage to get a partial plate number, storing that information until she could run a check on it on Monday. *Well, Deanna, if your nape hairs are running true to form, you just may have to give up your career.* She eased the Boxster into the flow of rush hour traffic on I-395.

"So, what do we do now?" Katie asked.

"Nothing."

"Nothing?"

"That's right, nothing at all."

"But—"

"Katie," Dean tossed a stern look at her partner, exasperation obvious in her voice, "there's nothing we can do, so just drop it!"

The look on Dean's face and the tone of her voice stung Katie, and tears began to well. She just wanted to help, to protect Dean, to protect them. She turned her face to the window, seemingly to watch the passing landscape, but really to hide the blinking back of the tears. Dean never backed down from a fight, and Katie didn't understand how Dean could take a potential threat with such... such uncharacteristic calm. Regaining control of her emotions, Katie stole a look at her partner and saw an expression she'd never seen before. It almost looked as if Dean was accepting defeat. The remainder of the ride home was made in silence, driver and passenger lost in thought. The only sounds were coming from the surrounding traffic and the wind whipping around the vehicle as it sped down the interstate.

The women entered the house to the sound of a ringing phone. As Dean entered the security code, Katie ran to pick up the receiver, and was just in time to hear a click followed by a dial tone. Replacing the handset, she checked the caller ID. The call had come from Reverend Lewistan.

"Dean, it was Martha."

Dean nodded and headed down the stairs to their den, opting for the solitude of that space.

Katie took note of her lover's slumped shoulders. She knew that since Martha hadn't left a message on their machine, the news the reverend wanted to relate was probably not good. "I'll get dinner going," she called. Katie looked around the entry and saw that even the cats were subdued as they watched their mistress walk down the stairs. "C'mon, girls, let's get you fed."

Katie had just finished preparing the grilled chicken Caesar salad when Dean came up the back stairs. One look at the reddened eyes and Katie wiped her hands on the paper towel and slowly walked over to Dean. She put her arms around her soul mate and held her. No words were needed to express her empathy. As they stood embracing each other, the cats joined them, softly rubbing against each woman in turn.

Finally, Dean took a deep breath, exhaled slowly, and pushed away from Katie. "He passed away about an hour ago."

"I'm so sorry."

Dean nodded. "We were just..." Tears welled again as Dean remembered the last conversation she'd had with her father. They had finally been able to come to terms with the past, and she was able to forgive him for the death of her brother Thad. It hadn't been easy, but she'd had Reverend Martha's support and Katie's love to help her over the final barriers.

Katie pulled Dean close, embracing her as she released the tears she had been trying to hold back. "I know, love, but at least you were able to find your way back to each other before it was too late." She stroked Dean's hair.

As her tears subsided, Dean pulled back from Katie. She looked into Katie's watery eyes and smiled weakly. "I'm sorry," she said softly as questioning emerald eyes looked back. "I shouldn't have snapped at you in the car."

"Eh, you had every reason," Katie responded with a quick shrug. "I shouldn't have pushed."

"No, no reason in the world gives me the right to snap at you. I'm sorry. Life is too short to be acting so foolishly."

"Don't let it bother you," Katie said with a shake of her head. "C'mon, let's sit down."

Katie led Dean to her chair at the kitchen table, then went over to the counter to get the salad and the bottle of wine she'd opened earlier. Dean slid her chair out from under the table and sat heavily, watching as Katie returned with the salad bowl and the wine. As Katie placed the bowl and bottle near Dean, Dean reached out and took Katie's left hand. She held it, studying the diamond and sapphire ring for a moment before lifting it to her lips where she placed a gentle kiss on the knuckles. "I love you, Katie O'Malley."

"And I love you, Deanna Peterson."

Len Russell moved quietly down the hallway. The rest of the family had already gone to bed but he wanted to complete his business before the morning. He closed the door to the den and walked over to his desk, where he had deposited his briefcase earlier in the evening. He pulled out his PDA, selected his address book from the file, and accessed a phone number. Closing the PDA, he picked up the receiver and dialed. The phone rang twice before it was answered.

"Yeah?"

"Kurt, it's Len Russell."

"Hey, Len. What's up? You ready to join my operation?"

"No, not yet, but maybe when I retire."

"One of these days, Len, you'll realize what a deal you're passing up." He made a clucking sound and sighed. "Okay, so, what's up with the call?"

"I've got a job for you."

"Civilian contract?"

"No, it's a personal job."

"Uh, oh...wife stepping out on you?"

"No, Kurt—"

"Kid in trouble?" Kurt added quickly.

"Kurt, for crissake, just listen a minute."

"Sorry. Go ahead," Kurt replied.

"I need you to do some surveillance on someone for me."

"Okay, give me the particulars."

Chapter Eight
June 9

"I've got your bag!" Dean shouted as she headed toward the door.

Katie looked around the kitchen and rechecked the note she'd left for Bill and Dirk. "Food, water, litter, vet's number... That's it." She slipped the note under the stack of cat food cans and then looked around for the cats. "C'mon, girls; come say goodbye." At the sound of their mistress' voice they came bounding into the kitchen. Spice led the pack, jumping up on the kitchen chair, then the counter, where Katie's hand still rested near the note. Sugar and Butter stayed on the floor, content to wind between Katie's legs and leave a deposit of fur on her chinos. Spice nudged Katie's hand and received the desired head scratch in return.

"Now you girls behave for Bill and Dirk," Katie instructed as she picked up Spice and gave her a hug before setting her down on the floor next to her mates. "Dean and I will be back in a few days. You won't even know we're gone."

"Meow!" vocalized Spice, followed by more subtle chirps from Sugar and Butter.

Katie reached for the bag of treats and dispensed an equal portion to each cat. After watching them devour the treats, she picked up her backpack and went to the front door. She set the alarm, looked back at the watching felines, then opened the door and left, locking it from the outside.

Dean, parked in the Boxster by the front door, watched as Katie removed the key and placed it in the small compartment on the front of the backpack. "All set?" she asked as Katie deposited her backpack in the front boot of the car and closed the hood.

"Yep." Katie slid into the passenger seat, closing the door firmly. "Dirk said they'd be by this afternoon. They're looking forward to staying with the girls...well, that, and the use of our fitness equipment."

"Not to mention the use of our new hot tub," Dean added.

Katie chuckled. "That, too."

"We've got plenty of time to get to Dulles. I'll swing by Starbucks and pick up a couple of lattes to go." Dean turned the key in the ignition, bringing the sports car to life. She slipped on her sunglasses, put the car in gear, and pulled out of the driveway. In the front window of the house, three cats watched with sad eyes as the car pulled away.

After parking the car and picking up their boarding passes, Dean and Katie had thirty minutes to spare. The gate area was full of passengers and their friends and family, saying their goodbyes. As they wove their way through the throng of people, the gate attendant announced the availability for pre-boarding and First Class passengers to board the plane.

"Good timing," Katie said as they approached the gate behind a woman in a wheelchair. She had made the reservations the evening before, and was lucky enough to get the last two seats in First Class for the long flight, so they could board right away.

Dean pulled out their tickets and handed them to the agent as the skycap wheeled the woman down the ramp.

"Welcome aboard," the agent said as she handed back their boarding passes.

They waited patiently as the skycap assisted the woman out of the wheelchair and into the plane. As they entered the cabin, Dean placed their hanging bags in the First Class closet and the carry-on bags in the bin above their seats in the last row of First Class. Katie took the window seat and Dean, the aisle. First Class allowed Dean to stretch out her legs, which had been a rarity for her when she flew on military transport that paid little attention to the comfort of its passengers. Since she'd met Katie, Dean had slowly gotten used to being pampered by her lover and was beginning to like traveling First Class. Dean buckled her seatbelt and watched as the parade of passengers passed. She was aware of Katie moving closer and she shifted to meet her halfway.

"In the baseball cap...student returning home?" Katie whispered as they began their pre-flight guessing game.

"Nope. His hair's too short and he's too buff. He's a sailor going on leave."

"Sailor?"

"Yep, a SEAL."

Katie looked again and noted the barely visible Navy SEAL tattoo on his bicep where it peeked out from under the cuff of his golf shirt. "Missed that."

The next person they picked out was a middle aged, balding man in a wrinkled suit, who was perspiring heavily and talking constantly to the person behind him.

"I'll say a used car salesman," Katie said as she watched him go by.

"Good choice," Dean replied as she watched him pull out a NADA Used Car Guide.

They continued with the game until the last passenger had boarded, and then settled back as the flight attendant collected the glasses and coffee cups from the First Class passengers in preparation for departure. As they taxied to the end of the runway, the flight attendants took them through all the safety features, exits, use of oxygen masks and life vests.

"Dean?"

"Hmm?"

"I was thinking...yesterday when we left the Pentagon, when I asked if your neck hairs were twitching..."

Dean frowned over at Katie, not wanting to re-open that conversation.

"No, hon, just listen a minute. Maybe they were twitching because you were picking up some kind of cosmic message that your dad was passing." Dean's eyebrows rose a bit at the suggestion and Katie put a hand on Dean's arm as she continued. "Just think about it. It was right about the time that your dad died. Maybe...well, maybe Reverend Martha was somehow sending thoughts your way."

Dean looked into Katie's eyes and read the sincerity in them. She turned away and laid her head back against the headrest and closed her eyes. "Maybe," she said in a whisper.

"Martha does have some kind of mystical powers that even she can't explain, so..." Katie let the sentence hang as she watched Dean open her eyes and return her gaze. She waited as Dean seemed to mull over the possibility. Martha Lewistan was, after all, a truly remarkable woman. With Martha's help, even though she was over a thousand miles away, she was able to give Dean the clues needed to find Katie in the tunnel under Niagara Falls. "She helped you find me, Dean. Remember? It's not impossible."

The somber look on Dean's face slowly faded and was replaced by a more relaxed expression and a hint of a smile. "Yes, it is possible," Dean agreed as she gazed at her lover.

Katie broke into a grin that brought a vivid sparkle to her emerald eyes. The contagion of her joy crossed the synapse between them like a summer night full of heat lightning, and soon Dean too was smiling broadly.

Dean reached over and placed her hand over Katie's where it was still firmly gripping her arm. She leaned closer and whispered, "I love you, Katie O'Malley."

The flight landed right on schedule. They had carried their bags on, so they went immediately to the curb to wait for the car rental bus. Within a few minutes, the Hertz bus arrived at the stop to pick up the waiting passengers.

"Afternoon, ladies," the driver said with a wide smile as he stepped out to load luggage. Behind Dean and Katie was a skycap pushing the wheelchair-bound woman that had been on their flight. They moved aside, allowing the driver and the skycap to assist the woman, with her luggage and canes, to enter the bus first. Katie watched with interest as the woman entered the bus. Except for the staggering steps she was taking to board, she seemed fairly nimble. From the general color of the jet black hair that was peppered with gray, and the wrinkles at the corners of her eyes and on her forehead, Katie guessed her age to be in the late sixties or early seventies, but the rest of her seemed youthful, save for the difficulty she had walking. Once the woman was settled on the bus, Katie and Dean boarded, depositing their carry-on luggage in the rack behind the driver. They took seats opposite the woman, who was now observing them through dark sunglasses.

"First time in KC?" the woman asked as the bus departed.

"No," they answered in unison.

"Ah, so you won't want any tips on the best places to stay or eat," the woman said.

Katie perked up at the woman's reference to eating. "Best places to eat?"

"Ah, so you're a food junkie, eh?"

Katie blushed and Dean chuckled. "You could say that," Katie replied. "I do enjoy a good meal." Dean's chuckle burst into a laugh and Katie poked her partner in the ribs. "Hey, you do too!"

Dean nodded, still laughing. "Yes, I do," she agreed as she suppressed her laughter.

The woman smiled. "Do you like Mexican dishes?" They both nodded. "Have you tried Patricio's on Troost Avenue?"

"No, never heard of it," Dean said as Katie shook her head.

"Well, it's a bit hard to find...the original one, that is. It's just a little hole in the wall kind of place. There's another satellite out north of KC, but it's not as good as the original. Best Mexican dishes outside of Mexico, in my opinion. You should try it."

"We may just do that if we have time," Katie replied. "Thanks for the tip."

"My name's Victoria...Victoria Delanore," she said. "I really can get around pretty well on these." She tapped her canes together. "I just let the airlines cart me around in a wheelchair so I don't miss my flights...and I get a little extra service, too." She chuckled as she extended her hand.

Katie shook it gently. "I'm Katie and this is Deanna."

The woman nodded. "Nice to meet you," she said, just as the bus pulled into the Hertz lot and parked at the office. "Perhaps we'll meet again."

The driver stepped out and assisted Victoria out of the bus, then deposited her luggage near the front door. "You can just leave it there, I'll get it on the way out," the woman said as the automatic door opened and she stepped into the rental office.

"Nice woman." Katie grabbed her bag and stepped off the bus. "Want to try that restaurant she suggested?"

"Well, she says that the food is good, and I like little off-beat places."

They entered the rental office and waited for the next available agent. Dean watched as a lot agent brought a vehicle to the curb that bore a handicapped license plate. He picked up Victoria's bag and placed it in the trunk, then entered the office and walked over to the woman as she signed the paperwork for her vehicle.

"I put your bag in the trunk, ma'am."

"Thank you."

"Are you familiar with the hand brake system in our cars?"

"Yes, I am. Thank you for asking."

"Okay, well, have a nice stay in Kansas City. The keys are in the car." He favored her with a smile and went out to collect the next rental.

Victoria picked up her paperwork and made her way out to the car, Dean's gaze following her progress.

"Dean?" Katie whispered, "We're up."

They approached the agent and gave her their reservation number, initiating the process to get their vehicle.

The ride to Crown Center took nearly an hour, but compared to the traffic in the greater Washington area, the traffic into KC was light. Kansas City International was built quite a distance north of the city proper in what was once cow pastureland. Now the area around the airport was developing into a small suburb, and the result was an increase in traffic. Kansas City itself was a lovely place, with numerous boulevards that had park-like separations between the roadways, lots of flowers, and more fountains than Paris, France. It still had its less desirable areas, especially downtown, where Reverend Lewistan's center was located, but other areas were beautifully kept and had undeniable eye appeal. Dean had opted to make reservations at the Crown Center Hotel south of downtown rather than at one of the convention hotels located in the downtown district, even though that would have been more convenient to Martha's city mission.

Dean was becoming increasingly silent as they hit the city limits, and Katie knew the impending stress of the next two days was weighing heavily on her partner. Dean had barely had a year to adjust to having her father back in her life, and many of the issues surrounding their relationship were still raw and painful, but the reconciliation had been progressing and she had enjoyed the time they had spent together.

Dean pulled the rented Mustang up to the hotel entrance and hit the trunk release before getting out. Katie joined her at the trunk and they removed their luggage.

"We'll be back for the car in about thirty minutes. Can you park it someplace close?" Dean asked as the valet handed her a ticket.

"Yes, ma'am."

Dean handed him ten dollars and followed Katie into the lobby.

Dean unlocked the door to their room and tossed the room and car keys on the desk. They unpacked and freshened up from the flight, then changed out of their traveling clothes into black slacks and short-sleeved blouses.

Katie watched as Dean silently hung up the conservative black dress she'd brought for the viewing and funeral. She moved behind her lover and slipped her arms around her, laying her head on Dean's back. "You okay, love?" Katie placed a kiss on Dean's shoulder.

"So-so." Dean picked a cat hair off of the jacket of the dress and hung the clothes on the rack. "Funerals are not my favorite thing." She shrugged and turned in Katie's arms to face her lover. "But I'm glad you're here with me. I don't think I could go through it alone. It took me weeks to recover after Mom passed. That was a really rough time. I was barely twenty-five and I had no idea how to make funeral arrangements." Dean shook her head and blew out a breath. "I was a real basket case when it was over."

"Joshua's arrangements are all taken care of, right?"

"Yes. When he told me about the cancer, I took care of everything then. I didn't want Reverend Martha to have to make those decisions, even though she offered. I'm just grateful that she agreed to put them in motion for me when the time came."

"The service is going to be at the church down the street from the shelter?"

"Yeah, that's what Martha suggested. She said the chapel in the shelter would be too small. I guess Dad accumulated a lot of friends at the shelter and in the neighborhood." Katie released her hold allowing Dean to move to the window that looked north toward the city skyline. "Martha assured me it would be a simple service. She said Dad wanted it that way."

Dean looked at her watch. "It's about time we meet Martha at the funeral home. We'll get the paperwork finalized and then get something to eat. The wake will be tomorrow night, so perhaps we can find that little Mexican restaurant tonight. What was the name of it again?"

Katie tilted her head back as she thought. "I think Victoria said it was called Patricio's, or something like that. Maybe Martha has heard of it. We can all go to dinner and maybe we can ask Martha about performing our ceremony while we're at it."

Dean picked up the two sets of keys. "C'mon. Martha is probably waiting for us."

Martha and two men were standing outside the J. & J. Jones and Family Funeral Home when Dean and Katie arrived. Martha gave Dean a hug as she stepped onto the sidewalk. "Dean, I'm so sorry you weren't able to spend more time with him."

"Me too, Martha, though I am glad we had what time we did."

Martha released Dean and took Katie into her arms, whispering into her ear, "How's she doing?"

"As well as can be expected. How are you doing?"

"I'm always saddened by the passing of a soul, but knowing that Joshua has found peace is a comfort." Martha released Katie and turned to make introductions. "This is Jeremiah Jones and Reverend Jeffery Mitchell from the Angels of Heaven church."

"Shall we go inside, folks?" Mr. Jones held open the door. As they entered, the group was met by another gentleman who looked to be Jeremiah's twin. "This is my brother John."

"Please follow me," John requested, leading the group into a spacious office.

The antithesis of the funeral home's plain exterior, the office was paneled in rich mahogany, with a large mahogany desk at one end. The far end was designed as a sitting area, with a deep blue damask-covered couch that was at least eight feet long and covered in a small floral print. Two enormous wingback side chairs faced the couch. Between the chairs was a mahogany framed side table with a beveled glass top. A box of Kleenex was sitting conveniently at the fore. A large matching mahogany coffee table was placed between the seating arrangements. It held several catalogs for caskets and flower arrangements, and a hymnal, along with more tissues.

"Please have a seat while I get the paperwork." Mr. Jones smiled politely and turned to the desk.

Reverend Martha and Katie sat on either side of Dean on the couch; Reverend Mitchell sat across from the women. When Jeremiah entered, he sat in one of the wingback chairs. "My brother John will go over the paperwork, but I want to make sure we've prepared everything for tomorrow's viewing." He looked at Katie and Dean, who were new to him. "Ms. Peterson?"

Dean lifted her hand slightly. "That would be me."

"Please accept our condolences for your loss," Jeremiah offered. "I understand that the only viewing will be tomorrow from 7:00 to 9:00 PM. Is that correct?"

"Yes."

"And the church service will be at Angels of Heaven on Monday morning?" He looked at Dean and then to Reverend Mitchell. Both acknowledged with a nod. "There will not be a graveside service?"

Reverend Mitchell shook his head. "No, only the church service. Mr. Peterson will be buried next to his wife in Lawrence, and the family will attend the interment. I believe you've taken care of the site requirements and the transportation of the casket?"

Jeremiah nodded, "Yes. We have arranged transportation to the cemetery immediately after the church service." He turned his attention back to Dean. "Reverend Martha brought over a suit for your father. Is there anything you wish to inter with the departed?"

Katie looked at Dean with a raised eyebrow and Dean reciprocated with the same, then turned her attention to Jeremiah. "No, I don't believe so," she said slowly.

"I know it seems a strange question, but often times loved ones send a keepsake along with the departed." He hesitated. "After the paperwork is taken care of, I will take you to the private viewing room where you can spend some time with your father before tomorrow."

"I don't—" Dean stopped when Martha and Katie both reached over and placed a hand on her arm. Martha leaned over and whispered in Dean's ear, and Dean nodded at Jeremiah.

"Fine," he said. "John will take you through the paperwork and finalize the legal details, death certificate and all, before you go to the viewing room."

Dean, Katie, and Reverend Martha followed Jeremiah into the private viewing room. He walked over to the casket and looked back at the women. "Please feel free to stay as long as you like. If you need me, just pull this cord." He indicated a heavy maroon cord that hung at the side of the drapery that was a backdrop for the casket, and then he quietly left the room.

"Dean, I know this is difficult for you. If you would like, Katie and I can wait outside," Martha offered quietly.

"No, please stay. I really don't know what to do now." The emotion of seeing her father in the casket was a bit overwhelming.

"You don't have to do anything, but it might be a good time for you to reflect and think about your father...the father you know now...the father you allowed back into your heart. It is a chance for you to say your goodbyes, with your family at your side." She took Katie's hand and put it into Dean's. "I'll wait outside."

Dean grasped Martha's hand and held tight. "You're family to us, too, and you were family to Dad, so please stay and say your private goodbye with us."

"Thank you, Dean. I'd like that."

The three women stood hand-in-hand before the casket, each silently saying her farewell.

Dean looked down into the casket at her father and saw a man she was just beginning to know and love. He wasn't the same man she remembered from her teen years. That man had been full of anger and the images of him beating her brother Thad to death one tragic night had slowly been replaced with the gentle, loving man that lay before her. She had forgiven her father for the rage that overcame him in his hour of darkness. She was no stranger to that emotion herself and it saddened her all the more that she would learn no more about the man she had begun to love and accept. Dean blinked back the tears that appeared as she came to grips with the fact that she was now the last of her family line. Releasing Martha and Katie's hands, she whispered a final farewell and turned away from the casket.

When the women exited the room, Jeremiah and John were waiting in the foyer with Reverend Mitchell. John stepped up first and extended his hand to Dean. "If there is anything else we can do, please call."

They shook hands, and the women and Reverend Mitchell left the funeral home. Martha grasped the minister's arm and squeezed it gently. "Thank you for coming along, Jeff."

"My pleasure, Martha. Are there any additional songs or passages you wish to have included in the service?"

Dean shook her head. "No, Reverend. I'm sure Martha has told you Dad's favorites."

"Will you want to say anything at the service?"

Katie squeezed Dean's hand and Dean replied, "No. Thank you."

"Fine." Reverend Mitchell nodded. "I'll see you on Monday morning. If you should change your mind, just let me know." He smiled and grasped Dean's hand in both of his. "Your father was a brave and gentle soul...more than you realize. I hope your memories of him will be good ones." He released her hand and turned away.

Dean's eyes followed the reverend as he retreated toward Angels of Heaven church. She wondered what his comment meant. Martha recognized the questioning expression and took Dean's arm, locking it in hers. Katie flanked Dean on the other side, taking Dean's other arm. The trio walked in silence, each with her own thoughts whirling in her head as they walked back to the shelter.

Chapter Nine
June 9

Martha pointed. "There it is!" Patricio's was sandwiched between two other non-descript buildings, with only a small sign above the one tiny front window. "Park anywhere you can find a spot," she directed as Dean slowed the car.

"There's one." Katie pointed to a space across the street. "Think you can do a U-turn without getting a ticket?"

Dean was already checking the traffic in front of them, as well as glancing in the rearview mirror. "Do birds fly?" she said with a grin as she pulled the steering wheel hard to the left. The vehicle was soon neatly parked in the spot Katie had indicated. As they got out of the car, Dean stepped between Katie and Martha and slipped her arms around their shoulders. "Sure glad you were with us, Martha. We never would have seen that sign."

"Sure you would. It just would have taken a few trips up and down the avenue before you did," Martha joked.

Katie slipped away from them and held open the door to the restaurant. She was greeted by the aroma of Mexican food and her stomach immediately growled.

"Guess we'd better get a seat quick, eh?" Dean teased.

"The sooner the better," Katie agreed.

Luckily, although there were only about twenty tables in the entire restaurant, the early dinner crowd was just finishing up and there were several open tables. Most were set for four, though a couple of larger tables near the front of the establishment were set for eight.

The waitress greeted them with a smile and led them to a small table near the back of the small room, then handed each of them a menu. "Can I get you something from the bar?"

Katie nodded. "I'll have a margarita...hold the salt."

"Frozen or regular?"

"Frozen."

She turned to Martha. "And for you?"

"Make mine a Dos Equis."

"Bottle or tap?" the waitress asked.

"Tap."

When the hostess looked at Dean, Dean pointed at Martha. "I'll have the same."

Before the waitress left, she placed a basket of tortilla chips and two kinds of salsa on the table. "The green salsa is very hot and the red is more on the mild side. I'll be right back with your drinks."

As soon as the waitress turned away, Katie dug into the chips and scooped up some of the green salsa.

"You might want to..." Martha cautioned as Katie slid the overloaded chip into her mouth, "...try a small bite first."

Dean laughed and nudged Martha's arm. "Not a problem, Martha. She loves it hot."

Munching on the salsa-laden chip, Katie rolled her eyes in pleasure and emitted sounds of approval. She finally swallowed, and scooped up another chip. "This is awesome salsa. Do they sell it?"

"I guess we could ask." Martha dipped some of the red salsa onto a chip.

Dean tasted the green salsa. "Yep, they should sell it."

By the time the waitress returned with their drinks, most of the chips and salsa had been devoured, which drew a warm smile. "Guess you need more chips and salsa?"

"You guess right," Katie said as she scooped up the last of the green mix. "Do you guys sell this stuff? It's awesome."

"No, unfortunately, we don't."

"Too bad," Dean said with a grin. "You could make a bundle selling it to just us."

The waitress laughed. "You don't know how many times we're told that."

"Maybe the owner would consider it," Katie suggested hopefully.

"Nope. He won't budge. It's an old family recipe and he won't let it go. Besides, it keeps the customers coming back. Now, are you ready to order?"

Katie slid her chair back from the table and groaned. "Ugh, I shouldn't have eaten all that!"

"I tried to warn you that dish was enough for two," Martha said in mock admonition.

"My eyes are always bigger than my stomach, but I still manage to pack it all in." Katie giggled as she patted her full stomach.

"So, there's no room in there for dessert." Dean took Martha's hand. "Guess it'll be just you and me." She looked back at Katie, knowing Katie would rise to the occasion and order something anyway. "Or, we could split something." As she released Martha's hand, she noted that Martha was beaming joyfully, apparently having a good time.

"You're on. What'll we have?"

When the waitress returned to the table with the dessert menu, they placed three orders for flan and churros. "Good choice," the woman said as she collected the menus. "It'll be out in a few minutes."

"Take your time," Katie said to the back of the retreating waitress, earning laughs from her tablemates.

After a short silence, Dean turned to Martha. "Martha, there's a favor we'd like to ask of you."

Martha smiled and took Dean's hand. "I'd love to," she answered before the question could be asked. "Here, or back in Virginia?"

"How do you do that?" Katie asked as she pulled her chair closer to the table.

"When Dean took my hand a minute ago, I could 'feel' the question swirling in her mind. Sometimes my gift is a blessing and sometimes it's a curse. I never know when I'll pick up on something by touching someone, but it's usually when the emotion is strong." She reached out for their hands. "I'm so glad you two are making this commitment. From the moment I first met you, I was overwhelmed by the force of your love for each other. It would be a terrible travesty not to acknowledge this love in a lifelong bonding." She smiled at them and gently squeezed their hands. "So, when and where? Just let me know and I'll be there!"

Katie's eyes teared and Dean's were sparkling with a bit more moisture than usual. "Thank you, Martha. I'm...we're so glad to include you in our little family," Dean said quietly.

"I'm the one who is happy to be a part of your family." Martha squeezed their hands once more before releasing them. "So, have you set a date?"

"Not a firm date," Katie said as she looked over at Dean. "We're looking at early to mid September. Virginia is lovely that time of year."

"Okay. September it is. That would actually be perfect for me. I usually have a meeting in Washington for our shelter's annual grant review at that time."

"Perfect," Katie said as the dessert arrived.

"How do I look?" Dean asked as she viewed herself in the full-length mirror, tugging on the hem of the short-waisted jacket that accessorized the sleeveless black dress.

Katie walked up alongside and gazed at the image in the mirror. "You look absolutely beautiful, love."

Dean smiled and turned to face Katie. "You'd say that if I was standing here naked as a jay bird."

"Oh, no. If you were standing here naked, I'd say...well, I probably wouldn't say anything, because I'd be too busy ravishing your body." Katie bumped Dean with her hip. "Seriously, you look great. Not too sexy, not too austere, but very...respectful."

"Respectful, huh?" Dean looked back at her image in the mirror. "Guess that'll do." She checked her watch. "We'd better get going. We promised Martha we'd pick her up by six." Dean tugged on the jacket hem and mumbled, "I just can't seem to get used to these short jacket styles."

"With your height, love, it looks terrific. Trust me."

Dean shrugged and picked up her small purse and car keys. She stopped at the door and turned to face Katie. "Katie, thank you for being here with me. I don't know how I would have done this alone."

Katie reached up and gently stroked Dean's cheek. "Sweetheart, I would never have let you do this alone. That's what family is all about."

Dean turned to kiss Katie's palm, closing her eyes. "You and I are the only family either one of us has left," Dean whispered as she opened her eyes. Her eyes looked like small ocean pools as they filled with a glaze of tears.

"That's true, love, but we're also blessed with a lot of friends who love and care for us." The assurance brought a small smile to her lover's face.

"You can always find the silver lining," Dean said as she kissed Katie's palm again. "C'mon. We'd better get going."

Another group of mourners entered the funeral home just as a large group left. They looked like most of the other folks who had come to pay their respects to Joshua Peterson. Most of the men were unshaven but clean; the women were covered in heavy makeup that failed to mask the lines and wrinkles on their faces. They all looked as if they had been beaten down by life at one time or another. Their attitudes were softer than their harsh appearances portrayed. Their clothing, although well worn and more than a few years out of fashion, was clean and neat, some even properly ironed. As they entered, each person stopped to exchange a few words with Reverend Martha, who was standing at the foot of the coffin, and each seemed surprised as Martha indicated Dean and Katie standing at the head of the casket. Each passed in review, stopping one by one to pay their respects to the two women. When they came to Dean, their faces were streaked with tears and they could barely mumble a word or two of condolence. Every one, though, told about the compassion and love that Joshua had shared with them. How his personal sorrow and shame helped to bring them through the darkest times of their lives and how much he would be missed. Some took a seat in the chairs provided, talking softly in small groups, but most just came and went, passing quietly into the warm summer evening, the night calling them elsewhere.

By 2100, most of the mourners had left. Only a few couples were still sitting near the back of the room.

"Looks like we're near the end of the line," Katie said, scanning the room. "Your dad sure had a lot of respect in this neighborhood." Dean nodded and shifted a bit.

A young woman entered, dressed in the summer uniform of an Army private. She was about Katie's height and had beautiful dark skin. Her hair was black as night and had a silken sheen.

Katie noticed her first and bumped Dean's elbow. "Anyone you know?" she said, indicating the newcomer with a subtle inclination of her head.

Dean shook her head slightly and watched as the young woman approached Reverend Martha and gave her an ardent hug rather than a handshake. They spoke softly for a minute, with the woman turning quickly to look at Dean then back to Martha. At the coffin, she stood looking down at Joshua a lot longer than most. She placed two fingers on her lips and transferred them to his hand in a final gesture, then removed a tissue from her pocket and wiped her eyes before moving away.

When she stood before Dean, she stopped and stood at attention but refrained from saluting, offering her hand instead. "Colonel, please accept my sincere sympathy for your loss. Your father was a very good man and I will miss him. He...he saved my life, and in a way, so did you."

Dean looked at the woman's nameplate and accepted the proffered hand, an eyebrow raised. "Thank you, Private Hawadi." She looked around the room. "It seems many people will miss him." She released the private's hand. "Do I know you?" she asked, wondering why the young woman had addressed her by her military title.

"No, ma'am, we have never met, but I did see you once at Fort Belvoir, and...I feel like I know you. Your father, you see... Well, let me start from the beginning." She looked at Dean, tears welling.

Dean looked around the room and saw no one else in line. "Why don't we sit down and you can tell us." She introduced Katie and the threesome moved to the side of the room where a small coffee table was surrounded by four stuffed chairs. Dean and Katie sat and waited for the woman to begin her story.

Private Hawadi cleared her throat. "If your father had not been there to help me, I would probably be dead by now. My boyfriend was pretty abusive, and I was young... Well, only a little younger than I am now." She laughed, blushing, "I had a hard time adjusting to the freedoms of this country. I had nowhere to go after my mother died, no safe place to escape to." She paused and looked around, almost embarrassed.

"But that is another story. Anyway, I met your father on the street behind the convention center. Frank...my boyfriend...was hitting me, and your dad just stepped right between us and took the next punch. It landed on Joshua's upheld Bible. When Frank saw the Bible, he went crazy. He started to hit him harder, but your father stayed between me and Frank...never flinching. He was so brave." The young woman looked back toward the casket and the frail corpse lying within. Returning her gaze to the two women, she continued. "Finally a police officer saw what was happening and Frank ran off like the coward he is. When the officer saw the bruises and cuts on your father's face, he called for an ambulance. I was going to sneak away then, too, when the policeman started talking to your father, but your father kept watching me. I noticed that he had dropped his Bible during the attack and when I picked it up, a newspaper clipping with your picture fell out. I stood there, holding that clipping...just staring at it. The next thing I knew, your father had me by the elbow and he brought me over to Reverend Martha's shelter."

As if on cue, Reverend Martha joined the group and sat in the empty chair. "I see you've met Saleeda," she said with a smile. "How long will you be in town, Sally?"

"Just today and tomorrow, Reverend. I have to leave right after the service."

"Oh, that's too bad. I was hoping you would be able to stay with us a little longer." Reverend Martha turned to Dean. "Saleeda just finished training for her job."

Saleeda said proudly, "I have been assigned to Fort Belvoir as an interpreter for the Intelligence Branch. I just started two weeks ago, that's why I don't have the leave to stay longer."

"Sally...that's Joshua's nickname for her...is Joshua's best work," Martha said with a gleam in her eye, causing Saleeda to blush. She reached over and took the woman's hand and gave it a gentle squeeze. "And, in a way, it's all because of you," she said to Dean.

Dean raised an eyebrow in question. "Me?"

"Yes," Saleeda interjected. "Your father was very proud of you. Not only of what you accomplished in your career, but the person you have become." She lowered her voice in an attempt to imitate Joshua's deep voice, "'Sally, you do not have to depend on anyone except yourself. You are an American citizen now, and no one can make you do anything you do not want to do. Now, take my Deanna, for example...' And then he would go off on how intelligent and independent you are, and how you excelled and got promoted through the ranks, and on and on."

Dean was becoming very uncomfortable with the young private's enthusiasm and tried to deflect the conversation. "I think my father over-rated me a bit."

"Oh, no, Colonel. He admired everything you had become!"

What I had become? Dean reflected, as she remembered some of her early assignments. *The Army encouraged me to use my rage to their advantage for covert ops.* She turned away from the woman, not wanting her to see that truth in her face — the truth about the hard assignments she had completed, the death she had dealt with her own hands. She knew that if her father had truly known the reason for her early military successes, he probably would not have been so proud of her. She wished she could have told him everything before he died, but even now, those assignments were not to be disclosed to anyone. *But I told Katie...every gruesome detail...and Katie still accepted me, loved me. Why couldn't I tell Dad? Was I just too ashamed?*

Katie felt Dean's discomfort and tried to change the direction of the conversation. "So, you weren't born in this country?" she asked, pulling the young woman's gaze in her direction.

"No, we...my mother and I...came to this country ten years ago...from Iraq. I was only ten at the time. Father sent us away...just before he was killed."

"Killed? What happened?" Katie asked, absorbed by the woman's story.

"My father was a doctor, a very good man. He would treat anyone who came to his clinic, no matter what religion they followed or who they supported politically. Unfortunately, one day he treated a cleric that was known for denouncing Saddam and was found out. He feared for our lives, so he made arrangements with a Saudi cousin to sneak us all out. We had to do it one at a time, so as not to draw suspicion. I was the first to leave, and then Mother. Once he knew we were safe, Father was to follow, but he never arrived. Ahmed, our cousin, found out that as he left the clinic, Father was stopped and led away. We learned later that he was shot by a firing squad in the town square." Tears welled in the woman's eyes and she pulled a tissue from the box on the coffee table.

"I'm so sorry, Saleeda," Katie noted that Dean was listening intently to Saleeda's story.

Saleeda inhaled deeply and shrugged. "It has been over ten years and it still gets me upset." She tossed the wadded tissue into the wastebasket. "It took us another eighteen months before we found asylum here in the United States. A distant uncle on my mother's side of the family sponsored us to come here. They were very strict, and being female and young, I had to be submissive to all males...even my cousins. They were very Old World in their ways, and extremely cruel to my mother and me. The toll on Mother was great and she died three years ago. That's when things got really difficult for me. When I met Frank in school, I thought I was in love. Frank wasn't Iraqi, and my sponsor family forbade me to see him and threatened to send me back to Iraq. So, Frank talked me into running away with him and we wound up here in Kansas City. When our little bit of money ran out, Frank changed. He got really hateful and started to take it out on me. I guess my upbringing, and the thought that I was in love with Frank kept me from fighting back when he hit me." She looked at Dean. "Your father...he was very kind to me." She looked at Reverend Martha. "And you too, Reverend."

Martha smiled and picked up the story. "When Saleeda came to the shelter, she was pretty scared. She had no one to turn to and was afraid her sponsor family would send her back to Iraq, where she would be considered a criminal and more than likely shot like her father was. So, since she was eighteen, we took her in. Joshua helped her study for her American citizenship, and we all helped her learn that in America, she did not have to be submissive to anyone. It took a while to get that point across," Martha said with a laugh.

"Yes, it did," Saleeda agreed, joining in Martha's laughter. "But once I figured it out..."

"...there was no stopping her!" Martha completed.

"I had heard so much about you, Colonel, that I decided that I wanted to follow in your footsteps and learn to be more independent and serve my new country like you do. So, I entered the Army last year, and here I am."

"Do you like it so far?" Katie asked.

"Oh yes. I was the best in my class at basic training, and in my MOS class, too. I really like the work at Fort Belvoir; everyone has treated me like a person and not a woman." She took in the surprised look on Katie's face and corrected herself. "What I mean is that I am a part of a team and valued as a member of it. I am not just a woman but a *valued* woman. Does that make better sense?"

"I see what you mean. Yes, I feel the same about my job," Katie agreed. "But, just so you don't think this country is perfect, there are pockets of folks out there who would still like to see women as wives and mothers who are reliant on a man, and not strong, intelligent women who can rely on themselves."

"Oh, I have run into a few of those already," Saleeda said with a chuckle.

"The military is still a class system, Saleeda, so you need to be careful about exerting your newly found spirit," Dean said in a cautionary tone.

"Yes, ma'am," the private answered sharply. "I understand the chain of command and know how to follow orders. I am just not going to let myself fall into a passive role in my private life ever again, or be degraded just because I am a woman." Saleeda checked her watch. "I guess I had better go. Thank you for talking to me, Colonel. Again, I am sorry for your loss." She stood to leave and Martha stood also. The two embraced for a long moment before releasing one another.

"I'll see you back at the shelter," Martha said as she released the young woman.

Saleeda nodded and turned to Dean and Katie. "Good night, ma'am...Ms. O'Malley." The women watched as she walked away, her self-confidence showing in each step she took.

Martha sat back down with a sigh. "I really miss her," she said, wiping a tear from her eye. "She's turning into quite a capable young woman."

"Thanks to you and Father," Dean interjected, earning a smile and a pat on the knee from Martha.

"Well, I'll go get my jacket and we can leave." Martha stood and looked around the room. "Looks like we're the last ones here."

"I'll get the car," Dean said, digging the keys from her pocketbook as she stood. "Meet you out front."

Katie got up from her chair and touched Dean's arm, "I'll be right with you. I need to make a stop in the ladies room. I'll meet you two in the car."

Three minutes later, Katie exited the ladies room and noticed a lone woman standing at Joshua's casket; she could hear the woman weeping softly. "Are you all right, ma'am?" Katie called quietly.

The woman didn't turn her head, but nodded in response. Katie looked at the black overcoat and large brimmed black hat. She thought it was odd that the woman was wearing the overcoat on such a hot evening, but figured that perhaps it was the only black attire she had.

"Would you like me to stay with you for a while?" she asked in concern.

Still not turning, the woman shook her head. "No, I'll be fine. You run along; you've probably had a long evening."

"Yes, it has been long," Katie replied. "But I could stay a bit with you, if you like."

Jeremiah Jones entered the room and walked over to Katie. "I'll stay with her. Go and get a good night's sleep and I'll see you in the morning."

Katie nodded and walked to the door, trying to discern why the woman's voice had sounded vaguely familiar.

Chapter Eleven
June 11

Katie's arm snaked out from under the covers and explored the other side of the bed, looking for its mate on her lover's body. Eyes still closed, the hand searched in vain, finding only rumpled sheets that had been vacated by the occupant, the warmth already replaced by the cold, air conditioned air. One eye opened and searched the room, like an emerald beacon looking for lost travelers. The room was dimly lit, with only tiny shafts of sunlight trying to slip past the edges of the heavy curtains. Katie rolled onto her side, searching for her absent partner.

"Dean?" she called softly, hearing only the hum of the air conditioner as she listened for a response. "Hon?" she tried, with the same result. She got up and opened the door to the bathroom and found it, too, was empty. She stopped to pull on the terrycloth bathrobe before returning to the bedroom. On the desk, she found a sheet of hotel paper laid prominently in the center. She clicked the light on and picked up the note.

Couldn't sleep so I went for a run. I'll bring back coffee.

"Okay, mystery solved," Katie said to the empty room. She set the note back on the desk and returned to the bathroom, opening the shower door and turning the shower on to warm up the water. She slipped off the robe, closed the bathroom door, and stepped into the shower.

Finished with her morning cleansing ritual, Katie was standing under the pulsating water, enjoying the massage mode on the showerhead, when she heard the room door close and the room key hit the desk. "I'm in here. Want to join me?" Katie called as the cooler air from the bedroom wafted in when Dean opened the bathroom door.

"Love to," Dean answered, closing the door and stripping out of her soggy running clothes. She quickly entered the shower and ducked her head under the spray.

"Have a nice run?" Katie asked as she re-lathered the nylon puff.

"Not bad. There are some moderate hills around here, so it made the run more interesting."

"I'd have gone with you if you had woken me." Katie turned Dean and started to scrub her back.

"I know you would have." Dean allowed Katie to work her way around to her front side. "But you looked like you were enjoying your sleep. Besides, it was pretty early and I did a little extra mileage today."

"Is something bothering you?" Katie asked as she rinsed the puff.

"No...yes...no, not really."

An eyebrow shot up over an emerald eye and Katie looked deep into Dean's eyes. "So, which is it — yes, no, or not really?"

Dean just shook her head and shrugged. "I don't know. I just couldn't sleep."

"And?" Katie gestured for Dean to continue.

"And...I was thinking about how Saleeda said Dad was so proud of me." Dean lowered her head under the shower, getting her hair completely wet. She picked up the shampoo and rubbed some into her hair before continuing. "I got to thinking that I never told him about all the ruthless stuff I did; he only knew about the good things that could be put in print." She rinsed her hair and added more shampoo for a second wash. "Dad would never have been proud of those things—"

"Love, are you proud of what your dad became?"

Dean stopped washing her hair and looked at Katie. "Well...yes. He did some really good things here. Last night attested to that. All those people he helped..."

"But, he also did a really horrific thing...something that you aren't proud of, right?"

Dean sighed and wrapped her arms around Katie. "Yes. But I knew what he did, and he never knew what I did."

"It doesn't matter, love. The outcome for both of you is the same. Hell, we've all done things we're not proud of, but we've also done a lot more that we can be proud of." Katie reached up and wiped soap from Dean's face and kissed her. "He loved you and was proud of the woman you became, just like you loved him and are proud of what he's accomplished."

"You..." Dean said, kissing Katie softly, "...are my proudest accomplishment."

"Accomplishment?" Katie said with a wary look. "Hmmm, I think you can do better than that."

Dean laughed and wrapped her arms tightly around her lover. "Supposing I show you?"

"That'll do for starters." Their lips met and hands began a familiar dance on curves and breasts and...

"Do we have time to grab a bite to eat?" Katie asked as she slipped into her black heels.

Dean looked at the clock on the nightstand. "I think we can squeeze in the breakfast buffet. We still have an hour before we have to be at the funeral home." She held open the room door and followed Katie out.

"So, what did you find in Saleeda's file?" Katie asked as they walked down the hall to the elevator.

Dean raised an eyebrow, then punched the down button for the elevator. "She's pretty smart. Top of the class in her MOS training, just like she said." The elevator arrived and they entered. Katie pushed the lobby button and the doors closed silently.

"Think she'll do well?"

"The Army will always provide opportunity for advancement if you're good at what you do. Only time will tell if she has the will to stick to it."

The doors opened at the lobby and they went into the restaurant, where they were seated near the front. A waiter brought over the coffee pot and two menus.

"Coffee, ladies?" he asked as he set the menus down.

"Yes," Katie replied and he turned over her cup and poured, then filled Dean's cup, which she had already turned up.

"We'll just do the breakfast buffet," Dean said as she handed back the menus. "And we'll need the check quickly."

The waiter nodded. "Help yourself to the buffet, ladies. The check will be here when you return."

They got up and made the rounds, returning to the table with plates of breakfast items. Katie looked longingly at Dean's bowl of biscuits and gravy with a side of cheese grits, bacon, and wheat toast, then back at her plate of fruit and bowl of oatmeal.

"Kinda heavy on the breakfast?" Katie said as she spooned up some oatmeal.

"Well, I did get up and run this morning," Dean said with a devilish grin. "Pays off when you want to splurge now and then."

"Yeah...just have to kick myself in the butt for being a lazy bum." Katie stabbed a piece of fruit and popped it into her mouth.

They finished their meal in silence, each contemplating the day to come. Katie thought about her parents' funeral which had taken place many years earlier, reliving the sorrow and pain of that day. She had been fairly young at the time but the hurt was still there, although not as sharp, and she still missed her parents.

As Dean signed the check and added their room number, Katie reached out and touched Dean's hand. "You know, it'll get easier with time. There's not a day that goes by that I don't think about my parents, but the sorrow is bearable now."

Dean placed her hand on top of Katie's. "Yes, that's what I remember from Mom's passing. I wasn't there when she died; I was on assignment somewhere on the other side of the world, but it hurt...still does, but as you said, it's bearable." She checked her watch. "C'mon, we'd better get going."

Angels of Heaven church was small, as churches go, more like a large chapel than a church. There were only ten rows of pews on each side of the main aisle and every seat was taken, with several people standing in the back and along the smaller aisles on the sides. The front pew on the right was empty, reserved for Dean, Katie, and Reverend Martha. They followed the casket in and took their seats, nodding to Saleeda who was sitting in the pew immediately behind them. Reverend Mitchell stood in front of the altar, taking his cue to start when they sat down.

"My dear friends...we gather here today to say goodbye to Joshua Peterson, a man who was a sinner and a man who was devout. Many of you knew Joshua the pious man, few knew Joshua the sinner. But like all men on this earth, we all have our weaknesses..."

Katie reached over and held Dean's hand and they settled in for the short service that Reverend Mitchell had promised. The day was supposed to become a very hot one and the temperature inside the church rose quickly. The effects of the sweltering temperature outside plus too many bodies filling the small space were not helped by the lack of air-conditioning. It became very hot and sticky in a brief time.

As Katie listened to Reverend Mitchell, she looked around the small church at the abundance of mourners. She noted that everyone in the room was beginning to perspire, and hankies were being used for mopping brows as much as mopping tears. As she turned back toward the pulpit, she thought she saw the woman from the previous night sitting in the rear of the church on the far end of the last pew. She was still in her black overcoat and large brimmed hat, which now bore a black veil across the front, obscuring the wearer's face. Facing forward, she hoped the woman would not suffer heat stroke. She looked over at Reverend Martha, who was also perspiring freely, then at Dean, who seemed amazingly oblivious to the heat. When she looked back up at Reverend Mitchell, she noticed that he too was perspiring and seemed to quicken his eulogy to bring the service to an end.

"...may the good Lord have mercy on your soul." Reverend Mitchell looked out at the crowd. "Thank you all for coming. I know Joshua's daughter appreciates your prayers for her father."

The pallbearers took the casket down the aisle and out to the waiting hearse. Dean, Katie, and Martha followed, and then the rest of the mourners exited.

Dean turned to Martha. "I can see why Reverend Mitchell didn't mind the request for a short service." She unbuttoned her jacket and slipped it off.

"He's been trying to raise enough money to air condition the building. Unfortunately, every time he thinks he's got enough to do it, something else gives out. This winter it was the boiler."

"How much would it take to do the job?" Katie asked as she pulled out her sunglasses.

"He's short ten thousand dollars."

Katie raised an eyebrow. "That's all?"

Martha took her hand and motioned to their surroundings. "That's a lot for this area."

Katie nodded. "Ah...well, I'll see what I can do to help." Katie's parents had left her with a very good portfolio of stocks and a sizeable bank account. She would never have needed to work a day in her life, but her calling to work for the DEA was stronger than her desire to live like a millionaire, so she often used her money to help others. Helping Reverend Mitchell achieve his goal of air conditioning the church would be another one.

As they waited for the casket to be loaded into the hearse, several of the people coming out of the little church came by to offer their condolences. The last person to stop was Saleeda. She was dressed in her uniform, ready for her military flight back to Virginia. As Dean spoke with the private, Katie watched the crowd exit, looking for the woman in the overcoat and hoping she had not collapsed. The woman was nowhere to be seen.

With the hearse loaded, the women walked to the car for the family where Mr. Jones stood holding the door open for them. They got in, glad to be seated in air conditioning.

"Martha, did you see the woman in the veiled black hat in the back of the church?"

Martha thought for a minute. "No, I don't recall anyone like that. Why?"

"No reason. I saw her last night on my way out of the funeral home. She had on the same black overcoat and hat. I just thought it was unusual, considering the heat today and especially given the heat inside the church."

The vehicles pulled away from the curb and Katie looked back, hoping to catch a glimpse of the woman. As they turned the corner, a woman emerged and Katie barely saw her as more than a dark blur, but sunlight glinted off something silver the woman held in her hand.

Mr. Jones lowered the clear window between the driver and rear compartment of the limo and turned slightly, eyeing the occupants through the rearview mirror. "There's water in the bottles and glasses back there. Please help yourself. The ride to the cemetery will take about forty minutes." He turned back to focus on the highway and returned the privacy window to the up position, alternating his watchful eye between the road and the rearview mirror.

The silence in the back of the vehicle loomed heavy as the miles clicked by. Dean continued to gaze out the window, seemingly content to say nothing. Martha looked over at Katie, who was holding Dean's hand, gently brushing her thumb over the scarred knuckles. Martha could sense the tension in Dean and decided to break the silence. "How long has it been since you last visited the cemetery?"

Dean continued to look out the window at the passing scenery, a long silence hanging in the air. "I haven't been there since the first time...when I got back from my overseas assignment to bury Mom."

"Ohh, I...I'm sorry, I didn't mean to..." Martha leaned forward and touched Dean's knee. That simple contact initiated a sudden wave of nausea that came rushing up from her depths, causing her to drop back into her seat.

Katie released Dean's hand and moved forward, grabbing a water bottle, quickly twisting off the cap and offering it to Martha. "Are you okay? Do you need the air conditioning turned up?"

"No...no, I'll be fine." She took the bottle from Katie and looked over at Dean, who was watching her with a knowing look.

Dean lowered her head and inhaled slowly, and exhaled just as slowly as though purging herself of bad air. When she inhaled again, she lifted her head and nodded almost imperceptibly. "I'm sorry, Martha."

"No, Dean. I should have thought first, but sometimes I just do first and think later." She grimaced, taking a swallow of the cool water.

Katie caught up with the conversation and looked at her partner. "Anything I can do for you, love?"

"Sure," Dean said softly. "You can hold my hand some more."

Katie smiled and picked up Dean's hand, bringing it to her lips and placing a soft kiss on the knuckles. "Your wish is my command."

Martha caught the sparkle off the sapphire and diamond ring on Katie's hand and changed the subject to a lighter one. "So, September is the big month?"

"Yes, September," Katie replied, relieved to be thinking about something happier.

"Ah, yes...early in September, right?" Martha smiled as she watched Katie and Dean gazing affectionately at each other. "And will it be a large gathering?"

Dean shook her head. "No, just a few close friends."

"We're going to keep it simple," Katie added.

"At the house or somewhere else?" Martha asked, still trying to keep the conversation light.

"At the house," Dean responded, eyeing Katie for confirmation and getting a smile in answer. "It's large enough for what we need."

"You said you would be in Washington in September. Do you know when?" Katie pulled her PDA from her purse.

"My grant meeting starts on September third and runs until the fifth, so the weekend before or the weekend after would be ideal for me. Would either of those dates work for you?"

Katie turned on her PDA and brought up her September calendar, showing it to Dean. "Honey, what do you think?"

"Well, since you end your review class the weekend before Labor Day and don't have to start training the next group until September twenty-fifth, I say we go for the ninth or tenth and then maybe take a little trip for the next few days...or even a week."

"Only one week?" Katie said with a faux pout, then broke into a smile when Dean grinned broadly, shaking her head.

"You are a spoiled brat, you know that?" Dean put her arm around Katie and gave her a hug, then added a tender kiss on her cheek.

Katie reached up and held Dean's face in place as she leaned in and returned the kiss. She didn't linger there, just wanting to share a simple gesture of love and devotion with her partner.

The action did not go unnoticed by Martha...or Jeremiah Jones.

The rural cemetery outside of Lawrence, Kansas was set on rolling acreage of neatly mowed land with an ample population of deciduous and coniferous trees, flowering shrubs, and shady benches for communing with departed loved ones. When they passed through the wrought iron gates, Dean noted a few empty cars parked about. Most of the owners of those empty vehicles were visiting gravesites, while a few seemed to be walking the grounds, perhaps in search of tombstones lost through time. One couple was using the grounds as a quiet place to walk their dog, where they could dismiss the fear of speeding vehicles and concentrate on the beauty of this final resting place.

Driven by John Jones, the hearse slowly traversed the small lane, eventually pulling over next to a majestic weeping willow tree with boughs reaching down to the grass. A group of grounds workers waiting in the shade of the willow came forward when the vehicle stopped. They helped unload the casket and carried it to the gravesite they had prepared. Jeremiah's vehicle pulled up and parked behind the hearse. He exited and held open the door for the three women, then led them to the gravesite where three chairs were waiting for them. As Reverend Martha said a few prayers, Dean watched the cemetery crew lower Joshua Peterson into his earthly resting place next to his beloved wife.

As she listened to Martha's soft intonations, Katie focused on the headstone. It was a simple stone of gray marble with the Peterson family name in bold at the top. No fancy angels or embellishments, just the vital statistics of birth and death in weathered chisel strokes under the name of "Christine Deanna, Beloved Wife" and freshly chiseled death statistics under the "Joshua Thaddeus, Devoted Husband" inscription. Katie looked at the next gravestone and read the name of the individual occupying that plot. The first name had both birth and death statistics in worn stokes, but the second only had the birth listed. She glanced up to read "Thaddeus John, Beloved Son" and inhaled sharply at seeing her lover's name inscribed above "Beloved Daughter".

At the sound of the sharp intake of breath, Dean looked over at Katie and followed her gaze to the adjoining tombstone and realized the cause of the reaction. She reached over and took Katie's hand, squeezing it gently to reassure her that she was still among the living and brought Katie's attention back to her. "Sorry, love," she whispered. "I completely forgot about that."

Katie nodded and whispered back, "It just took me by surprise." She closed her eyes for a long moment before returning her gaze to their surroundings. Without relinquishing Dean's grasp, her eyes continued to sweep the cemetery while Martha completed a short prayer she recognized from her childhood. In the distance, Katie caught the glint of sunlight that reflected off of a shiny object held by a figure standing next to a group of gravestones on a far hill. The person was too far away for Katie to get a good look, but she definitely recognized the large brimmed hat as it flopped gently in the breeze.

"Hmm." Katie squinted to get a better look.

"What?" Dean asked quietly.

"I think it's that woman again...the one I saw in the back of the church."

As Dean followed Katie's gaze, the lone figure turned and moved away, slipping over the crest of the small hill and out of their line of sight.

When Martha finished, she took Dean's hand and brought her attention back to the graveside. She sat quietly, allowing Dean to take the time she needed to come to terms with the loss of her father. As they sat there, lost in their memories of Joshua, Martha was relieved to feel a sense of calm closure in Dean's thoughts and knew that the past had finally been laid to rest and that Dean was at peace with her father. Dean released her grip on Martha's hand, and Martha stood to leave. Dean whispered a good-bye to her parents. Still holding Katie's hand, her free hand brushed a tear from her eye.

"I guess it's time to go," Dean stated as she stood and started to move away. She stopped for one last look at her brother's grave, smiled a final homage, then turned and walked away.

Katie kept to her side. Releasing their handclasp, she slid her arm into the crook of Dean's elbow and they all walked back to the waiting limousine. On the other side of the hill, a car with handicapped license plates eased away from the curb and slowly passed through the wrought iron gates of the cemetery, pausing for traffic to thin. The driver pulled off her sunglasses and looked in the rearview mirror. The eyes staring back in the mirror were a startling sapphire blue.

"Are you sure you can't stay another day or two?" Martha asked as Dean packed the few belongings of her father's that she wanted to keep.

"I wish I could, Martha, but there's a lot of stuff going on right now that I really need to keep on top of." Dean put the final piece into her carry-on bag.

"I need to get ready for the next training session, too." Katie walked over to Martha. Dean joined her and they took turns giving Martha a goodbye hug.

"We'll be in touch," Dean said as she released the reverend.

"Yeah," Katie chimed in. "Before you know it, September will be here!"

"Oh, I hope not," Martha chuckled. "I'm one of those folks who really enjoys summer, so I hope it goes by slowly."

"You'll keep working on Pedro for us, right?" Katie asked as she walked arm-in-arm with Martha.

"I sure will. If he won't sell that salsa, maybe I can figure out what's in it."

They walked out of the building and across the parking lot to where their rental car was parked. Dean placed the carry-on bag into the trunk with the other suitcase. Katie released Martha's arm and walked around the car to the passenger side, opening the door and sliding into the seat. Dean opened her car door and slid behind the wheel, gently closing the door behind her. She turned on the ignition and pushed the switch to roll down the window. "Thank you, Martha...for everything."

Martha reached her hand in, gently cupping Dean's cheek. "You're welcome, Deanna." She smiled, despite the tears that welled in her eyes. She closed her eyes to fight back the tears, and suddenly a cold chill ran up her hand and pierced her heart. Opening them quickly, she looked deep into Dean's sapphire eyes, her mind wondering what message was behind that chill. "You two take care, and please, keep safe." She drew back her hand and wiped away a tear that had escaped, then stepped back onto the sidewalk.

"We will, Martha. See you in September." Dean smiled and waved as she pulled away from the curb.

They drove to the airport in relative silence, each reflecting on the events of the past two days. As they neared the terminal, Katie looked over at Dean, who seemed to be much more relaxed than she had been since they'd arrived. Reaching over, she laid her hand on Dean's thigh, giving it a gentle squeeze before returning her gaze to the passing scenery.

"Thanks again for being there for me," Dean said softly.

"I wouldn't have wanted to be anywhere else."

Dean reached down and took Katie's hand, lifting it to her lips and placing a soft kiss on the palm. No more needed to be said as they pulled off the interstate and followed the car rental return signs to their destination. They stopped at one of the several gas stations to fill the tank first, then drove the short distance to the lot and pulled in, parking the car in the return lane. Katie had already taken the rental form from the glove box and a pen from her backpack. She marked down the mileage on the form, then handed it to Dean.

"Why don't you take our backpacks and get in line," Katie said. "I'll get the rest of the luggage out of the trunk."

Dean nodded and punched the trunk release. By the time Katie removed the two carry-on pieces and walked over to the office, Dean was nearly finished with the check-in process. Katie waited outside by the transport van while the driver placed the two pieces of luggage inside. The sun was bright in a cloudless sky and a warm breeze blew through her hair. Katie looked around the area, noting the rolling hills in the distance. There was still a lot of farmland surrounding the area, and she could see a herd of Angus cattle ambling toward a huge roll of hay that had just been dropped off by a farmer on his tractor.

"Think you could handle being a cattle rancher?" Dean asked as she watched Katie study the scene before her.

"Well, it sure would be a lot simpler than the work we do now; a lot more physical, though. Get up, feed the cattle, fix some fences, make sure the water troughs are full, drop off more hay and feed." She sighed. "I'm sure they have their crises too, but..."

Dean watched the rancher move on to the next drop site. "When I was a kid, I wanted to raise horses...maybe a few cattle, too."

Katie turned and faced her lover, a look of surprise on her face. "Really? You've never said anything about this before."

Dean shrugged. "Guess being out here just stirred up those old feelings." She gave a wry smile. "C'mon, we've got a plane to catch."

The flight wasn't full and First Class was nearly empty. As they sat and waited for the rest of the passengers to file in, they played their game again, guessing the occupation of each person.

"Lawyer," Katie guessed as the man charmed the young flight attendant into allowing him to sit in first class. "Smooth talker."

"Nope, he's in life insurance. See the seal on his laptop case."

Katie looked at the case and nodded. "Well, he's still a smooth talker," she said, watching the final passengers board. "Hey, there's that sailor again; the one with the SEAL tattoo on his arm." Katie smiled at him as he walked past, but he didn't seem to notice.

Dean watched the man as he moved past into the coach cabin, the hairs on her neck starting to prickle. She thought he was working too hard at avoiding any contact with them, so she discreetly watched as he took his seat, memorizing his features. He didn't have the baseball cap on today. Today he was wearing a straw cowboy hat and a long sleeved western shirt, complete with pearl buttons.

Katie picked up on Dean's interest and moved toward her lover. "Someone you know?" she whispered.

"No. Just a feeling."

Katie reached up and softly scratched the back of Dean's neck. "One of *those* feelings?"

Dean shrugged and smiled at Katie. "Overactive imagination."

"Umm hmm," Katie said softly as she turned to give her attention to the flight attendant as she started the review of aircraft safety procedures.

Chapter Thirteen
June 22

"I'll get it, Dad," Terrance yelled as he went to answer the knock on the front door. The man standing in the doorway was a tall blond in jeans and a tight fitting tank top that accentuated his body builder physique. A Navy SEAL tattoo stood out prominently on his bicep. As Terrance recognized the caller, a broad smile lit up his face. "Captain Kurt! Wow...I haven't seen you in a long time!" He opened the door wider to let the man in.

"Hey there, Ter, how're you doing?" Kurt Ruskin looked Terrance up and down. "You've really grown up." He feinted some boxing jabs at Terrance and the two of them play-boxed into the living room.

"Dad! It's Kurt!" Terrance yelled as his father stepped into the room.

"I can see that, Terrance." Len Russell stepped over to greet Kurt. He reached out a hand. "It's good to see you."

Kurt Ruskin nodded his head and met the outstretched hand with his own. "Yeah, Len. Good to see you, too."

There was an awkward pause between them, then Len jerked his head toward his den. "C'mon in the den. We can talk there."

Terrance started to follow the two friends to the den, but his father stopped him in the hallway. "Terrance, your mother needs some help with the dinner dishes."

"But..." Terrance stopped at his father's stern look.

"Don't worry, there'll be time for you to talk to Kurt later. Oh, and Terrance, have your mom put in one of those apple pies she keeps in the freezer for company."

"Okay." He looked at Kurt. "See you in a bit."

Len waited until Terrance had turned the corner and entered the kitchen, then he led his visitor into the den, closing the door behind them. He went over to his wet bar and took down two glasses. "Still drink scotch?" Len asked as he motioned for Kurt to sit in one of the chairs by the fireplace. Kurt nodded and Len poured two fingers of scotch into each of the glasses, handing one to Kurt as he moved to the indicated chair.

"So," Len began, "what do you have for me?"

Kurt sipped the scotch and sat down. "Your colonel's not going to be an easy person to tail."

"Kurt, let's just refer to her as the target, okay? Just to keep things cleaner."

"Okay. As I was saying, your target isn't going to be easy to tail. It's almost as though she's got a sixth sense or something. I could've sworn she pegged me on the plane."

"The target is good, I'll admit that, so you'd better be careful, Kurt, or this could come back and bite me in the butt. You do have someone on their tail now, right?"

"Yeah, yeah, they're covered. And spying on one of your own isn't a good thing to be doing, Len. Even if she is the way you say she is. You could be getting yourself marched out of the Army instead of her." He paused to take another sip of his drink. "I did a bit of research on her and I sure wouldn't want to be on the wrong end of her paybacks, if you know what I mean."

"Yeah? The Army is no place for homos...and in her position, a hell of a lot of intelligence could get compromised. So, what do you have so far?"

Kurt reached into his back pocket for his notebook. "Well, she and the blonde took off for Kansas City last Saturday. I wasn't expecting to have to buy a last minute ticket to KC, so that'll be on your expenses." He drank the last of his scotch and Len took the glass and returned to the bar for a refill.

"They went to a funeral...her dad's. He was some kind of Bible thumper that went bad, spent some time in prison for killing his own son, and then got religion again when he got out. I asked around with some of the mourners that came to pay their respects. It wasn't hard to get them to talk. Most of them would sell their mother for some decent cash, but it seems they all liked the dude."

"Interesting." Len immediately began to consider how he could leverage the information. "Go on." He handed Kurt the refreshed drink.

"I got a couple of shots of her and the blonde holding hands and walking arm in arm, but I don't think they'll do the trick. They could easily be explained as her friend comforting her at the funeral."

Len looked disappointed. "Anything we can use?"

"Yeah." Kurt smiled. "As a matter of fact, there are a couple of things, and I've got some other tricks up my sleeve, too."

"Good. I want as much as possible so there will be no way to explain any of this away." Len smiled and the two men continued their discussion behind closed doors for another twenty minutes before they went out and sat with the rest of the family, talking over old times and eating apple pie.

"Duck!" Dean yelled to Bill as Katie spun and kicked out at Bill's padded headgear. He did duck, but unfortunately, right into her foot as it came up. The resulting blow knocked him on his butt and he collapsed backward and stayed down, slapping the mat three times.

"Uncle!" he gasped.

The two women walked over to him and sat down on the mat and then, in unison, fell back into a prone position.

"Wow, that was a good workout!" Katie wiped the sweat from her brow. "I really needed that. These last two weeks of inaction have taken their toll on me."

Bill lifted his body up to rest on his elbows and looked at her in disbelief. "Coulda fooled me, cupcake."

From her supine position, Katie snapped out with her right arm and popped him in the gut. "Don't call me cupcake!"

"Owww, okay, okay," he said with a laugh.

Dean grunted and sat up, looking at her two best friends in the world. She smiled and slowly got to her feet as she looked at the clock on the wall. It was 2000 hours. "Think Dirk's got that computer glitch solved yet?" She reached down with both hands and offered a lift to her two friends, which they gladly accepted. As they stood, Bill's cell phone chirped.

"That's probably him now," he said as he jogged to the bench where the phone was.

"See if he wants to get something to eat," Katie called as she picked up her towel and a half empty bottle of water.

Bill looked over his shoulder. "You buying?"

"Sure. You deserve a reward for the butt-kicking you just got," she said, laughing.

"Hey!" Bill flipped open the phone.

"Just kidding," Katie said. "I've got to get my licks in while I can. Once you're back in shape, it won't be so easy."

Bill pointed a finger at her. "Just don't you forget that, cupcake!"

Thirty minutes later, the foursome was entering a local steakhouse in Georgetown. The place was jam-packed with late evening diners.

"Good thing you phoned in the reservation," Bill said as the hostess checked the waiting list. His comment was seconded by grateful nods from Dirk and Dean.

Katie smiled and blew on the fingertips of her right hand, then brushed them on her shoulder. "Yep. That's me. Always thinking ahead."

Dean groaned at Katie's retort. "Yep, she's right. Whenever there's food in the mix, Katie's always a step ahead of anyone!" That earned her a good-natured poke in the ribs.

As they waited in line at the hostess podium, a young man wearing jeans and a pale blue polo shirt brushed up against Katie as he reached for one of the menus that were stacked on the stand.

"Sorry, miss," he said as he backed away, pushing up his glasses as he picked up a menu. He watched as the hostess seated the group near the bar in a booth with high wooden backs. Taking the menu, he turned and sat in one of the chairs in the waiting area, removed an iPod from his belt, unwound the earpieces from around the case, and then plugged them into his ears. He fiddled with the buttons for a bit, then began bobbing his head to a tune that was playing. Satisfied, he opened the menu to scan its contents.

The bar was separated from the restaurant area by a wall with a wood bottom and glass top. The glass portion was etched with various scenes of cowboys roping and branding cattle with a mountain range etched into the background. The loud noise levels from the bar overflowed into the restaurant area as a group of young Capitol Hill aides were having a heated discussion of the results of a recent legislative vote. Bill and Dean shared one side of the booth and Dirk and Katie shared the other. Dean looked around the room and scanned the patrons, who were in various stages of consuming their meals or appetizers. She looked through the glass into the barroom and saw a young man with an iPod still listening to his tunes as he sipped a beer at the bar. Shaking her head, she turned her attention to the waitress who arrived at their table, order pad in hand.

"My name's Erin and I'll be your waitress tonight." She smiled and made appropriate eye contact around the table. "Would anyone care for an appetizer?"

"Dean, do you want to share some buffalo wings?" Katie asked, and received a nod of agreement from Dean who had yet to look at the menu in front of her.

"Mild or hot?" Erin asked.

Katie grinned. "Hot."

"Make that two, please," Dirk added, while Bill said, "jalapeno poppers," when Erin looked at him.

"Anything to drink?" Erin asked next. She recorded their drink orders and put her pad away. "I'll be right back with those." She hurried off toward the bar.

"So," Dirk started with a glint in his eye, "Bill tells me you two are planning a nuptial?" Dean grinned broadly while Katie blushed, then showed off her ring. Dirk gave a low whistle. "Wow, that's beautiful."

"You'd think it was part of the crown jewels the way she flashes it," Dean said with a chuckle.

"Is that a white gold setting?" Bill asked as he took Katie's hand for a closer inspection.

"No, it's platinum," Dean answered quietly.

It was Bill's turn to whistle. "Nice job, Colonel."

The waitress returned to the table with their drinks and set them down in correct order before asking, "Are you ready to order?"

Katie started and they went around the table quickly, each one ordering the same item though in varying degrees of doneness.

"Well, that certainly makes it easy on me. Two rare, one medium rare, and one well done," Erin said as she finished recording the orders. "I'll be back in a bit with your appetizers."

Dirk made sure the waitress was out of earshot before resuming the conversation. "Do you have a date set?"

Katie fielded that one. "We're hoping to have the ceremony at our house in September. Reverend Martha agreed to perform it, and she'll be in D.C. for a grant meeting around that time. We're hoping to do it on the ninth or tenth and then take off for a week or so."

"Sounds like a good plan." Dirk grinned. "Do you have anyplace in mind for the honeymoon?"

"We haven't gotten that far," Dean said, "but I'm sure we'll come up with something."

"Dirk and I went to Hawaii for our honeymoon and we could recommend some really nice secluded places."

Dirk and Bill took turns providing descriptions of quiet sandy beaches, exotic drinks, extraordinary scenery, and warm nights for exploring intimate pleasures.

Across in the bar, the young man with the iPod grinned broadly. "Oh man, two for one! The boss is gonna love this."

Captain William Jarvis sprinted up the staircase, exiting into the corridor on the C Ring. He took Corridor 5 back to the A Ring and Colonel Deanna Peterson's office. Outside the door, he stopped to straighten his jacket and shift the file folder from his right hand to his left. Knocking on the door, he waited for the colonel's response.

"Enter," Colonel Peterson called.

Jarvis opened the door, entered, and closed it behind him, then took up a position in front of the colonel's desk and stood at attention.

"At ease, Captain," Dean said, finally looking up from her computer screen. "Do you have the latest from Belvoir?"

"Yes, ma'am." He extended the file.

"Have you had a chance to review the information?" Dean asked as she accepted the folder.

"Just skimmed it," he said.

"Have a seat, Bill, while I run through it myself." She indicated the small round table in the corner. Bill walked over and sat down, watching his mentor's face as she opened the file and looked through the papers. The intensity of her concentration was a sight to see, still he knew instinctively that she was totally aware of her surroundings.

Dean flipped through the last page, picked up the pile of papers, and joined Bill at the small table. "Nice compilation here. Who did the background work?"

"A young private named Hawadi," Bill replied. "She's new at Belvoir, so she's eager to please."

Remembering the young woman from the funeral, Dean smiled. "I'm sure she is. Keep an eye on her, Bill. We can always use a good researcher that can interpret too."

"How'd you know she's an interpreter?" Bill asked in amazement.

"Lucky guess," she said with a smile. "Now, let's take a better look at what she's gathered."

They spent the next two hours reviewing the information that had been gathered from filed reports of the intelligence community. The "community" consisted of all the major agencies such as the CIA, FBI, NSA, all four military intelligence groups, and other government departments like Treasury, State, Energy and National Reconnaissance, and the National Imaging and Mapping agencies.

"Let's start with the 1995 CIA report from the Philippines. That seems to be the start of a common thread for threats." Dean pulled out the report and placed it on the table.

"Right. And it looks like the most dangerous group is bin Laden's network." Bill pulled the reports that warned of terror cells developing in the U.S.

They continued sorting the reports into piles of commonalities, hoping to see a trend develop, but kept coming across reports from different agencies that would contradict what they were seeing.

"I keep seeing airline hijackings as a big denominator in the equation," Dean said.

"And the FAA has issued three warnings to the airlines," Bill added. "But I wonder how seriously their warnings are being taken."

"Hopefully, damn seriously," Dean said as she picked through the files. "This one really makes my neck hairs stand up." She handed it to Bill. It was a 1998 FBI report on a terror plot to fly an explosive-laden foreign plane into the World Trade Center. The FAA indicated that the plot was unlikely, given the state of foreign airline programs.

"That one caught my eye, too." Bill shook his head. "I sure hope the FAA is right, because that could wipe out the whole complex and then some. I can see why your neck hairs are standing on end. Most of these reports show the targets as New York City and Washington, D.C.," Bill said as he reviewed the piles yet again.

"There are several indicating American citizens on foreign soil, too," Dean commented. "And even Langley. Wonder what the folks there think about that one."

"Well, this one didn't come off." Bill held up a report that indicated a possible attack during the New Year's millennium celebration. "Could you imagine the loss of life if terrorists were to hit Times Square on New Year's Eve?"

Dean closed her eyes and shook her head. There certainly wouldn't be many survivors in a situation like that. She had often wondered what drove people to Times Square on New Year's Eve. Katie said she had always wanted to bring in the New Year in Times Square, but so far Dean had managed to dissuade her. It wasn't the thought of a terrorist attack that had Dean persuading Katie otherwise, it was the thought of all that humanity in one place. All of them celebrating loudly, pushing and shoving, on top of one another, and more than likely, the majority of them drunk. Dean had little tolerance for people who allowed alcohol, or any substance, to rule their lives. She knew that alcohol and other drugs were addictive, and once someone became an addict, they were considered to be medically ailing with a disease. Still, she firmly believed that people should never get into that situation in the first place, that it was a sign of a weak person, someone who could not control their lives — grief, losses, whatever the reason that caused them to become addicted. They should have been able to address the cause in a positive way and get help if they needed it.

"Okay, this is a good start. Send the matrix over to Hawadi and have her plug in all of these reports. Somewhere there's got to be a solid clue we can use. I think we can agree that al Qaeda is the candidate most likely to be planning something; we just need to figure out when and where the next attack is supposed to occur. I'm afraid it's going to be soon and we're going to get caught with our pants down."

Bill collected the reports and replaced them in the file. "Anything else, Colonel?"

"Yes. Tell Hawadi she did a nice piece of research. Oh, and once Hawadi has the information added to the matrix, let me know. I want to get Major Russell involved in this too."

"Will do, ma'am," Bill said as he turned and left the office.

Back in the IOC, Major Russell picked up his phone and dialed a now familiar number. When the phone was answered on the other end, Len queried, "Anything new today?"

"Not yet, Len. Give me a chance to get my people in place."

"Did you get that tape made from the other night?"

"Yes. I'll drop it off tonight, but I'm not sure how useful it will be. Yeah, they alluded to a wedding, but it could easily be argued that there isn't any evidence linking it to the two women. They could have been talking about a double ceremony...stuff like that."

"I'll check it out when I have it. I want to get this over as soon as possible," Len added. "My next...and final chance at promotion is coming up in September, and I want to have my ducks in a row before then."

"No problem, Len. Just give us some time, okay?"

"My career's riding on this, Kurt."

"Yeah, yeah. I don't know why you want to stay there when you could be making twice as much with me, but I'll get you what you want."

"All right." Len paused, then added, "Thanks, Kurt."

Chapter Fifteen
July 13

There was a knock on Colonel Peterson's door and she quickly responded, "Enter."

As Major Russell and Captain Jarvis entered the office, Dean moved to the table in the corner and indicated that the men should join her. She opened the file that was on the table.

"Major, I want to compliment you on the job you began with this matrix. With the additional information, I think we have some work ahead of us to decipher what's going on and hopefully thwart another attack on U.S. assets."

"Thank you, Colonel." The major accepted the compliment graciously while inside he bristled with disgust, knowing the woman before him and his junior officer were perverts and had no right to wear the uniform of command. His ability to control his hatred of them was accomplished only through the knowledge of the personal attack he was piecing together to destroy them both.

"I'd like you to put together a task force to tear into these reports and to scour the intelligence community for more information. Something's up and we need to get on top of it."

"Do I have permission to select my own people?" Major Russell asked.

"Yes, of course. All I ask is that Captain Jarvis remain on the project, since it was his persistence that brought us to this point."

Russell was angry at the thought of keeping Jarvis in the loop, but figured that he could keep him in line, so he smiled and nodded. "Yes, certainly." Then he thought of something else. "Will I need to get your permission to access all of our material assets, or may I issue the orders for their use?"

Dean thought about his request for a bit then decided if she was going to show good faith by trusting the man, she wouldn't be insistent on this issue.

"Normal requests can go through you, but I will still need to sign off on any satellite use or if there is something that is going to go over our normal DOD budgeted items."

Major Russell smiled at the knowledge that what he wanted to requisition was going to be within the scope of his powers. "Yes, ma'am. Understood."

Dean stood, indicating an end to the meeting. "I'll expect regular updates." She went to her desk and picked up her calendar.

"Every morning at 0830 in my office. Even if there is nothing new, I want to be so informed."

The major and the captain stood. "Yes, ma'am," they answered in unison, and turned to exit the office.

When they'd left, Dean returned to her desk and sat heavily in her leather chair. She spun around slowly to look out the window. She made a tent with her hands, bringing the tips of her fingers to her lips, and gently rocked in her chair. "Okay, Russell. Let's see what you're made of." She continued to look out into the courtyard a few minutes longer before turning back to tackle the next file on her desk.

"Hey," Katie cooed as Dean picked up the phone.

"Back at ya," Dean replied. "What's up?"

"Interested in a road trip?" Katie asked.

"Tomorrow?" Dean inquired.

"Nah, tonight."

"Hmmm, okay, I'll bite. Where to?"

"Trust me?" Katie asked.

"Implicitly," came the quick reply.

"Great. What time will you be home?"

Dean looked at her watch. "I have a meeting at 1400." She considered the agenda. "It'll take about an hour. Then a quick check on a new project, and a short session with Dirk on the new computer program he's working on..." She paused again while she checked her calendar for any other obligations. "Guess I'll be pulling in around 1700. Will that do?"

"Yep. I'll give you ten minutes to change and then we're off."

"So, you're not going to tell me where we're going?"

"Nope." Katie chuckled.

"Not even a hint?" Dean persisted.

"Well..." Katie giggled again. "Nope. No hints. See ya at five!"

Before Dean could say anything, there was a dial tone in her ear. She looked at the phone in her hand then gently replaced it in its cradle. "What does she have cooking in that pretty little head of hers now?"

At 1635 hours, Dean was weaving in and out of traffic, trying to get ahead of the weekend rush heading for home and parts unknown. She had the top down, the stereo cranked up, and the wind whipping through her hair as she sped home, anxious to see what was in the works for the road trip. As her exit came up, she slowed down and took the turn nice and easy. At the bottom of the ramp, she picked up her cell phone, slipped on her headset, and speed dialed Katie. Katie answered on the second ring.

"Hello?"

"The battery is dead on my garage door opener. Will you get the door up; I'm almost home."

"Wow, you're a little early. That's great. Maybe we can beat the worst of the rush hour traffic."

"Yeah, then we can get to...?"

"Ah, ah, ah...nice try, Colonel. Just get your cute little butt home. I'll open the door." Katie hung up and jogged to the front door and down the short walk to the garage. Inside, she pushed the button for the automatic opener and watched as it slowly rose. As the door stopped at the end of its cycle, Katie could hear Dean's Boxster rumbling up the road. She waited and watched as Dean drove up the lane and onto the driveway, slowing only slightly as she entered the garage, then hitting the brake and coming to an abrupt stop right in front of Katie. Katie stood calmly, hands on hips, watching as Dean turned off the engine, opened the car door, and slid out gracefully. As Dean reached in to grab her jacket and briefcase, Katie moved around the car and stood behind her.

"Now, wouldn't you have felt bad if you'd broken my kneecaps?" Katie said in a whisper.

Dean turned and looked at Katie's kneecaps and then at the front of the car. "Nah, would've hit your shins. Cleaner break that way."

Katie gave Dean's stomach a gentle punch. "You still would've felt bad."

Dean led the way to the back door and punched the garage door control, sending the door down. As the door started to come down, Katie reached up and put her arms around Dean's neck, pulling her down to meet her lips.

Outside and across the lane, from under a thick bush, the sound of a camera's automatic advance whirred several times.

"So, where are we going?" Dean asked as they entered the house.

"You'll see. Go get changed. I've laid your clothes out on the bed."

Dean looked at Katie with a grin. "Sure you don't want to help me change?"

Katie gave Dean a swat on the butt. "No. Now, go change while I finish packing my car."

"You driving this trip?"

"Yep. I'm going to keep you in the dark for as long as I can. Now, go!"

Dean snapped to attention and saluted. "Ma'am, yes, ma'am!" and then double-timed it to the bedroom.

Katie broke into laughter as she watched Dean leave the room. Once she was sure her lover was out of sight, Katie went to the couch and picked up the suitcase she had packed and took it out to the car, depositing it in the front trunk. She went back into the kitchen and grabbed the small soft-sided cooler she'd packed with snacks to tide them over until they arrived at their destination. She also grabbed the backpack that was on the kitchen table and took the final two items out to the car and set them behind the seats. "Now I just need my sweetie," she said to the waiting car.

"Here I am," Dean said as she put her arms around Katie's waist.

"Arrgghh!" Katie jumped at the touch. "You are sneakier than the cats!" she groaned as she turned in Dean's grasp. "Okay, let me just do one more thing in the house and we're off."

Katie placed a quick kiss on Dean's lips, then slipped out of her arms and went back inside the house. She refilled the cats' food bowls, freshened their water, and laid out some treats for each of the felines who were eagerly awaiting them. "Okay, girls, now be good. We'll be back tomorrow evening." Sugar looked up and meowed softly. "Well, by Sunday morning for sure." Spice seemed to nod in approval, while Butter munched on the treats. Katie reached down and gave each a scratch on the head before returning to the front door. She keyed in the security code, then went out and locked the door behind her.

Dean had raised the garage door and was patiently sitting in Katie's white Boxster, head back on the rest, sunglasses on, and a grin on her face. She couldn't wait to see what Katie had in store. She heard Katie close the front door and walk down the path then enter the garage. "So, where to?"

"You'll see. Buckle up." Katie slid in behind the steering wheel and placed the key in the ignition, turning it and getting the Boxster to purr. The car was already facing out, so she put it in drive and moved beyond the garage door, then keyed the button to send the garage door back down. Once the door was settled, Katie grinned over at Dean, slipped on her sunglasses, then accelerated down the drive and onto the lane.

The figure in the bushes keyed a mic and said quietly, "The birds are moving your way, I'll check on the nest."

"Affirmative. I have the birds in view," came the reply. The sound of an engine starting could be heard in the background.

Katie accelerated onto I-95 North, heading back toward D.C. She took the exit for I-495 East, crossed the Potomac, and took the first exit south. Dean looked over at Katie, curiosity in her eyes as they headed down 220. Ten minutes later, Katie pulled into Washington Executive Airport and parked the Boxster in front of the Executive Air offices. She turned off the engine and turned to Dean. "Would you get the bag out of the trunk and put the top up while I go inside?"

Dean smiled. "Your wish is my command." She got out, opened the front trunk, and removed the bag.

Katie took the soft-sided cooler and her backpack from behind the seat and went into the office. It took Dean ten minutes to secure the top and lock the Boxster, then she entered the office carrying the small bag.

"Just in time," Katie said, motioning Dean to follow her out into the private hangar.

Dean followed her through a nearly empty hangar and out the other side to the tarmac, where several small aircraft were parked. Katie and the man from the office were walking to a Beechcraft King Air C90GT. A mechanic was just closing up the engine cowl and he gave the man from the office a thumbs-up.

"She's fueled up and ready to go, Chuck," the mechanic said as he stood by the short staircase into the plane.

Chuck and Katie entered the plane and Dean followed with the bag she was carrying. Katie put the backpack and the cooler on the second seat back from the cockpit. Dean followed suit, placing her bag on the floor of the second seat and sitting in the front seat.

Chuck looked at Dean. "Would you like me to put those in the luggage compartment?"

Dean looked at Katie, an eyebrow raised in question.

"No, they'll be fine there, thanks."

"Well," he said as he looked around the cabin, "the flight plan has been submitted and the weather, as we discussed, is perfect for your flight. One-five thousand should be just about right for a smooth flight."

"Thanks, Chuck. Oh, pre-flight check?" Katie said as the man stepped out of the plane, giving her an okay sign.

Katie followed, walking around the aircraft doing a brief pre-flight to double-check what Chuck had done. Everything looked fine, so Katie returned and waited for Chuck to help secure the cabin door. While she waited, Katie went and placed a kiss on

Dean's lips. As their lips parted, they heard Chuck outside lifting the door. Katie went over and pulled it in the rest of the way and secured it for the flight. When she stepped back, she winked at Dean, then moved into the cockpit, sat in the pilot's seat, and strapped herself in.

"Wanna join me up here?" Katie said, looking over her shoulder, amused to see Dean's jaw drop.

"You can fly?" Dean said as she unbuckled her lap belt and moved into the cockpit.

"Yep." Katie turned her attention to the instrument panel and put on her headset. After getting the latest airport information, she went down her preflight checklist. Finally, the engines were started. When she was satisfied, she looked out the side window, then the front windshield, and eased the throttle forward, following the directional batons as the mechanic waved her out. "You might want to put on that headset and buckle up." She pointed at the set. Dean did as she was told and sat back, amazed.

"Hyde Traffic. Executive Air 342, taxiing runway Zero Five," Katie said into the headset. Departures from Washington Executive, the small airport also known as Hyde Field, were a bit easier without a control tower. As she neared the active runway she announced, "Hyde Traffic, Executive Air 342 taking the active runway Zero Five." She was letting the other aircraft in the immediate area know of her intentions to take off.

Katie eased the throttle forward and the Beechcraft picked up speed as it hurtled toward the far end of the runway. Katie eyed the instruments and the runway, made adjustments and, at optimum speed, gently pulled the yoke back. The plane lifted off smoothly and began its speedy climb to cruising altitude.

Expertly maneuvering the aircraft into a turn and then leveling off on a course to the east southeast, Katie watched the compass on the instrument panel and smiled as she turned to her planned course of One Zero One to intercept the airway which would take them northeast to their destination.

"So, when did you take up flying?" Dean asked when Katie looked her way.

"A long time ago," she replied. "My dad had a private pilot's license. He'd fly us to all our vacations and took me up on weekends when he had the chance. I pretty much knew how to fly before I took my first official lessons. My first solo flight was on my twenty-first birthday."

Dean nodded and then said with just a hint of caution, "I never heard you say anything about being able to fly. Guess there's still things we don't know about each other."

Katie heard the concern in Dean's voice and looked over at her. "Hey, I wasn't trying to hide anything from you. It just never came up. I mean—"

Dean shook her head, "No, I wasn't...I mean... It's just, I guess I haven't really worked hard enough at getting to know you...not like you've worked at getting to know me."

"Hey, and when did I stop talking long enough for you to do that?" Katie said with a grin. She reached over and held Dean's hand, giving it a squeeze.

Dean looked down at Katie's hand and returned the squeeze. "So, just how many skills do you have?" Dean asked, breaking into a grin.

"Oh...I have many skills," Katie said with a laugh. "In fact, if you go back into the cabin and grab the cooler, I'll demonstrate how I can fly a plane and eat a sandwich at the same time."

It was nearly 1900 when Katie started to descend. It was a beautiful evening, the sun was still fairly high in the west, and they were cruising over the ocean. In the distance, Dean could see a finger of land.

"Are we heading to Cape Cod?" she asked as she got an inkling of where they might be headed.

"Close. We'll pass over it soon, then drop down a bit further."

Dean thought a bit, then said, "Okay, Boston?"

"Nope. We're going to P-town."

"Provincetown? Cool. I haven't been there in a very long time."

"I have an old family friend that runs a bed and breakfast there. He's really excited about meeting you." Katie made a few adjustments before continuing. "He's got a great place that still has quite a bit of privacy...including beachfront."

"Sounds great. It'll be nice to be able to relax on the beach."

"And, he's gay, so we can just hang and be ourselves."

"How gay is he?" Dean asked, a bit concerned.

"You mean: is he a flaming queen?" Dean grimaced and nodded. "Well, it's been a while since I've seen him, and he was just out of the closet with his family. I can't imagine him as a queen, though. He was always a very reserved kind of guy...like Bill and Dirk." Katie looked over at Dean. "Are you worried about being around folks that are gay?"

Dean shrugged. "It's not that. I'm just a bit cautious with folks I don't know."

"Yeah, I know just how you feel. I'm pretty much the same way myself." She paused, then added, "Half of P-town is gay anyway... but then there are a lot of straight tourists there, too."

Dean shrugged. "Yeah, that's true."

Katie patted Dean's thigh. "On a good note, his partner is a four star chef, so be prepared for some terrific eating."

"Any chance we'll get some lobster?"

Katie just laughed as she called the Providence tower for landing preparations.

Chapter Sixteen
July 13

"Yoohooo, Katie!"

Katie heard the voice and scanned the thinning crowd inside the airport. It didn't take her long to locate her friend. Jeff Garver, taller than Dean by a good six inches, was dressed in very short shorts that hugged his muscular legs, a wild flowered shirt, clog type shoes, and a bright yellow straw cowboy hat. Katie laughed and pointed him out to Dean. "Umm, maybe he's a wee bit of a queen now," Katie allowed with a grin.

"Just a wee bit?" Dean said wryly.

As they approached him, Katie's friend ran up and wrapped his arms around her, lifting her off the floor. "Oh, girlfriend! You look marvelous!" He put her down but held on to her hand.

Katie looked him up and down and laughed. "You sure look different than the last time I saw you."

"Well," he said with a grin, "I'm now in touch with my inner self." They laughed and hugged again. "Actually, I just dropped off some Fag Hags that were staying at our B & B this week, and I didn't have time to go back and change before picking you up." His voice was much more normal than the falsetto with which he'd greeted them. He took off his yellow cowboy hat and placed it on Katie's head. "There, that looks much better on you."

When they broke apart, Katie said, "Jeff, this is Deanna Peterson."

Jeff tilted his head and looked at Dean, checking her out from head to toe. Dean looked around the now empty lobby, discomfort showing as she shuffled from foot to foot. "Girlfriend," Jeff said with a beaming smile and a return of the falsetto, "she is gorgeous! Where on earth did you find her?"

"Long story," Katie said, eager to end Dean's uneasiness. As she led them out the door, she said, "Dean, this is Jeffery Garver."

"Don't forget the 'the Third'." Jeff took the suitcase Dean was holding and the backpack and cooler from Katie.

Dean stopped in her tracks. "Jeffery Garver? Are you any relation to Admiral Jeffery Garver?"

Jeff looked a bit surprised. "You know my dad?" Dean nodded. "Wow. How is the old coot?" he asked in his falsetto.

"He's well," Dean said, wondering how the cantankerous Chief of Naval Intelligence could have such an unconventional son. She shook her head at herself. *For that matter, how could a southern evangelical minister have a lesbian for a daughter?* "It's a pleasure to meet you, Jeff," she said, holding out her hand.

Jeff shook it firmly, then grinned and said in a very normal tone, "The pleasure's all mine." He winked and led them to his van.

"Provincetown?" Len closed the door to his den. "How the hell did they get there?" He listened as he paced. "Damn, must be nice to be rich. Yeah, go ahead and get up there. This may be a good thing." He laughed as he listened. "Yeah, that's for sure. We're bound to hit paydirt this time. By the way, I'll have some interesting toys for you to use next week. Come by my house Monday." He smiled as he hung up the phone. "Going to hang with the perverts in Provincetown, eh? Thanks, Colonel. You just made my task easier."

Jeff opened the back of the van and placed the backpack, cooler, and suitcase into his van. Dean opened the door for Katie and she slid into the back seat. Dean sat in the front, grateful for the additional leg room. Jeff closed the back door and got into the driver's seat. He looked at Dean, who was quiet. "Can you imagine what my dad would say about my outfit?" He laughed and started up the van. "I don't normally dress like this, but when you're in business for yourself, you do what you have to do. Entertaining Fag Hags brings in the bucks."

Dean nodded, then asked, "What's a Fag Hag?"

"Ah, those are straight chicks who like to hang out with gay guys, especially flamboyant gay guys. Like the women I just dropped off at the airport." He pulled out of the parking lot and headed out to the main road. "A guy's gotta do what a guy's gotta do. Hope I didn't embarrass you."

Dean shook her head. "No, but you weren't quite what I expected."

Katie piped up from the back, "I just got finished telling Dean how reserved you were and then...well, you even made me gulp a bit." The three of them laughed and the tension of the greeting began to dissolve.

"So, you gals hungry?" Jeff asked as he pulled onto the main road.

Dean laughed and Katie answered for them. "Do bears poop in the woods?"

"Good. Jack's putting together one of his spectacular seafood dishes for you. You should have just enough time to freshen up before its ready." Jeff turned off Route 6 onto Snail Road, then took a left on Commercial Street. On a triangle of land and beach, he pulled into the drive of a classic old home that appeared to have been built back in the late 1700s. "Here we are. Home sweet home."

Dean and Katie looked at the picture perfect Federal home and whistled in unison.

"I'm stuffed," Katie said as she slipped between the silk sheets on the bed.

Dean stepped out of the bathroom holding her stomach. "You and me both, love. It's a damn good thing we're only going to be here the weekend."

"So, I take it we can stay tomorrow night, too?" Katie asked. When she'd made the arrangements with Jeff, she'd told him to hold Saturday night, just in case.

"Yep...as long as I get my lobster."

"Oooo...how can you even think about food?" Katie pressed two fingers against her lips and puffed up her cheeks with air.

Dean grinned and took three long strides toward the bed, hopping in next to Katie. She rolled onto her left side and rested her head on her hand. "So, are we going to get up early and take a run on the beach?" Katie rolled away from her and started to snore. Dean moved closer and put her mouth closer to Katie's exposed ear. "Okay, I'll go by myself, but remember...no second desserts for the lazy."

Katie groaned. "Arrgghh. I hate it when you're the voice of reason. Okay, okay...I'll get up and go running with you."

"That's my girl." Dean rolled onto her back. "By the way, your friends are nice. Jeff has quite a sense of humor. His Carmen Miranda imitation is a hoot."

Katie laughed. "You should have seen him when we were kids. He was always doing funny stuff. I thought for sure he could go toe to toe with Robin Williams in Improv." Her voice turned serious, "Then his dad would come in and Jeff would go still and get real quiet. When my parents died, I moved in with my aunt, and Jeff and I didn't see much of each other after that. We stayed in contact, but mostly by email. When he said he was going to the Naval Academy, I couldn't believe it. He always wanted to go to the New York Film Academy and study acting. Guess Daddy put an end to that, too."

"He didn't stay in the Navy long, did he?"

"Nope. When he finished the Academy he was posted to San Diego on a vice admiral's staff. Nice posting, thanks to his dad.

Anyway, that's where he met Jack." Katie smiled as she remembered. "Jack was a chief petty officer and the vice admiral's personal cook."

"Ah, the plot thickens," Dean said, realizing where the story was going.

"Yep. One thing led to another with the two of them, then the inevitable happened and they were outed. His dad managed an honorable discharge for Jeff, but not for Jack. Jeff hasn't forgiven his dad." Katie rolled onto her back and sighed. "He and Jack came back East and Jack enrolled in the CIA."

"CIA?"

"The Culinary Institute of America...in upstate New York. He graduated at the top of his class, got picked up by a hot restaurant in New York City, worked his way up to four stars, and then quit. Jeff did some theater in New York City while they were there, but never got to break into the big time. His day job on Wall Street was his main paycheck. They saved their bucks and bought this place two and a half years ago. The first year was spent on renovations, and the rest is history. They're booked solid practically every weekend. I was lucky to get this time slot for us."

Dean rolled nearly on top of Katie, "I'm glad you lucked out." Dean brushed a stray hair away from Katie's eye, then leaned in and gently kissed her. "Tired?"

"Not that tired." Katie placed her hands along Dean's face and pulled her down for another kiss.

When they parted, Dean reached across Katie and turned out the light. "Mmm, good."

Saturday morning dawned bright and clear. Temperatures were in the low seventies at 0730 hours, and Dean and Katie took advantage of the empty beach to get in a little exercise.

"C'mon, slow poke," Dean chided. "Let's pick up the pace!"

"Hey," Katie puffed out, "I've got shorter legs."

"Wimp!" Dean started to pull away.

"Kiss my ass!" Katie kicked into gear and passed Dean.

Dean watched her pull past. "Works every time," she said with a grin, and then sped up just enough to stay a pace behind. "Race you to that dock and back?" she said with a breathy voice.

Katie looked over her shoulder and nodded. "Last one back is a rotten egg!" she said, then picked it up a notch.

With a broad smile, Dean maintained a stride that kept her a step or two behind. Every time Katie looked over her shoulder and sped up, Dean did the same, keeping the separation. They made it to the dock and turned back. The return found Katie losing speed but retaining the lead.

"Feeling old?" Katie panted as they neared the B & B with Dean now several steps back.

"Nah, just pacing myself," Dean said as she estimated the final distance between them and the house.

"Okay, then pace this!" Katie sped up to her fastest.

Dean finally picked up the slack. It only took a few yards before she passed Katie, her long black hair flying in the wind, laughter floating back to tease her mate.

"You creep!" Katie called as she tried to catch up. Her efforts were in vain as Dean increased the distance between them, slowing only when she reached the B & B then danced in a circle while Katie caught up.

Dean never saw Katie coming because she was still doing her celebratory dance and her back was to her partner as Katie executed a perfect tackle and took Dean down into a small sand hill. They rolled in the sand, coating their damp bodies in a layer of grit and laughing while they wrestled playfully, totally absorbed only in each other. Exhaustion finally got the best of them and they lay back on the sand, still laughing.

"I think the guys might be upset if we drag all this sand into the house," Katie said as she carefully wiped her eyes.

Dean checked out her coated body. "Ya think?" She sat up and peered at Katie. "I don't know which one of us is worse."

Katie looked at her own body, then Dean's. "I'd call this one a tie. How about we hose ourselves off?"

Dean looked at the bay before them, then the hose curled up by the side of the house. "Wonder which one's colder," she muttered.

"I bet it'd be another tie," Katie offered. "But, if we hose off, we're closer to the hot tub on the deck."

"Ah, I see a plan hatching in that blond head of yours." Dean chuckled as she stood and offered a hand to Katie.

"Umhmm, and there's those big fluffy towels there for when we get out," Katie added with a grunt as she allowed Dean to pull her up.

"So, what are we waiting for?" Dean jogged over to the hose.

Katie grimaced at the glint in Dean's eye as she picked up the hose. "Uh oh."

"Hey, gals," Jack said as he stepped out on the deck. "Have a nice run?"

Jeff appeared next to Jack. "Hmmm, by the looks of these," he poked at the wet clothes on the deck with his shoe, "you gals worked up quite a sweat."

"Anyone ready for breakfast?" Jack interrupted.

That put a smile on Katie's face and she raised a hand in response. "Can someone toss me a towel?"

Jeff handed her the requested towel. "Hey, there's no skinny dipping in the hot tub. Didn't you read the posted rules? Naked bodies running around the deck offend our neighbors!" He picked up another towel and tossed it to Dean. "Unless," he laughed, "they're sexy, buff, naked men."

Jack, who had moved toward the house, turned and said over his shoulder, "You'll have to meet them."

"Who?" Dean asked. "The sexy, buff, naked guys, or the neighbors?"

Jack laughed. "The neighbors. They're the sweetest old ladies you ever met. Make a heck of a corn chowder, too." He stopped at the sliding glass door. "C'mon, Jeff. Give them some privacy so they can hop out of that tub."

Ten minutes later they were all sitting at the table in the breakfast nook, plates of goodies spread out in front of them: fresh hot cranberry scones, Eggs Benedict, bacon and sausages, homemade jams and jellies, muffins, quiche, and coffee that smelled outrageously good. Katie's eyes roved amongst the selections and Dean could just see the indecision on her face — so much great food; where to start? Dean's chuckling got Katie's attention.

"And just what's so funny?" Katie said, a smirk appearing on her face as she watched Dean break into full-fledged laughter.

Between guffaws, Dean gasped out, "Sorry, love, it's just that," she inhaled and tried to control herself, "the look on your face: like a little kid at Christmas that doesn't know which present to open first."

Katie gave an indignant, "Hmpf," but then started to giggle.

Jack finally cut in. "If you girls don't get yourselves under control, all my work will get cold and go to waste."

Dean and Katie both looked at him and said in unison, "Nuh, uh," and they began placing food on their plates.

Outside, a tourist walked past the B & B for the fifth time, taking photos of the homes along the beach, seagulls, and the protected deck of the B & B.

Jack, Jeff, Katie, and Dean strolled along the sidewalk, enjoying the weather and the shopping. Dean was walking with Jack and they were both carrying several bags containing Jeff and Katie's purchases.

"Hey, Dean," Katie called over her shoulder as she pointed at yet another shop window, "what do you think of that one?"

Dean looked in the window and shook her head. "Nope, I don't think she'd like it."

"Really? I think it would look terrific on her," Katie countered.

"Hon, do you really think that Tracy would wear a hot pink pants suit?"

"Okay, so what do you suggest for her birthday?"

Dean sighed and looked around at the shops, then pointed at one across the street and down the block. "Let's try over there."

Katie looked at the shop and shrugged. "Whatever."

As they crossed the street, a young man stopped Jack and asked him for the time. In thanks, he gave Jack a pat on the butt, deftly slipping a small coin into his back pocket, then went on his way.

Jack watched the young man as he walked over to the small park and sat on a bench. "Now, now, Jacko," Jack whispered as he turned to catch up to his friends, "he's way too young for you." He crossed the street and entered the shop, where Dean was admiring a piece of sculpture.

"Now that would be something she'd like," Dean pronounced with finality.

The piece was a wood carving of three intertwined dolphins. They lifted out of the water as though performing an intricate dance. The wood was dark, with a beautiful grain and smooth finish. Including the base, which was a solid piece of black marble, the piece was almost two feet tall.

Katie touched the fine piece, enjoying the smooth texture of the wood. "Wow! That is beautiful. What kind of wood is it?"

The proprietor came up to them, a smile on his face. "That's walnut. It's a beautiful wood with a very rich grain, don't you think?"

"It certainly is gorgeous," Katie said with a nod. "The artist really did a great job carving the dolphins. You almost expect them to come to life, they're so perfect."

"Thank you." He held out his hand. "My name is Oscar, Oscar deVicento."

"You're the sculptor?" Katie inquired as she shook his hand.

"Yes. And this is my favorite piece." He released Katie's hand and looked at Jeff and Jack. "Well, it's about time you boys made it to my shop!" He gave each a hug. Turning back to Katie, he said, "Are these gentlemen friends of yours?"

"I'm afraid so," Katie said, shrugging.

Oscar smiled and gave Katie a hug. "Thank you for finally getting them through my door." He shook a finger at the men, then looked back at Katie with a smile. "So, can I wrap it up for you?" Katie nodded and he picked up the piece and took it to the back of the room, motioning for them to follow.

The foursome did as requested and watched as Oscar wrapped the piece in layers of bubble wrap and placed it in a sturdy box. While Oscar packed, introductions were made, as were arrangements to meet later for dinner and some local nightlife.

Outside the shop, a young man was sitting on a bench across the street, earphones in his ears and an iPod in his hands. As he watched the wood shop, he pulled out a small video camera and started to take pictures of his surroundings. Just as Dean, Katie, and the guys came out of the shop, he panned the camera toward them, capturing their conversation on the listening device he had slipped into Jack's pocket. "Well, let's hope we can get some incriminating photos tonight." He packed up his camera and kept listening, casually strolling behind the group as they headed back to the B & B.

Chapter Seventeen
July 16

"What have you got so far?" Dean asked as she took a seat at the small conference table.

Major Russell nodded slightly, indicating that Jarvis should begin, then sat back and watched as the captain opened his folder and began a review of the intelligence gathered over the weekend. He had been ordered to work with Jarvis on this project, and over the weekend he had come up with a few ideas about how he could make this work in his favor...especially with General Carlton. He had already made an appointment to talk to the general that afternoon to run some of his suggestions by her. A thin smile appeared on his face.

"Are you finding this humorous, Major?" Dean asked.

Major Russell sobered quickly. "Um, no, Colonel. I was just thinking..." He paused as he hastily tried to come up with something. "I think we can all agree that bin Laden is the most dangerous terrorist we face, so what about using one of our undercover teams to do some extra digging in the sand?"

Dean sat back and looked at Russell. "Already done, Major. We already have teams in Yemen, Afghanistan, Saudi Arabia, and even a small group in Iraq. They've been sending regular reports."

"Yes, yes. But how about sending in another team? I'm sure they could use some help."

"Send in a new team?" Bill asked.

"Yes, exactly." Russell looked at Bill, then back at Dean. Both were looking at him with blank faces. "More teams, more information."

Dean leaned forward in her chair and rested her arms on the table, never losing direct eye contact with Russell. "You see any problems with that suggestion?"

Russell sat back in his chair, totally unaware that the backward move showed he was intimidated by the colonel. "Well," he began, "it'll take time to get the team infiltrated."

"Months," Bill interjected solemnly.

"And they could jeopardize the few human resources we have in the area...maybe even blow their cover." Dean sat back and folded her arms across her chest. "Besides, as much as I'd like to have more operatives in the field, it won't pass the Joint Chiefs.

We'll need to continue mining the data that's out there and rely on technology to help us out."

Bill nodded and looked at Major Russell. "Should we send more spiders out on the internet?"

Knowing he was not going to be able to press for his own plan with the colonel, Russell acquiesced. He'd get what he wanted after his meeting with the general. "Yes, let's grab everything we can. I'll push the Land Information Warfare Activity group at Fort Belvoir for more information." He paused, then added, "Colonel, we've got oceans of data already. Belvoir could use more analysts to wade through it."

Colonel Peterson nodded. "I'll see if I can send more help over to LIWA. We've got six new analysts coming on board in a couple of weeks. I'll transfer half of them over to Belvoir on temporary assignment." Russell nodded and Bill returned his files to the folder when Dean stood, ending the meeting. "That will be all, gentlemen."

The two subordinate officers stood. "Yes, ma'am."

The two officers returned to the IOC in silence, each retreating to his own office upon entering. Major Russell closed his door and hurried to his desk, barely sitting in the chair before picking up his phone. He looked out into the main section of the IOC, scanning the personnel as he placed his call. The phone on the other end was picked up on the second ring.

"Kurt...Len here. Look I need you to come by my house tonight." He paused and listened. "No, make it around 2300 — and don't ring the bell. I'll be waiting for you by the garage. I'll fill you in tonight." Russell replaced the handset and leaned back in his chair, a smile on his lips. He sat there a moment longer, then turned on his computer monitor and pulled up the proposal he was preparing for the general. Looking it over, he added a few more sentences, checked the document, and printed a copy for his meeting that afternoon. He reached into his briefcase and pulled out a completed requisition form, then placed the document he had just printed into his briefcase, locking it so no prying eyes would see it. He didn't think that Captain Jarvis would dare to enter his office when he wasn't around, but he felt better knowing that at least the clandestine proposal wouldn't be easy for the colonel's toady to find. He read over the requisition and nodded approval. Getting up from his desk, he took the paperwork, folded it, and placed it in his inside jacket pocket. Then he left his office and walked over to Jarvis'. "I need to run over to Belvoir. I'll be back around 1200." Without waiting for a response, he turned and left the IOC.

Bill looked up in time to see the major turn and walk away, then shook his head and went back to reviewing the new data that had been placed on his desk. He kept at it for nearly three hours before he came upon an FBI memo regarding the possibility of foreign individuals involved in flight training at several facilities in the U.S.

"If I were a terrorist looking to strike within the U.S., I'd certainly want to know how to fly one of the big birds," Bill said softly, setting the memo aside. "What better way to facilitate a hijacking than to be able to fly a commercial jet yourself?"

Bill pulled up the computerized version of the matrix of the data that had already been gathered, along with the current warning levels issued by the FAA, FBI, and CIA. Security had been increased since the U.S.S. Cole incident and the worries about new attacks with the advent of the new millennium, but Bill knew there were still many holes through which terrorists could attack. With the exception of the World Trade Center bombings back in February of 1993, terrorist attacks had taken place on foreign soil or in foreign ports, but Bill was convinced that the data now being collected was indicating an attack on American soil. The problem was putting a finger on where and when and, most importantly, how to stop an attack before it happened. Bill added the new information to the matrix and emailed it to Colonel Peterson, then sat back and reviewed it in much the same manner as his mentor in her office, two floors above.

The electronic surveillance supply sergeant checked the list and nodded. "This is some pretty sophisticated equipment, Major. Got a hot op in the works?"

"Not your concern, Sergeant. Just get it boxed up for me," Major Russell said curtly.

"Yes, sir. Do you want to wait for it or have it delivered to the Pentagon?"

"I'll take it with me. How long will it take?"

The sergeant looked at the list again. "'Bout a half hour, sir."

"Fine. I'll be back for it in precisely thirty minutes." Major Russell eyed the sergeant sternly, then turned and left the room and the supply building. He walked to the Operations building and stepped into a room that was a duplicate of the IOC at the Pentagon, only on a much larger scale.

"Hey, Len," a voice called out. "You slumming?"

Major Russell turned to see his former superior coming toward him. He put a smile on his face and stepped toward Lieutenant Colonel Hayes.

"Good to see you, Colonel." He looked around the bustling room. "Busy as usual, I see."

"Pentagon wants us to dig deeper into the data, so we're pulling double duty. So, what brings you here? Did they send you back to help us out?"

"Um, no. Just needed to pick up some equipment." *Damn, I should have stayed in the supply building,* Len thought belatedly.

"They've got you doing grunt work, eh?" He laughed and slapped Russell on the back. "I tried to tell you that majors are a dime a dozen in that place. You should have stayed here, Len. This is where the real work gets done."

"You're right, Colonel. But, not everyone gets the chance to be a Major grunt!" Len laughed.

"Well, hopefully the posting will help with your next promotion round." Colonel Hayes smiled, knowing that the only reason Russell asked for the transfer was to try to suck up for the next promotion board. Russell wasn't a bad officer, but he was out of his league in intelligence work. He would have had a better chance at promotion in just about any other area of the Army. He was glad that Russell was now the Pentagon's problem and not his.

Major Russell smiled back. "Colonel, I don't think there will be a problem with my promotion this round." He pointed at the silver oak leafs on the colonel's lapels. "I'm confident that I will be wearing those come October."

"I'm glad for you, Len." Hayes looked around the room and saw a young lieutenant looking at him. "You'll have to excuse me," he said as he walked toward the lieutenant. "Feel free to pitch in while you're here."

Major Russell walked around the perimeter of the room, trying to take in the frenetic energy inherent to the collection of intelligence data, but all he could think about was the colonel's comments about his promotion. He knew that Colonel Hayes' remarks in his file contributed to his inability to get promoted. Russell looked around the room again. He felt distant, lost. Things were moving too fast and he couldn't keep up. He couldn't concentrate on his job anymore. He was overwhelmed by his failures. He knew they weren't *his* failures, but the failures of the people around him. They didn't — no, *couldn't* take orders properly. That's why he couldn't get promoted. It was the system that failed him and he was consumed with fixing it so he would make the grade. He had to; he had no other life to turn to. Kurt's job offer was as nothing more than a glorified private detective. He knew it was good money, but to him it was a major step backward. He had no desire to do fieldwork. That was a job for someone who didn't have leadership abilities. Len knew that he was destined to be a great leader; all he needed was the promotion. That would make everything right.

"Can I help you, Major?" a young female private asked.

Russell shook off his thoughts and looked at her nameplate, not recognizing her. Irritated with the interruption, he snapped, "No, Private Hawadi. Get back to your work." He looked around the room once more, then headed back for his consignment.

"All set, Major," the supply sergeant said as he picked up the box of electronics. "Do you need help taking this out to your vehicle?"

Still irritated, Russell barked, "No. I've got it," and grabbed the handles of the plastic crate and slid it off the counter.

"Sir!" the sergeant called. "Sir, I need you to sign for them."

Russell stopped at the door and set the crate down and motioned for the sergeant to bring the forms to him. He waited as the sergeant came around the counter with the requisition form and a pen. He quickly scrawled his name and handed it back to the sergeant. Picking up the crate, he waited until the sergeant opened the door for him, then headed out to the parking lot where he placed the crate in the back of his van. Looking at his watch, he determined he had time to run the crate home before returning to the Pentagon.

Colonel Peterson's door was ajar, but Bill knocked and waited for permission to enter.

Dean was facing the window, a pile of papers in her lap. She raised her hand, waving him in without turning to see who was there. "Got something, Captain?"

Bill smiled and entered, amazed as always at her uncanny ability to know everything about her surroundings without having to look around. He didn't know how she knew it was him and hoped that one day he'd be able to tune his senses to the same level. He'd already learned much from her but knew it was just a fraction of what she was capable of teaching him.

Dean swiveled around and waited for him to begin. "Colonel," he said slowly, "I've been reviewing some FBI memos about reports of Arabs coming to the States to take flight lessons..." He paused for effect and watched as Dean's eyebrow rose. "...to fly jets...big jets...passenger jets."

Dean sat forward and rested her arms on her desk. "You have a theory?" Bill nodded. "Okay, go ahead and convince me."

"I got to thinking...what's so special about taking lessons here in the States as opposed to say in Europe or Asia or any of the Arab countries? A big jet is a big jet anywhere in the world. Most of the aeronautics would be the same in aircraft that were made by Boeing, or Airbus, or Lockheed, or Embraer. Maybe there would just be different languages on the controls and dials, right?" He smiled as he got ready to present his theory. "So, why come for lessons in the United States? What would be the pull?" Bill paused for effect before giving his answer. "They would come here because our flight schools would provide lessons in U.S. civil aviation procedures."

Dean realized that her protégé was definitely onto something important, something *very* important. "You're absolutely right. This puts a whole new spin on these reports." She indicated that he should take a seat and then she turned to her computer and pulled up the computerized matrix. She entered a few key strokes to narrow the search. The computer did its sorting and produced a list of reports that narrowed in on flight lessons. There weren't many, but enough to make her neck hairs begin to itch. "Have you talked to the FBI about your theory?"

"No. I wanted to run it by you first."

"It's a damn good piece of logic," Dean said. "I think you should get in touch with them."

"Me? Wouldn't it be better coming from you?"

"It's your hypothesis, Bill. You should be the one to present it. Besides, this is a civilian issue right now. The FBI needs to be the lead on any investigation of civilian flight schools." Dean put her phone on speaker phone and dialed the number for her friend Walter at the FBI.

The ringing filled the room, then the click of Walter picking up on the other end of the line was followed by his standard response, "Agent Cummins."

"Walt, this is Deanna Peterson."

"Hey, Colonel. What's up at the Pentagon?"

"I've got you on speaker phone, Walt. I have Captain William Jarvis here with me. The captain has been mining data on possible terror threats and has come up with something very interesting. I'll let Bill explain."

The captain reviewed his thought process with Walter, ending with his theory. "So, my thinking is that the Arabs are coming here not only to learn to fly the big planes, but to learn about U.S. civil aviation procedures." There was silence on the other end of the line which made Bill look at Dean for a long moment.

Walt finally replied, "That makes a lot of sense, Captain, a hell of a lot of sense." After another pause, he said, "Captain, do you mind if I run your idea past my superiors?"

"Not at all. That's why we're calling."

"Walt," Dean interjected, "what's the possibility that some of your field agents could start looking into the flight schools across the country and trying to get a fix on any possible suspects, see if they can figure out what they're really up to?"

"I'll have to run it up the line, but it makes damn good sense to me to investigate this further."

"You'll keep us informed?" Dean asked.

"You bet, Colonel. Nice job, Captain."

"Thank you, sir," Bill said with a pleased grin.

"Thanks, Walt." Dean disconnected the call. She sat back in her chair and tented her fingers in front of her, tapping the tips together lightly. Bill seemed to finally relax as he exhaled and rolled his head around in a slow circle, releasing the tension that had built up in his neck. "So, we're looking at the possibility of a homeland hijacking," Dean said quietly.

"That would be the scenario," Bill agreed.

Dean rocked in her chair and closed her eyes. The hairs on her neck seemed to be getting itchier and itchier the longer she rocked. "We're missing something, Bill," she finally said, opening her eyes to look directly into his. "It's time to think outside of the box, my friend."

Bill nodded and clasped his hands together and began twiddling his thumbs. Dean used her rocking to help her think; Bill twiddled his thumbs.

"Okay, so why do people hijack airplanes?" Dean began.

"To get something they want," Bill answered. "Like money, or to get comrades released from prisons, or to get someone to do something they want done."

"Okay, those are inside the box. What would a terrorist gain by grabbing a plane in the U.S.?"

"Not a whole hell of a lot. We don't negotiate with terrorists," Bill replied quickly.

"Right. So why hijack a plane?"

"Media coverage?" Bill asked.

"Could be, but would it be positive coverage in the U.S?" Dean asked.

"No, probably not."

"So, what is there to gain? What would be the outside the box thinking in the world of terrorists?"

"Death and destruction," Bill answered quickly. "And of course...seventy-two virgins."

"There's that," Dean said with a wry grin, "but I think you're on the right track with the first part of your answer."

Bill thought a moment longer. "But crashing a commercial airliner won't bring about a lot of deaths with two or three hundred passengers and crew and maybe a few more on the ground." He thought for a moment. "But they could wrack up more death and some serious destruction if they aimed right."

Dean stood abruptly. "That's it," she said excitedly. "That's outside the box, all right!" Dean paced her office. "Think of it, Bill. What if they're going to hijack a plane to use as a weapon! A weapon of mass destruction."

"Oh my God! The possibilities are unthinkable!"

"The general will be right with you, Major. Please have a seat." Sergeant Major Tibbits motioned Russell toward a group of leather chairs in the corner and then picked up a file folder and entered the general's office.

Major Russell sat down, opened his folder and thumbed through the pages, insuring that his proposal was complete. He needed to make a really good impression on General Carlton, especially if he was going to be bringing charges against Colonel Peterson in the near future. He was hoping that during this meeting he would be able to get a better read on just how General Carlton felt about the colonel. He needed to find out if he was going to be walking into an active minefield or a deactivated one where Peterson was concerned.

He looked over his notes one more time, fairly confident about his ideas. Closing the folder, he looked around the room. It was pretty staid for a general's waiting area. Oil paintings depicting military battles hung on the south wall, along with signed photographs from two past presidents and a nice display case with two crossed swords dating from the Civil War. Major Russell stood and walked around the room to inspect them and was surprised to see they were the property of the sergeant major. He was moving back to his seat when Tibbits re-entered the room. "Nice," Russell said, pointing at the sword display.

"Those belonged to my great grandfather. He was a cavalry sergeant with General Grant during the Civil War and then served with General Custer after. He retired just before Little Big Horn. They've been passed down to the oldest child ever since."

"Are you passing them to your son?"

"Nope. These will be going to my daughter. She's a first lieutenant with the 50th Medical Company, 101st Airborne Division. She flies one of the Black Hawks."

"Impressive, Sergeant Major. You must be very proud of her." Russell mentally marked Tibbits down as an ally of Peterson.

"That I am, Major." Tibbits smiled broadly and then motioned toward the door to the general's office. "The general will see you now."

Russell went back to the table and picked up the file folder. "Thank you," he said, and proceeded into the general's office.

Len Russell looked at his watch, noting that it was almost time to meet Kurt. He folded the newspaper and set it on the floor by his chair. The twins were already in bed, Connie and Terrance were getting ready for bed, and his wife Alice was sleeping in the recliner next to him. Quietly he stood up and padded toward the kitchen, taking his coffee cup with him. Dashiell, the family dog, rose and followed eagerly, his tail swishing in anticipation of a late evening walk.

"Can I get you something?" his wife asked in a sleepy voice.

"No, dear. I'm just going to take the dog out for a last walk. Why don't you get ready for bed? I'll be back before you know it."

"Mmm, sounds like a good idea. I'm really tired tonight. The twins just take the life out of me some days." The twins were five, and they were a handful. They were real boys, through and through — always into something and never into anything good. Their daughter Connie was always a good helper, but she was a teenager, like Terrance, and needed her own time to do homework and chat with her girlfriends on the phone. There were days when Alice wished the twins hadn't come along when they did and then she would look at their angelic faces and know life wouldn't be the same without them. Then there were days she wished for a more simple life, one with just her and Len in it, one that didn't have any worries associated with it, worries about where they would be stationed next month, or whether Len would be pulled out into a dangerous field operation...or, God forbid, whether a war would break out. She knew that all the wishing in the world wouldn't change what was. Len was Army, through and through. He lived and breathed Army, and if he were ever wounded, his blood would be olive drab rather than red. She was just thankful that the posting to the Pentagon had come through. It was a stable time for them, a time they could enjoy. Sitting up, Alice rubbed her eyes. "Don't be long," she said as she turned off the TV.

"I'll be back before you can say—"

"Yeah, yeah...I've heard that line before. Now scoot, so you can come to bed."

Len smiled at his wife, then took the dog leash off the hook by the back door and clipped it onto Dashiell's collar. "C'mon, Dash, let's go for a walk." Dash was short for Dashiell Hammett, the creator of the *Thin Man* mystery series. Alice thoroughly loved the series and insisted on naming the black Labrador after the author.

Len and Dash went out the front door and turned down the road that led into their cul-de-sac. Only one way in to their house and Kurt was not yet waiting outside, so they walked to the intersection and then turned back. Dash marked every bush and tree along the way and kept his senses on the alert for any stray squirrels or rabbits that might scurry out from under a bush or car. They were nearly back to the house when Kurt drove up along side them, headlights off.

"Hey," Kurt greeted.

Dash recognized the voice and wiggled his way to the Jeep and its open window, whimpering softly.

"Right on time," Len said as he checked his watch. "Park here and we'll carry the stuff over."

Kurt parked the Jeep and got out to a greeting from Dash's warm nose and wet tongue.

"Hey, boy!" Kurt gave the dog's head a quick rub. "So, what've you got for me?"

"The latest in high tech surveillance equipment," Len said as he led the way to the open garage.

"No shit? How'd you pull that off without anyone questioning you?"

"Just a little bit of maneuvering on my part. We're working on a big project right now and I asked for control of all requisitions relating to it."

"And the colonel agreed?"

"Yeah. For some reason she's playing nice." Russell grinned and Kurt gave a low chuckle. "So, I'm going to play nice right back until I get what I need to kick her ass out of the service."

"Good move, Len. Show me the toys you brought me to play with."

Katie closed the front door and took off her light jacket, hanging it on the coat hook by the door. She turned back to the security control pad and keyed in the code to secure the door for the night.

"Have a good time?" Dean asked as she entered the front room from the kitchen.

"Yes, actually, I did. I never thought a baby shower would be much fun and I was afraid it was going to turn out to be a real drag, but it turned out to be a hoot of a time."

Dean raised an eyebrow in disbelief. "Yeah? And how'd McKenna pull that off?"

"Instead of playing the typical baby shower kinds of games, she set up a mini casino."

"Really?" Dean was intrigued.

"Yeah. She had a blackjack table, a roulette set up, and even a mini craps table."

"Those are my kind of games," Dean said as they walked into the kitchen. "I just brewed some chamomile, want to join me?"

"Sure, it'll help me to wind down. I'm still running on a high from the shower. McKenna set it up so that the top four chip winners at the end of the evening won the door prizes. Sandy was laughing so hard the entire evening that we thought she was going to give birth right then and there."

"Did you wind up one of the winners?"

"Hah! No, I actually wound up with the least number of chips. I did win a prize, though...the *booby* prize!" Katie reached into her pocket and pulled out a gift certificate and handed it to Dean.

Dean looked at the certificate and frowned. "A free consultation with a plastic surgeon?"

"Yeah." Katie laughed. "McKenna's husband is a plastic surgeon who specializes in breast implants."

"Hmmm, well..." Dean put her thumbs together, steepling her index fingers to form a picture frame then holding them out to examine Katie's chest. Katie put her hands on her hips and sighed, and Dean smiled and put her hands down, "Nah. I kinda like them just the way they are."

"Good answer," Katie said with a laugh. "Now, how about that tea?"

Dean fixed two cups and Katie pulled out a package of Lorna Doone cookies, taking out several and putting them on a plate. They carried their snack to the table and sat down, enjoying a comfortable silence as they sipped their tea and ate cookies.

There was one cookie left on the plate and they eyed each other like two gunslingers in the Wild West sizing up an opponent. Both reached for it simultaneously, but Dean's longer arm reached the prize first. She snapped it up with a satisfied grin and took it halfway to her mouth then stopped, snapped it in two, and handed Katie half. Rather than taking it from Dean, Katie took the hand holding the cookie and brought it to her lips. She opened her mouth and guided the cookie in, sucking on Dean's fingers as she pulled the cookie from them.

"Mmm," Dean purred. "Want the other half too?"

Katie winked and swallowed. "No, you deserve your prize." Dean laughed and popped the cookie half into her mouth and chewed it. "So, how was your day?"

Dean's expression turned serious and she swallowed and drained the last of her tea. "Bill came up with an interesting out of the box theory today."

"From the matrix he's working on?" Katie picked up the teacups and cookie plate and took them to the kitchen sink.

"Not from the matrix itself, but from a piece of data he found in an FBI report. It seems that there has been an influx of persons of interest from the Middle East that are here in the U.S. taking flying lessons."

"What? They can't get a pilot's license in their own countries?"

"Not with the information they can get in the States."

"And what information can they only get in the States?" Katie asked, completely into the discussion.

"U.S. civil aviation procedures."

Katie thought about that for a bit. "He thinks they're planning a hijacking here in the States?"

"That would be part of his theory." Katie looked puzzled so Dean continued. "The rest of his theory would be that they would use the hijacked plane to inflict as much destruction as they could."

"My God, Dean, let's hope this remains a theory. Are any of the agencies privy to his theory?"

"We called Walt over at the FBI. He's going to get some field agents out to eyeball some of the training facilities."

Katie could tell just by the tone in Dean's voice and the slight slump in her shoulders that Dean wanted to be out in the field herself. "Will Army Intelligence be involved in the surveillance?"

"Nope. This is a civilian operation for now, but we're keeping an eye on it. The FBI did have the FAA issue another hijacker warning to all the airlines."

"You mean the FBI, CIA, and NSA are all cooperating on this?"

"They'd better be." Dean frowned, knowing that the possibility of such cooperation actually happening was very slim. "Look, I'm going to go out for a run. You want to join me?"

Katie knew the offer was sincere, and also knew that Dean hoped she would decline. Dean had a habit of needing to move while she thought. In her office, it was rocking in her chair; at home, it was either working out or going for a run.

"I think I'll pass." Katie gave Dean's arm a squeeze. "There's that show on the Food Channel I wanted to watch. He's doing seafood tonight."

Dean smiled and gave Katie a peck on the cheek. "I won't be out long," she said, and went to the bedroom to change.

Katie watched Dean as she left the room, then went over to the sink and washed up the dishes, gave the cats their nighttime snacks, and snuggled into her favorite chair to watch her show.

Katie smiled in satisfaction, confident that she could prepare the new recipe on the weekend. She put down the notepad where she had scribbled out the directions for the seafood dish and picked up the remote control. "Dean?" Katie called as she clicked off the television.

"Yes?" Dean purred in Katie's ear.

"Arrrgh!" Katie said as she jumped in place. "Where did you come from!"

"Hmm, well, once upon a time, my mom and dad..."

Katie turned to face Dean, a semi-serious look on her face, but when she looked into the sapphire pools innocently looking back at her, she just shrugged, got up on her tiptoes and planted a kiss on Dean's lips. "You are incorrigible, Deanna Peterson."

"So you keep telling me," Dean said, returning the kiss.

"I take it your run was good?"

"Yep," Dean said simply. "Now, what did you want to ask me?"

Katie slowly lowered her heels back to the floor, mesmerized by the intensity of color in her lover's eyes.

Dean waited, then waved a hand in front of Katie's face. "Earth to Katie," Dean whispered softly.

"Uh, yeah, sorry. Sometimes I just fall into your eyes and can't seem to get myself back out, ya know?"

"Mmm, yeah, I know. I have the same problem sometimes with yours. Now, what were you going to ask?"

"I wanted to know what you thought of inviting the guys over for dinner next Saturday. I have some killer recipes I'd like to try out."

"It sounds like a good time to me. I'll ask them tomorrow. Now, how about we pick up where we left off?"

Katie frowned. "Where did we leave off?"

"Right here," Dean said as she lowered her head and placed her lips on Katie's, lingering a bit longer than usual. When they parted, Dean took Katie's hand and led the way to the bedroom.

"This is some fine equipment, Len." Kurt finished putting the last piece into his trunk.

"And it better come back in fine condition too."

Kurt nodded and closed the trunk. "I'll treat them with kid gloves."

"I can't tell you how important this is to me. I need to get some hard proof as soon as possible. My paperwork will be going to the promotion board at the end of next month and I want to insure a good recommendation this time."

"Len, I'm telling you, this just doesn't feel right. Why don't you just resign and come to work with me? It's a hell of a lot more fun on the outside and you'll be your own boss."

Len shook his head vehemently. "No! The Army is my life. It's been in Russell veins since the Civil War. I need to get this promotion and I need you to get the dirt on Deanna Peterson. The general will have no choice except to approve me as Peterson's replacement."

Kurt held up a hand in capitulation. "Okay, Len. Leave it to me. I'll get you what you need."

The two men shook hands and then Len led Dashiell back to the house while Kurt turned his car down the lane.

"Hi, guys, c'mon in." Katie swung the door open wide and Bill and Dirk stepped in. Bill was carrying a small cooler and Dirk had his hands full with a large salad bowl filled with chunks of fresh melon, berries of all sorts, citrus sections, and grapes. "Wow, that looks good," she said as she led them toward the kitchen.

"Bill has us eating healthy again," Dirk said with a thin smile as he placed the salad into the refrigerator.

"What's in the cooler?" Katie asked as Bill set it on the counter by the sink. Bill opened the cooler exposing two pitchers of Sangria nestled in crushed ice. "Now those can't be healthy," Katie said with a chuckle.

"Au contraire," Dirk said with a grin, "red wines are actually good for you, and look, there's fruit, too."

Bill laughed and shook a finger at Dirk. "But only one or two small glasses a day."

"Well, we haven't had any all week, so we can have them all today." They all laughed and Bill closed the top on the cooler.

"I like your logic, Dirk, but I don't think it works that way," Dean said as she entered the kitchen through the sliding door that opened to the back deck.

"Maybe not, but we're going to drink it all anyway," Katie said as she patted Bill's arm gently. That elicited a smile from her guests.

"So, are we going to leave that cooler on the counter or bring it on out to the deck?" Dean asked as she grabbed a plate of hors d'ouvres from the refrigerator.

Dirk obligingly grabbed the cooler while Katie took some wine goblets from the stemware rack and followed the others to the deck. They were soon settled with plates of finger food and glasses of Sangria, looking out across the backyard where it sloped down toward the Occoquan Reservoir. It was a perfect day. The temperatures were in the low eighties, with a light breeze coming up through the trees from the water and plenty of sunshine shining down from a clear blue sky.

Dirk lifted his glass. "Here's to good friends." They all tapped their glasses together with a satisfying clink, then sipped at the wine. They sat without speaking for a while just soaking in the sun and taking in their surroundings. Bill was the first to break the silence.

"So, what's up your culinary sleeve today, Katie?"

"I thought we'd start off with some steamers, and then I'll do some marinated salmon on cedar planks. I got some new marinade recipes from that grilling show on Thursday nights. I'm trying one on the salmon and another on some veggies for roasting. Dean made a nice salad for the side. We can have the fruit for dessert with homemade ice cream."

"Homemade ice cream? That sounds terrific. I'm hungry already, and let's start with dessert," Dirk said.

Katie laughed and took another sip of her wine. "You and Dean," she said with a grin, "are both hopeless when it comes to sweets." That earned her a sly smile from Dean.

Dirk pointed to a fisherman in a boat anchored just off shore from the house. "Wrong time of day for fishing, isn't it?"

"Maybe he just wants to enjoy a day on the river." Dean adjusted her sunglasses and took a longer look at the boat, alarmed by the owner's disregard for the dam warning signs. She had selected that particular site to build on mainly because it was perfect for her house design, but it was also at the junction of the Occoquan River Dam that formed the Occoquan Reservoir. Boats weren't supposed to come within a specified safety perimeter of the dam, which afforded her even more privacy. "Guess he can't read warning signs either. Boats aren't supposed to go beyond those marker buoys," she said, pointing at the bobbing items in the distance. "We'd better keep an eye on him, just in case he gets into trouble."

Kurt swore softly as he listened to the conversation through the earpiece and tugged at his fishing pole as a bluegill nibbled at the bait. He knew he was taking a chance by anchoring so close to her shoreline, but the boat traffic on the reservoir was too heavy to filter out the noise and made this anchorage his only viable choice. He reached into the tackle box sitting on bench seat in front of him and adjusted the sound on the receiver. "C'mon," he whispered at the box, "just give me some damn crumbs I can follow up on and I'll call it a day."

"So, how are the plans for the nuptials coming?" Dirk asked as he reached for another cheese puff.

"Martha agreed to do the ceremony, but we're going to have to move the date," Katie said. Bill raised an eyebrow in question.

"Martha has to come to D.C. earlier than originally planned, so we're going to have the ceremony a week earlier — on the first instead of the eighth."

"You two will still be available, won't you?" Dean asked. "Martha just called last night and we figured we could let you know about the change when we saw you today. We're still going to have it here; it'll just mean getting the place ready sooner." Dean looked over at Katie, who smiled and nodded in agreement.

"No problem, Dean," Dirk said, looking over at his partner.

"No, ma'am," Bill echoed, "not a problem at all. Are Tracy and the crew from New York coming?"

Dean just grinned and Katie laughed. "You mean you didn't hear Linna's hooting way down here?" Katie said as she caught her breath between giggles. "They'll all be here. You can bet the farm on that."

"Well," Dirk stood and held his drink high, "here's to the future. May all your mornings be cheer filled, your afternoons peace filled, and your nights..." He tapped his index finger on his lips then smiled broadly, a wicked twinkle in his eye. He looked at his partner, who gave him a stern look. "What?" Dirk said in mock outrage. "I was just going to say...and your nights, bliss filled."

"Yeah, right," Dean, Katie, and Bill said in unison, touching their glasses together and then taking a sip, sealing the toast forever.

Dean slipped her hand into the pocket of her shorts and fingered the tattered piece of paper she had been carrying for weeks. *Your destiny lies before you. Choose wisely.*

Kurt smiled and began making his plans. September first was just a few weeks away. He packed up his gear, started the small fifteen horsepower motor, and raised anchor. He was lousy at fishing for fish, but very good at fishing for information. Now he needed to make plans for the first. Sitting out on the reservoir was not an option; he'd need a new approach. He either had to get in closer or get more toys from Len. He looked back at the property, taking in the details of the surroundings. It wasn't going to be easy, but he had time.

"Looks like our fisherman is giving up." Bill nodded in the direction of the small boat that was weighing anchor.

"It's too hot right now anyway. Fish won't be biting in this heat," Dean said, watching the boat depart. "He must be a newbie to the area."

"Maybe he just needed some time away from the wife," Dirk suggested.

"He sure had a lot of gear in that small boat if that's all he wanted to do," Dean replied. "Well, enough about him. Anyone hungry for steamers?"

Katie took the hint and got up and went into the house. "Light the grill," she said over her shoulder as she slid the door closed behind her.

Dean dutifully got up and went over to the grill. She turned on the tank, opened the top, and turned on the burners. She had to hit the ignition switch twice before the gas caught. Then she closed the top and surveyed the back of the house.

She had taken pains to capture the best elements of Wright's *Fallingwater* design in her own house. All she had needed to begin building her dream home was to find this piece of property on the hillside overlooking the Occoquan River slightly to the north and the Occoquan Reservoir in front of her. It took years and patience, but the final result was breathtaking. Because of the many windows and open floorplan, the entire house was full of light. She did most of the interior work herself — staining woodwork, laying and sealing the floor tiles, even installing the lighting, sinks, cabinets, and bathroom fixtures. She'd spent every spare dime on her home and it filled her with joy every time she walked through it. The deck off the main room was larger than the one at *Fallingwater*, but then she'd had to compromise on some of Wright's designs, too. The decks weren't made of concrete and slate, but of man-made decking and steel beams. There wasn't a comparable Bear Run to cascade from under the home either, but there was a small creek babbling close by that followed the stone walkway to the water where she'd laid out a flagstone patio. And she didn't have Wright's plunge pools, but did have a nice large hot tub sitting on the deck off the master bedroom. She had used as much native rock as she could find and haul to the site by herself to supplement the rock the contractor brought in, and he incorporated as much of the natural rock into the project as he could. He was also a fan of Wright and the opportunity to build something similar to *Fallingwater* was his dream, too. Between the two of them, they took Wright's basics and incorporated new techniques and materials that were more cost effective but still allowed the feel and flow of Wright's genius in the completed project.

The house was cantilevered out from the hillside, albeit without the waterfall, and the drive up to the house wasn't as hidden as Wright's was, but the back was similar, with all the trees and jutting rocks that filled the hillside as it dropped down toward the water. Because of the trees and the steep incline, the deck was very private and she had purchased the lot on each side of her home as soon as she could afford them. This ensured her privacy even more and she and Katie were looking forward to closing on the last two pieces in the cul-de-sac sometime at the end of August. Only the survey of the property boundaries needed to be completed along with the marking of the easement for the power authority. Once the new deed with the correct survey points was completed, they would be able to close on the property and file the deed. She and Katie would then own the entire cul-de-sac...their own Shangri-La in Occoquan, Virginia. A stone's throw from the nation's capital, but seemingly thousands of miles away from the encroachment of humanity. It was their home, their castle, and her safety net.

"Yo, Dean," Dirk said, holding the pitcher of Sangria in front of Dean.

"Oh, sorry." Dean held out her glass. "Guess I was just spacing for a minute."

"Or two," Dirk said as he refilled her glass. "Something on your mind?"

"Oh, no. I was just thinking about the ceremony. The deck will be perfect, don't you think?"

Dirk turned and looked around. "Yep. Perfect. Is there anything that Bill and I can do to help get things ready? We have the last week in August off."

Dean smiled at the generous offer. "Aren't you two going somewhere?"

"Eh." He shrugged his shoulders. "We were going to visit my folks, but we can do that anytime." He winked. "Actually, I'd love to stick around and help. Dad's been after us to paint the barn and it's just too darn hot in August to make that sound like a fun vacation."

"Tell you what," Dean said, "you help us with the wedding arrangements and we'll come help you paint the barn this fall. Deal?" She held out her hand.

Dirk quickly shook her hand, knowing he'd gotten the better end. "Deal."

"Wow...those were great." Bill chucked his last clamshell into the big bowl. Between the four of them, they had polished off six dozen clams and the discard bowl was overflowing with cast-off shells.

"We'll let those settle a bit before I start on the main course," Katie said as she drained the last of her Sangria. Looking at the bottom of her empty glass, she observed, "I think it's time to switch to iced tea."

"Got that right." Bill looked around the deck and noted the strategic layout of the house. In addition to it being a great design, the placement at the back of the lot on the steep slope toward the water afforded the two women optimal privacy. He hoped that some day he and Dirk would be able to build something similar, where they could relax and be themselves with no worries about nosy neighbors. In the meantime, they'd found a loft apartment in a converted warehouse just off of US 1 between Crystal City and Alexandria. The location was terrific and it had a great layout and decent privacy, but they didn't have the outside space that a house would.

"So, did you hear about the deal Dean made with Dirk?" Bill asked.

Katie nodded and grinned. "Yup," she said slowly. "And, I think Dirk got the better end of that one. There's not a whole lot to do here to get ready." She looked around the deck. "String a few lights here, some candles there, spread some flowers around the deck. It's not like it's going to be a big shindig, just a few close friends."

"No family?" Bill asked. Dean never talked much about her family and even less about Katie's.

"Nope. We're it now." Katie's flipped her sunglasses down over her eyes and sighed. "With Dean's father's passing, that's just about the end of the line for us. But, hey, you guys are our family," she said, regaining her spirit as she reached over and squeezed his forearm.

"Dean never talks about her family, or yours, for that matter. I knew she and her dad were estranged for a long time and just recently resolved some old issues, but she's not very vocal when it comes to personal stuff. Except for you," Bill added. That made Katie's eyebrows shoot up. "Uh, oh, no...not that kind of personal," he amended quickly. "Even when she does talk about you, it's because I've dragged it out of her, but when she does, her demeanor changes in a flash. Her eyes glitter and her smile gets broader; she oozes happiness from every pore of her body. It's like popping a champagne cork — she just bubbles over. You really have made her happy."

Katie blushed deeply. "That goes both ways, my friend. I can't imagine spending my life without her. I never dreamed that I could love someone so deeply and so completely. When we're together, she makes me feel like I'm the one and only person in the universe. Our connection is so intense, so finely tuned and powerful, it's like we're old souls united at last."

"Wow," Bill said in a whisper. "That's awesome."

"What's awesome?" Dean took a seat next to Katie and leaned in to examine the blush that was receding from her lover's cheeks.

"You are, my love." Katie leaned forward, gently putting a hand on the side of her lover's face and stroking her cheek. She moved in closer and met Dean's lips with hers, which relit the blush in her cheeks, but this time it came from the heat of passion and not embarrassment.

Later that night, Kurt watched until the two male guests left, then he drove around to where he had tied off his boat. He paddled over to the point and waited, watching through the trees until the last light blinked out in the house before paddling the rest of the way to the base of the cliff. Dressed in black from head to toe, he quietly tied off his craft just down the shore from the flagstone patio. Dean had been kind enough to cut back the brush about four feet, allowing him to stay dry and skirt along the brush line to the stone walkway.

He flipped down his night vision goggles and scanned the area, then he flipped on the Voice Actuated Sensor, fine tuning it and listening intently through the one earbud that was fixed into his right ear. The only sounds he picked up were the rustle of a breeze in the leaves, the trickle of water in the brook next to the walkway, and the buzzing insects and crickets. He crept up the walkway, constantly scanning and listening. At the top, he paused behind a string of large azaleas that lined the perimeter of the property. He assessed the exterior of the house and decided to pick out a path that would use the azaleas for cover.

Kurt swore under his breath as he stumbled over an exposed tree root and nearly tumbled down the steep slope. Only his quick reflexes saved him. The further he went toward the house, the worse his footing became. Soft ground turned to rock and the rock was picking up moisture from the cooler night air, causing it to be slick and treacherous. He made it as far as he could and decided that this would not be a viable approach. Reversing his direction, he returned to the walkway. He wasn't certain that there were motion sensor lights, but suspected that the colonel would have them. To be on the safe side, he stayed as far away from the buildings as he could, again staying in the perimeter of the woods.

This side wasn't as steep or as slippery and his footing was sure and silent. The problem was there was too much open ground between him and the front of the house. He stopped mid-way and surveyed the situation. He didn't see a good way to get to the back of the house without any cover. The landscaping at the front was formidable and could provide cover, but getting to it without tripping motion sensors would be impossible unless he shut off the electricity.

Electricity, he thought, *where are you?* He searched the exterior for the hook-up. He found one on the garage, but none on the house, also noting the several spotlights mounted on the house and garage. The garage had been built closer to the road leading into the cul-de-sac, but the entire lot was tree lined. With the house set toward the back edge of the property, the trees and garage helped to almost totally obscure it from the road. Kurt eyed the line attached to the garage and found the phone and cable lines entered through the same area of the garage. He assumed the lines must all be buried since he found no trace of exterior lines running from the garage to the house. "It's never easy," he whispered as he got up and slowly moved along the trees as far as he could to get a view of the back from this side. Halting when he started to lose his footing on the steep slope, he pulled out a small notebook and jotted some notes and a quick sketch of the property. He put the notebook away, retraced his steps, and quietly returned to the boat.

Among the night shadows inside the house, three pairs of eyes watched the intruder from window to window until his form slipped down the walkway toward the water. Spice led the troop back to the bedroom where their mistresses were entwined in blissful slumber. With the grace of her species, she jumped up on the bed, landing as soft as a feather near Dean's pillow. She trod her way gently to where Dean's head rested. Lying down by her ear, she reported her findings in an ancient language lost to humans. Just as stealthily, she moved to the foot of the bed to join her mates, where they took turns napping and listening in the still of the night.

Colonel Peterson sat in her leather chair facing the window that looked out into the courtyard of the Pentagon. Her eyes were shut as she slowly rocked and turned over the information that Captain Jarvis had handed to her. The fine muscles around her eyes appeared relaxed, but the tension in her jaw betrayed what she was feeling; the muscles there clenched and slackened rhythmically.

Captain Jarvis waited quietly, considering the extent of the impact his report had made on his commander. He had more bad news to impart, but wanted to wait until he could better judge his boss' mindset. He could tell she was really ticked off that Major Russell had succeeded with an end run around her and gotten the general's approval for his "readiness plan", as he called it. He looked at her reflection in the window, trying to gauge the best way to proceed. He was spared making the decision as the colonel turned around and faced him.

"So, what's the rest of the bad news?" Colonel Peterson asked without hesitation.

Bill swallowed. "The FAA warnings to the airlines keep stacking up." He handed an updated matrix to Colonel Peterson. "And," he continued, "the President asked for an updated report on al Qaeda during the intelligence briefing. He was told that the airlines have been warned to be aware of possible hijackings."

Colonel Peterson looked at the matrix and frowned. "They keep warning of hijackings, but they are still couching it using traditional thinking. Why the hell haven't they acted on the theory you gave them? Politicians! They're going to muck things up and back us into a corner that we're going to have to fight to get out of." She took a deep breath. Every time she thought of the elected officials on the Hill, she shook her head in disgust. "Have you talked with Walt at the Bureau lately?"

"Yes, ma'am. He passed along the theory the day we gave it to him, but he hasn't heard any rumblings on anyone taking it seriously. Every time he brings it up, they turn to another subject and ignore him. He's as frustrated as we are."

"Something is coming, Bill. I can smell it, taste it, feel it." She scratched the back of her neck. "I just can't see it." She slammed her fist on her desk. "Damn it, Bill!"

Captain Jarvis watched as she paced like a caged tiger treading back and forth in its confinement. He knew she would rather be in the field, gathering intelligence and sifting through the minutia herself — touching, listening, and interpreting. Those were her strengths. She was the best field agent the Army had and she was constrained by her position as aide to General Carlton. And then there was Major Russell to consider. His end run around her to General Carlton had the colonel spitting bullets. Bill shook his head thinking about the wasted resources Russell's readiness scenarios were going to involve. The major was in the wrong section if he wanted to play war games, but Russell had sucked up to the aide of Admiral Vincent Morris. Morris was the head of combined military intelligence and, with the help of the admiral's aide, Russell had sold his proposal to Admiral Morris. Russell was even allowed to pull some key personnel from the IOC to play with him. No wonder the colonel was so ticked. His shorthanded crew at the IOC was now processing less and less information as it came in. He just hoped they would be able to find a thread and follow it to something tangible. He hated to be blind.

"All right, Bill. Keep up the good work. Let me know if anything breaks."

Bill stood. "Yes, ma'am." He turned and left the office, closing the door quietly behind him.

Dean silently cursed her outburst in front of the captain. Walking back to her chair, she sat, staring at the desk and the piles of paperwork in front of her. She loathed being behind a desk and detested even more being out-maneuvered by Russell. She was so wrapped up in meetings with the general, preparing reports for the Joint Chiefs, and walking on eggshells trying not to piss off the Secretary of the Army, that she had completely missed his move. She hadn't even anticipated it. And that disturbed her most. The past few months were really taking a toll. Even that damned picnic at James River State Park was still nipping at her. She'd been kicking herself for letting her guard down and just knew that one infraction was going to cause her grief. That cadence the troop sang, the one her unit wrote, kept playing in her head. Only that unit used it and someone on that trail knew her. Then there was the kid. That kid definitely had a parent working at the Pentagon. Why else would he have been waiting at the entrance? She needed to look into him and get to the bottom of it. Just thinking about it made her neck start to itch.

And finally, there was her father's death. She had just started to re-connect with her dad and now he was out of her life again.

The last of her family was gone. She picked up the small photograph on her desk. It was a head shot of her with her dad. Katie had taken it at Christmas. The resemblance between father and daughter was remarkable. They had the same square jaw, dark hair, and clear blue eyes. She set the photo down and trailed her fingers across the top of the frame. She was alone now. "No, that's not true," she whispered. "I'll always have Katie." Just the thought of Katie brought a smile to her face and lifted her spirits. Katie had been the only bright spot in her life for the past several weeks. Her proposal was so awkward and so unlike her normal confident self, but Katie didn't seem to notice. And after she accepted, the butterflies settled and the expectation of life forever with Katie was her life raft in a sea of constant turmoil and treachery. And an uncertain future.

Katie paused in her dinner preparations as she heard the front door open, and smiled as the cats sped off to welcome their other mistress. She listened as Dean greeted each cat, then tracked her footsteps as Dean traversed the house to the kitchen. She anticipated the approach and welcomed the warm embrace as Dean slipped her arms around her waist from behind.

"Hey, love. How was your day?" Katie asked.

"Eh, same stuff, different day. How was yours?" Dean tilted her head down to place her lips on Katie's neck, gently caressing the bare skin that was exposed by the oversized tank top.

Katie groaned softly as Dean's lips and breath warmed her skin. "Mmm, not bad," she managed to say as she turned to face her lover. She raised her head and received the next kiss on her lips.

"Ah, that's some spice!" Dean licked her lips. "Creole?"

"Close. It's a Jamaican recipe."

Dean kissed Katie again, prolonging the kiss to get a better taste then gently running her tongue across Katie's lips. "Mmmhmm...I can taste the mango."

"It'll be ready in about twenty minutes. Go shower and get comfy," Katie said as Dean released her. I'll bring you an iced tea."

Dean smiled and shook her head. "Make it a Southern Comfort Manhattan instead." Then she turned and headed to the master bedroom.

Dean stepped out of the steamy shower stall and wrapped the bath towel around herself. She wiped the steam off the mirror with her hand and watched her figure wiggle in the rivulets that gathered and ran down the glass. Picking up a dry washcloth, she wiped the mirror dry and bent forward, peering in to get a closer look at her face. Raising her chin, she turned her head from side to side, examining her face closely. Moving even closer, her finger traced the age lines beginning to make a deeper, permanent appearance around her eyes, mouth, and forehead. Dean wasn't vain regarding her appearance — she believed aging was a natural process. She wasn't ready for the signs of it to show up so early, but at thirty-nine she had to expect some changes. This summer seemed to be taking a toll on her physically. She stood back and examined the rest of her body, flexing her muscles. She had the body of an athlete and was still suitably fit, but there were signs of recent weight loss. Her face was gaunt and her pelvic and collar bones were more pronounced. She decided to make a conscious effort to eat better and stop skipping lunches at work.

Katie watched silently as Dean frowned, pursed her lips, and finally shrugged in defeat as she picked up her body lotion and poured a liberal amount into her hand.

"This latest investigation is getting to you, isn't it?" Dean waggled her hand and Katie pinned Dean with a questioning look. "But it's not the only thing, is it?"

Dean paused in applying her lotion. She knew better than to hedge her answer with Katie, a top notch interrogator. Trying to dodge her questions never worked, so she came clean. "James River Park."

"Ahh. Okay, that explains it. What doesn't make sense is what it's doing to you."

Dean cocked her head and frowned. "What it's doing to me?"

"Mmmhmm." Katie stripped the towel away and traced the lines on Dean's face, her collar bone, abdomen, and hips. She stepped back and looked Dean over from head to toe. "What's your weight now?"

Dean shrugged. "Okay, I'm about five pounds light."

"Only five?" Katie challenged, gaze pinning Dean again.

"All right, maybe eight or...ten," she allowed hesitantly.

Katie frowned. "Nothing is worth worrying yourself sick over. You need to take care of yourself."

"I will, love. I promise."

Katie reached over and stroked Dean's body. "You still take my breath away," Katie said in a sexy whisper. She picked up the body lotion, poured some into her hand, and began applying it to Dean's back.

Dean smiled and started humming, then singing out loud: "'Will you still need me, will you still feed me, when I'm sixty-four?'"

Katie couldn't help giggling as she joined Dean for the remaining verses of the old Beatles song as they finished applying lotion and then danced out of the bathroom and into the bedroom. They both fell onto their backs on the waterbed, tears of laughter streaming down their faces.

When the giggles subsided, Dean rolled onto her side, smiled, and reached out to wipe a tear from Katie's face. "You are my life, my joy, my love. Thank you."

"You're welcome." Katie kissed Dean. "You're not sixty-four yet, but I'm still going to feed you. So put some clothes on," she tenderly patted Dean's butt, "and come to dinner." She winked at her partner as she rose to leave and added, "Your drink is on the dresser."

Dean rolled back onto her back and grinned. "Hon, you're a better pick-me-up than a Manhattan any day."

The evening was another one for the record books. The temperature was a comfortable eighty-four degrees. Puffy clouds dotted the evening sky and turned pink, then pinkish-purple, and finally gray as the sun set in the west. They had gotten into the habit of having their dessert while seated on the teakwood bench on the flagstone patio by the water. The birds were just ending their serenade for the evening and the reservoir was devoid of any boat traffic. The sounds of soft music could barely be heard as it skimmed across the water from a distant home.

"I love evenings like this." Katie snuggled closer to Dean now that the darkness of the night was upon them. Across the water they could see lights blink on as campers lit lanterns or campfires.

Dean settled an arm around Katie's shoulders. "Me too."

"So, James River Park," Katie prompted.

Dean let out a breath. "Yeah. It's been nipping at me ever since. I can't shake the feeling that something bad is going to happen because of it."

"But it's been quite a while now. If something was going to come from it, wouldn't it have happened by now?" Katie waited, judging Dean's silence. "It's the cadence, isn't it? You're thinking someone who knows you was there with the troop."

"That's about it."

"Dean, any of the scouts in that troop could have picked up that cadence from their father...or mother...or from someone's friend. It doesn't mean that there was someone there that knows you. Besides, the position we were in, no one would have been able to see our faces."

"You're right, you're right. But my neck hairs...they never lie."

"Well, there's that," Katie agreed. "But you've got so much happening at work right now, those neck hairs of yours..." Katie reached up and scratched them, "could be reacting to all sorts of stuff."

They sat in silence, each mulling over the possibilities. Dean finally broke the silence. "What's on your schedule for the rest of the week? Are you going to have to go to Kansas City?"

"Yes." Katie sighed. "I've been called to testify in the drug trial after all. The attorney for the defense is trying everything to get this jerk off; they're reaching for straws." She sat up and turned toward Dean. "I thought I'd try to spend some time with Reverend Martha in the evenings."

"She'll love that."

"Yeah. I called her today and told her I might be in town for a few days. She's lining up several new restaurants for us to try out."

"Better take some antacid with you."

"Already packed," Katie said with a giggle. "I learned my lesson last time."

"Do you have any idea how long you'll be gone?"

Katie snuggled closer. "Why, I believe you're going to miss me."

"You bet!" Dean said.

"I'm hoping I'll only be there a day or two, but I hear the defense lawyer is a master at drawing things out. Worst case scenario, I'll be back next Wednesday." Dean frowned. "I'll call you every night and we can talk dirty over the phone." This made Dean's head jerk around. "Oh, you like that idea, huh?" she said with a grin.

Dean smothered a giggle. "Phone sex, eh? Now, where would you have learned how to do that?"

Katie whispered into Dean's ear, "You haven't learned everything about me quite yet, and don't forget — I too have many talents."

The next morning was a frenzied rush as Katie tucked her suitcases into her car for the trip to Kansas City.

"Are you sure you don't want me to drop you at the airport?" Dean asked.

"No, love. For the tenth time — I'd rather leave the car at the airport since I don't know for sure when I'll be back." Katie picked up her backpack and slung it over her shoulder. "Are you sure you're going to be okay without me around for a bit?"

"For the tenth time, I'll be fine."

"You're going to make sure you eat and relax every night?"

"For the eleventh time, I'll be fine."

Katie put her hands on her hips. "I'll call you every night, so you better be ready to tell me every detail of your day, including—"

"Yeah, yeah...but don't forget about the sex talk."

Katie laughed, glad to see the humor twinkling in Dean's eyes. "Come here," she crooked her finger at Dean, "and give me a proper kiss goodbye."

"Proper kiss? You mean the earlier ones weren't proper?" Dean cocked an eyebrow as she pulled Katie to her. She dropped her head down toward her lover and met her lips, softly at first and then with an urgency she hadn't anticipated. As they finally broke apart, Katie's eyes went wide as she inhaled deeply while a blush rose nicely on Dean's face.

"Uh, mphf...uh, now that's what I call proper," Katie said, enjoying the tingle that was flooding through her body.

"Yeah, proper," Dean said as she leaned in for one more *proper* goodbye.

Chapter Twenty-one
August 15

Katie was due home late that night and Dean wanted to finish her project before Katie arrived. She walked down the stairs to the lowest level of their three level hillside home. The lower level could be reached by a series of stairs from the deck on the second level that connected to a small deck off the den, or by the stairs inside the house. The exterior of the house was a combination of local stonework and glass, and the sides that faced the river and reservoir had accompanying decks. The entire house was cantilevered out from the hillside with the exception of the first level, which extended onto the property more than the two lower levels.

It was misting lightly outside, so Dean used the interior stairs. She went into the den and first adjusted the windows to the opaque setting. Satisfied that she was free from observation by anyone from the outside, she went to her secured closet and punched in the code for the week. Opening the door, she entered and pulled out the drawer that held several electronic devices. She selected the bug detector and closed the drawer and re-set the alarm on the door. She switched on the device and began a sweep of the entire room. Finding it clear of any listening devices, she decided to sweep the house from the top to the bottom. As she entered each room, she first converted the windows to the opaque setting and then completed a thorough sweep. The top level held the expansive living room/dining room combination with a large stone fireplace and a decent sized kitchen with an eating space that was small and cozy. It had a small table with four chairs and was just right for most of their meals. A laundry room and a half bathroom completed the first floor. That level also had a large double deck, one on each side of the house. Dean found the entire level clear of any devices. The second level held the master bedroom with its large bathroom, and a guest bedroom. A small reading room, stairwell, and full bathroom separated the two bedrooms on this level. All the rooms were connected by a deck which wrapped around three sides of the house, with the fourth side built into the hillside. Again, the sweep was clear. The third and bottom level, toward which she was now going, held her den, a smaller guest bedroom, and an exercise room with a full bath. The final level was also clear and she was satisfied that the entire house was clear of any listening devices.

Her final sweep was of the exterior of the property that could be walked around, the garage, and the walkway down to the river. Satisfied the entire house and property were clear, she returned to the den and replaced the detection device in its drawer in the secured closet, resetting the code.

Next she went out to the garage to her workshop. One wall held a tall unit that was divided into smaller cube-like openings. The cubbies held pieces of wood organized by size, dowels of various sizes, and rolls of paper, as well as other assorted materials. Dean selected one of the rolls that contained the blueprints of her house and unrolled it on the workbench. She was going to install four wireless mini cameras and needed to determine the optimum location for each device in order to cover the largest area. She wasn't as concerned with the back side of the house since the natural terrain of the steep slope and the reservoir would provide privacy protection. Taking into account the range of the lenses and angles that could be covered, she selected the locations for the cameras: a tall oak at the top of the walkway that led to the patio on the reservoir; one on each front corner of the house; and one on the far corner of the garage that faced the road. It wasn't a perfect arrangement because it left a narrow strip of land behind the garage unobserved, but she could pick up another camera or two and then the entire property would be covered. She reviewed her selections, then rolled up the blueprints and returned them to their storage bin.

She opened the box she'd brought home and carefully ordered the contents on the workbench. Skimming through the directions, she gathered the tools she would need, put them in her leather work belt, and made sure she had extra screws. Grabbing the cameras, photoelectric cells to power them, and wiring, Dean went out to install the visual surveillance equipment. She had a full two hours before Katie was due, and that was plenty of time to place them and test them out.

While the software finished loading, Dean plugged the external receiver into the computer. She pulled up the screen images one at a time, satisfied with the first three. The viewing range of the one on the garage would need to be adjusted, but it would do for now. She entered a few keystrokes and the four views filled the screen, one in each corner of the monitor. She was eager to see how well they would work at night.

Checking her watch and realizing that Katie should be home any minute, Dean changed the monitor to show just the view from the garage camera and watched as it focused on the road leading to their property. She could see Lydia, the neighbor who lived at the beginning of their road, walking her dog. She watched as Lydia stopped and bent down to pick something up along the way. "Good woman," Dean said in a whisper as she realized it was the dog's excrement that Lydia was picking up. "Can't let the neighborhood go to the dogs." She watched another minute or two before the headlights of a car turned into the road and came directly into the cul-de-sac. Dean smiled as she saw Katie's face through the windshield. Her lips were moving and her head was bobbing from side to side while her right hand tapped a beat on the steering wheel. She went out of view as she pulled up to the garage door.

Dean selected the camera at the top of the walkway and saw Katie's brake lights brighten as she stopped the car and the garage door began rolling down. Switching to the camera at the right front, she barely caught the side door of the garage opening in the left portion of the screen. "Hmm, looks like there's another dead spot." She tried the other camera, but its focus was out into the yard and not toward the front door. "Maybe I'll pick up a wide angle camera too," Dean said softly as she clicked on the record mode and shut down the computer screen before hurrying up the stairs to meet her lover.

Dean scowled as she reviewed the personnel records. Things couldn't have turned out worse. The records she was reviewing were the latest on Army personnel working at the Pentagon, and Major Russell was the only person currently assigned that had also been in her company at Fort Huachuca that had a son approximately the age of the Boy Scout she'd seen at the park and at the Pentagon's main entrance. *Nearly two hundred soldiers in that company and thirty in my unit, and the only one that fits the bill is Len Russell. Just my luck.* She entered a few more keystrokes and Russell's file filled her screen. Scrolling through it, she came to the dependents page and there was a picture of the teen. It was definitely Russell's son that had followed them at James River Park. And, if the boy was a chip off the old block, she was sure that he reported everything he saw to his old man. She just couldn't understand why Russell hadn't yet acted on the information. *Unless Russell didn't notice us,* she thought. *Maybe he assumed we were a hetero couple?* Dean shook her head. "We can only hope for the best," she whispered.

She closed the file and went to look out the window. In the tree just below, she spied the female cardinal, camouflaged.

"That's it, little one," she cooed softly. "Make yourself a part of the background. Keep your head down in the foliage and an eye out for the enemy. They'll never see you coming until you're ready to spring out."

She watched the bird as it jumped from branch to branch, seemingly looking for the best cover as it moved along its decided path through the tree. Suddenly the bird dove to the ground, catching the prey it had been stalking in its beak in mid-flight, then just as quickly disappearing again in the thick foliage of the next tree.

Her thoughts went back to Russell and she wondered if he was hiding in the foliage, just waiting to spring out at her. From what she remembered, he never thought things through, always acted too quickly. That was his downfall in intelligence work: he never waited for the bigger picture to develop and that often resulted in badly planned and executed operations. If he was still operating that way, maybe she and Katie were safe because he would have stepped forward by now. He would have slapped her with a UCMJ

Article 133: Conduct Unbecoming an Officer, and she would be on her way out of the Army. But, he would have to prove the charge and she didn't think the word of his son would be damning.

She sighed. Even if she beat the charge in court, her military days would be numbered. Just the allegation would be devastating. General Carlton surely knew, but never stepped into the arena to "ask" because then she would be obliged to report. If anything came out about her relationship with Katie, whether it was proven or not, General Carlton would have no recourse but to reassign her. It would have to be out of intelligence work, because she would be considered a security risk. Her productive career would be over. She could have a successful career outside the military. Many of her former colleagues ran corporate security firms and she could easily get a job with one of them, but the Army was her life. It was there for her when she was lost and gave her a way of life she was good at...very good. The civilian world couldn't match the challenges of today's Army.

Dean watched the female cardinal slip out from her cover again and wing her way over the roof line of the courtyard. Dean smiled at her flight and watched until she soared out of sight, then she returned to her desk and opened the next file.

Captain Jarvis exited the IOC and took the stairs up two flights to Corridor 5 and then to the A Ring and Colonel Peterson's office. Arriving at the door, he hesitated for just a second before knocking. The past week and a half, his superior's disposition was definitely getting harder and harder to read. Every time he had a meeting with the colonel, he felt he was walking on eggshells. Everyone in the IOC was overloaded and the colonel was helping out as much as she could along with all her other duties, and it was taking a toll on her, physically and mentally. She was irritable and demanding, well beyond her normal parameters, and he could see the strain in her face. There were dark circles under her eyes and the gauntness of her normally striking features was worrying him. She could handle stress better than anyone he knew, but as the days went by, he was becoming more and more concerned. He'd seen her operate under worse conditions and never blink an eye. Something more was on her mind than just the enigma before them. He was glad that Katie was back from Kansas City and hoped that she would be able to pull Dean back from the depths of wherever she had been lately. He wished the colonel trusted him enough to talk to him, but he didn't want to step over the line, even though he considered her a close friend as well as his superior officer. Bill shook his head, sucked in a breath, and knocked on the door.

"Enter!" came the reply in a harsh tone.

Bill sucked in another breath and opened the door. *Maybe I should just bite the bullet and talk to her,* he thought as he opened the door. *What's the worst that could happen?*

"Good afternoon, Colonel." He walked to her desk and was waved to a seat. The colonel kept reading the file before her. He took a seat and waited a few seconds before she set the file down and raised her head to look at him. He cleared his throat and handed a file folder across the desk.

"Here's the latest information on post security updates for the European sector." Selecting a larger file, he passed it over the desk as well. "And here's the current information on our Stateside posts." Handing over a third file, he explained, "And these are the remaining post updates, including our independent operations."

Dean placed the files into a stack on her desk where they joined several other stacks.

"Also, Walt hasn't heard much else from that arrest that was made in the Midwest. The local bureau reapplied for a warrant to examine the guy's computer, but they haven't gotten a decision yet. The agent at that bureau who ferreted out the suspect thinks this guy is so full of hatred for Americans that he might be the type to crash an airplane into a metropolitan area to create the most death and destruction."

Dean raised an eyebrow. "Finally! Someone who's thinking outside the box! So what are they doing about it?"

Bill shook his head. "Not much. She originally asked for that warrant and didn't get it, but she sent a memo to D.C. and Walt saw that. Unfortunately, no one's acting on this agent's instincts."

"What's her name? We should get her to enlist," Dean said sarcastically. "We wouldn't ignore her like the Feds." Closing her eyes, she massaged her temples.

"Ma'am, are you okay?" Bill asked cautiously.

Dean opened her eyes and looked into the concerned eyes of her protégé. She debated crossing the line and confiding in her subordinate, especially as he might find himself in the line of fire if Russell was on her case for real.

"Frankly, Bill, I'm not doing too great."

"Is there anything I can do to help?"

Dean shook her head. "I'm not sure, but it would be nice to get your take on the situation."

"Situation?"

"I'm not sure if it's a situation for real or just something I'm imagining, but it's really getting to me." She stood and walked to the credenza, picked up the water pitcher and poured herself a tall glass. She looked at Bill and held the pitcher toward him in question.

"No, thank you, ma'am."

Dean replaced the pitcher and returned to her desk. She set the glass of water down and removed a bottle of aspirin from her top drawer, opened it, and tapped out four tablets. Popping them into her mouth, Dean washed them down with the water then looked up at Bill.

"This past May, I thought this was going to be the best summer of my life. Katie accepted my proposal and the future was looking bright. Then Dad died. Even though we expected it, it was still hard." Bill nodded and Dean took another drink of her water. "Now all this..." She pointed at the stacks and stacks of files that she had to review. "I know in my gut that something big is out there, but it's like finding a needle in a haystack. There's so much to look at and our interpreters can't keep up, and Russell has half the IOC out doing mock drills."

"But," Bill began, "this..." he waved his hand over the files, "is not unusual. We've had times like this before. Remember the attack on the U.S.S. Cole?"

"Exactly! We had a lot of this then, but this time it's worse!" She shook her head. "Bill, I'm not an alarmist, you know that. But I can't get past the feeling that this time, they, whoever *they* are, are coming after us. Up close and personal."

"I agree with you. And we've been working on that premise for months now. But, Colonel, forgive me, there's something else eating at you and I'm worried." He searched her face for a clue, then took the leap and landed with both feet across the line. "Dean, have you taken a good look at yourself lately? For a while now I've been seeing a noticeable difference in your physical appearance." He hesitated. "It got worse when Katie was gone. Things are okay with you two, aren't they?"

Dean was startled by his comment. "What? Yes, Katie and I are fine, just fine. Hell, we're better than fine!"

"Then what's gotten to you? What's ripping you apart?"

Dean lowered her head and let out a big breath. "Hmpf. If I knew the answer to that..."

"C'mon, Dean. Let me in. Let me help."

Dean nodded, taking her own leap. "You're right. This may be something I'm way off base with, but earlier this spring Katie and I went on a Saturday road trip and wound up at James River Park. It was beautiful there and we had a picnic lunch under a great old tree overlooking the river. Not a soul in sight all afternoon." She shrugged. "Katie fell asleep in my lap and when she woke, we sorta got carried away."

"Sorta got carried away? Like how?"

Dean blushed. "No...not like that. Anyway, we got to horsing around and I was on top of her and started to kiss her."

Bill raised his eyebrows in surprise. He'd been around Dean and Katie a lot and had never known the colonel to do anything in public that might even hint of impropriety.

"Yeah, yeah. I know what you're thinking. And yes, I let my guard down." She thought back to the moment. "Hell, there hadn't been anyone around for hours. Then all of a sudden there was this scout troop, double timing it up the path from the river right past us."

Now Bill was really amazed. "You didn't hear them coming?"

"No. We had the CD player on and I really wasn't tuning in to my surroundings. Like I said, I was caught off guard."

"Okay, so these Boy Scouts saw you. And someone recognized you?"

"That's just it. I'm not sure. When I heard them coming, we froze. I was...on my side and Katie was pretty much hidden from view. I had my hair tied back with my ball cap on in reverse. No one could have seen our faces."

"Okay, that's good. So what's got your knickers in a knot?"

"Two things. First, the troop was chanting an old cadence that was originated by my company back at Fort Huachuca earlier in my career. Second, after the troop ran out of sight, we started packing up. Then another scout came up the path and got a really good look at us. He even followed us back to the car."

"That's strange."

"Not as strange as seeing him at the west entrance of the Pentagon one day as I walked out with Katie."

"Ah, so you think he's related to someone here."

Dean nodded. "Not just *someone* here...he's Major Russell's son."

Bill's head dropped to his chest. "Shit."

"Couldn't have said it better myself."

"What's up with you and Russell anyway?" Bill asked quietly. "You two have a history?"

"You could say that." Dean stood and went back to the credenza for another glass of water. This time when she indicated the pitcher to Bill, he nodded and got up, retrieving a glass for her to pour into. They returned to their respective seats and sipped quietly for a moment. Dean set her glass down and folded her hands in front of her loosely.

"It happened back at Fort Huachuca. Russell was in my unit during our intelligence training. He wasn't married at the time and was feeling pretty cocky around the female officers. He was a first lieutenant at the time and I was a second lieutenant, so he was doing the 'God's gift to women' thing and all that."

"Trying to be the big man on campus?" Bill asked knowingly.

"Right. You've got the picture." She picked up her glass and took another sip. "Anyway, I've known about my orientation since high school and I just wasn't into his macho crap. Blew him right off when he came sniffing my way, only he wouldn't take no for an answer. Then he tried to get the other guys in the platoon to hit on me. I was pretty angry back then and didn't take the whole thing very well. One night, he came into my quarters drunk and proceeded to force his affections on me."

Bill let out a chuckle. "I'd have liked to have seen that. Or...should I say I'd have liked to have seen what happened to him."

Dean smiled. "I didn't punch his lights out but I was pretty forceful about putting an end to his advances, and the next morning I filed sexual harassment charges against him."

"And they didn't stick," Bill said, nodding in anticipation of the outcome.

"Right. I did file the charges, but the company commander got me to 'tone down' my accusations. He didn't want to see anything unpleasant come up on his watch. I was young and I followed his advice. Russell wound up with a letter of reprimand in his file, but no UCMJ charges."

"So, he's got a motive for holding a grudge."

Dean nodded. "Yes, he does."

"But if he knew anything, wouldn't he have filed charges against you by now?"

"That's what's driving me nuts. Maybe he knows, maybe he doesn't have a clue. If he knows, he's really playing it close to the chest. Maybe he's hoping to blackmail me in the future. His paperwork goes in for promotion in September. That would be the time to make his play, if he has one."

"You think he'd be satisfied with that?"

"Honestly? I think he'd rather try to bury me, but he'd need a ton of proof to do that...more than just his word or his son identifying us. I can feel the hate every time he enters this office, every time he passes me in the corridor, and every time he has to ask me for approvals. I think that's why he did the end run past me to the general."

"I'm sorry, Colonel. I know he's my superior officer but that was crap. I can't believe he did that."

"Yeah, sticks in my craw, too. But," she waved her hand, "it had a benefit. It's kept him out of my hair, even though it's been a double hardship on you and your unit."

"Okay, so what's the plan?"

"I don't have a plan."

"Well, let's put one together," Bill said confidently.

"Great dinner, Katie." Bill picked up his plate and carried it to the sink.

Dean had already finished her meal and removed her plate. Dirk was just finishing his third helping of mashed potatoes. "Absolutely," he said after he swallowed the final bite. "This is my all time favorite meal."

Katie had the afternoon off and prepared a huge meat loaf, garlic mashed potatoes, fresh green beans from a road stand on the way home, and an enormous salad loaded with other fresh veggies, also from the stand. She'd made enough for an army, so, she decided to invite the Army to dinner and called Dean and asked her to bring Bill and Dirk home with her. Her ulterior motive was to get Dean to relax and unwind a bit. She'd been working on her lover to do that since she got back from KC but to little avail. Tonight she was hoping with the help of the guys Dean might loosen up. So far, her plan didn't seem to be working. Dean ate better than she had the past two nights, but hardly said anything. Maybe her heads-up call that afternoon to enlist Bill's aid would help. If not, a serious talk was next on her list.

"I'm glad you liked it," Katie said as she looked at the scant remains.

"The meat loaf was superb. It wasn't just beef, was it?" Dirk asked as he set his fork down.

"Nope, it was a combination of beef, pork, turkey, and lamb."

"Ah, that explains it," he said knowingly. "You never do anything the simple way." Katie stood and started to clear the table. "Here, I'll give you a hand." Dirk grabbed several of the serving dishes.

As Dirk and Katie busied themselves with the clean up, Bill looked over at Dean who had remained fairly quiet through the meal. It had only been a few days since they had talked, but he'd noticed that she still wasn't up to par and was barely eating. Dean normally had a voracious appetite, especially for Katie's cooking, and she seemed to enjoy the meal but her normal quick wit was absent from their conversation. Her thoughts were obviously elsewhere.

"Katie, you don't mind if Dean and I go outside, do you?" He looked at his partner. "More than the two of you is really overkill for the clean up."

Katie winked at Dirk. "No, you two go ahead. We'll finish up and bring dessert out to the deck in a bit."

As Dean and Bill closed the screen door to the deck, Dirk looked at Katie and mouthed, "Man-to-man talk time?" as he picked up the last plate from the table and put it on the counter next to the sink.

Katie spoke softly. "Yeah, something like that. I'm hoping that Bill will be able to find out what's bugging her."

Dirk nodded. "Well, hon, something sure is. Her usual razor sharp wit is definitely in need of some honing. She didn't even blink when I brought up the latest escapade of the sexually deviant senator we all know and love so well."

Katie sighed. "She's had a lot to deal with this summer. Usually by the time she gets home, whatever is going on at work is left there, unless she wants my input or opinion on something. Trying to get her to let me in on this has been like trying to pry open a giant oyster with a plastic knife."

Dirk winced at the image. "That's not good. Maybe Bill can help. I know he's been stressed out about work, so maybe that's what's got your sweetie all tied up too."

Outside, Bill took the chair closest to the far rail of the deck. Dean followed and sat down heavily on the chair beside him. "Give," he said simply.

Dean looked up at him and frowned. "Nothing. I've swept the house every evening and every morning. No bugs. I don't see anyone following me and I've been varying my routes. I don't see strange cars on the streets, either. Everything seems normal around here."

Bill brightened. "That's a good thing, isn't it?"

"Yeah, I guess. But I keep having this feeling that something big is going to happen."

"It's probably related to all the intelligence data we've been collecting. I've got the same antsy feeling myself. I know we're missing something and that's bugging the bejeezus out of me. Dirk's been very patient, but he's getting worried about me now, too."

They sat in silence, watching the sky slowly darken. Dean got up and lit several citronella candles spaced around the deck.

"Those things really work?" Bill asked as she lit the last one on the table between their chairs.

"I'm not sure, but they look nice and Katie likes them."

As if on cue, Dirk slid back the screen door and allowed Katie through with a tray of desserts.

Dean stood and grabbed another side table for Katie to put the tray on, then pulled over a couple more chairs. All further discussion centered on the fruit tart and the work to be done during the next week to prepare for their wedding. Schedules had to be reworked since Bill and Dean would not be available to help as planned due to the staff shortage in the IOC.

Katie was in bed, propped up on her pillows and engrossed in reading her latest novel when Dean slipped under the bedcovers. "Thanks for dinner, love," Dean said. "I think the guys really enjoyed themselves."

Katie closed her book, keeping her place with her index finger. "I know Dirk certainly enjoyed it." She giggled at the thought of his third helping. "Who would have thought meatloaf was his favorite meal?"

"What's wrong with meatloaf?" Dean said in his defense. "Meatloaf was what I always requested for my birthday dinners."

"Really? Not steak or prime rib?"

"As much as I enjoy a good steak or cut of juicy prime rib now and then, meatloaf was always my favorite when I was a kid." Thinking back on that time, Dean laughed. "It was the only meal Mom didn't burn. You see, my mom wasn't the best at cooking dinners, but she was a terrific baker. Guess that's where I get my sweet tooth."

"I'm glad you enjoyed it." Katie slipped her bookmark into the book and set it on the side table. She watched Dean settle down under the covers. It was obvious from Dean's face that she was tense and Katie decided to try to get to the bottom of what was eating at her partner. Every night since she'd gotten home, Dean would be up wandering around the house shortly after Katie went to bed. The first night she came home, she and Dean went to bed together and things seemed normal, until she woke about an hour later and noticed that Dean wasn't in bed. She figured she had just gotten up and was in the bathroom, but after a few minutes she heard Dean closing the front door and going down to the den. She waited for her to come back to bed, but fell back to sleep before Dean returned. In the morning, she asked Dean about it, but never got a satisfactory answer. The second night Dean went through the same routine: wandering the house, going outside, and then down to the den. Tonight Katie was going to find out why.

"Dean?"

"Mmm?"

"Why have you been wandering the house at night?"

"Hmmm?"

"You heard me," Katie said, more forcefully than she had intended.

Dean rolled over and stared at Katie. "What do you mean?"

"Don't try playing that game with me. I know you've been wandering at night, going through each room and outside, then to your den." She softened her tone. "What's up?"

Dean rolled away from her and punched her pillow into a ball. "Nothing. Just making sure the house is secure."

"And...our security system doesn't do that?"

"Umm, just checking it."

Katie got up and went around to Dean's side of the bed and sat down next to her. She reached out and stroked Dean's dark hair, moving it away from her face, then caressed her cheek with a soft kiss. "Dean, you know you can't keep things from me, so you'd best come clean and tell me or we'll be up all night."

Dean rolled onto her back and stared into the green pools of her lover's eyes, seeing the determination there. She sucked in a deep breath and nodded. "I know who taught those scouts the cadence." Katie cocked her head in surprise. "And I know who the kid is that followed us to the car and who was waiting in the lobby at the Pentagon."

When Katie didn't say anything, Dean continued. "Turns out the missing link is one of the officers under my command, Major Len Russell. We were in the same company at Fort Huachuca for intelligence training." Dean explained what she had found out, her fears and suspicions, why he might have a grudge, and the plan she and Bill had come up with.

"I even installed cameras around the house to soothe my paranoia just before you came home on Wednesday. I've been sweeping the house for listening devices every night and then checking the recordings from the camera."

"Why didn't you tell me about this on Wednesday?"

"I didn't want to worry you." Dean sat up and grabbed her pillow and hugged it to her chest. "This may wind up just being a case of paranoia on my part, just a fabrication...a way to punish myself for my lapse of self-control at James River Park."

Katie pulled the pillow from Dean and replaced it with her body. She reached around her lover and hugged her, resting her chin on Dean's shoulder, inhaling her scent deeply. "What are your neck hairs telling you?"

The question might have seemed bizarre to anyone else, but Dean sighed and answered truthfully, "They itch like hell."

Len Russell signed the equipment request form and handed it to the waiting supply officer. The sergeant looked at the requisition and nodded, then turned and went into the storeroom. Ten minutes later, he returned with the electronics and placed them on the counter. He recorded the serial numbers for each item, had the major initial each one, and then added his initials beside each. When the paperwork was complete, he said, "These are the latest in micro technology, Major. Top of the line and barely out of I.S.I.S. These new mics are really something. They can't be picked up by electronic sweepers. They're the best product from the new Intelligence and Surveillance Instrumentation Systems unit. They come up with all these new high tech gadgets."

"I know about I.S.I.S., Sergeant. I work with them."

"Oh, yeah, I guess you would, Major. So, you got a new op in the hopper?"

"Just field testing, Sergeant," he said grimly.

The sergeant nodded and placed the items in the file box the major had brought in with him. "Need help getting these out to your vehicle?"

Russell picked up the box and shook his head. As he hurried out of the room, the sergeant scratched his head. "That's weird," he said to the clerk sitting at the desk in the corner. "They don't put that stuff on the shelf until it's been field tested to death."

"Maybe the major just wants to play with the stuff. He looks like a desk jockey to me," the clerk replied.

"Hmpf, yeah, you're probably right." He looked at the information on the request form. "He's with the IOC at the Pentagon. You'd think he'd be happy playing with the big toys they have there."

The corporal laughed. "Hell, the IOC? Then he's probably going to use the stuff to spy on his cheating wife." They both laughed and went back to processing paperwork.

Len Russell drove through Rock Creek Park and pulled off at the designated picnic area, parking under a large chestnut tree at the far end of the lot. He turned off the motor and watched in his rearview mirror as cars came and went, loading or unloading children and dogs and picnic supplies. He opened the morning paper to hide behind as a surveyor's truck pulled alongside his vehicle. As a result, he didn't see the driver come around to his car and he jumped when there was a tap on his window.

"Hey, Len. You're gonna die of heat stroke if you don't roll down a window."

Len opened the door but Kurt waved him back inside the car. "Ahh, Kurt. I wasn't expecting you in that truck."

"My cover for the day," he said as he got into the back seat. "Geez, Len, open a window or turn on the air. It's hotter than hell in here."

Len started the car and turned up the air conditioning, then turned to face Kurt. "They're in the box," he said, pointing to the file box on the seat.

Kurt flipped off the lid and peered inside. "Sweet." He picked up the micro camera. It was barely the size of a fountain pen and came with several options for mounting. "Wide angle lens?" he asked as he inspected the camera.

"Of course, and it can be fine-tuned from a distance of a mile."

"What about sound?" Kurt asked as he rummaged through the box.

"In the white box." Len pointed. "Everything is wireless, with a range of a mile."

Kurt picked up the box and opened it. Inside were several small devices a little bigger than a shirt button and several adaptors that could be placed around them to look like common items such as nutshells...from acorns to peanuts, pebbles, even moss shapes for outdoor use, and sugar cubes, pencil erasers, thumb tack heads, marbles, and many other shapes for indoor use. Kurt closed the lid and returned it to the file box and retrieved the monitoring equipment. Including the power source, it took up half the space of the file box. "How long does the power source last without a charge?"

"Twelve hours."

"That should cover it. I'll install the stuff today and then check out the reception from the reservoir. At a mile range I can easily stay out of sight. I'll recharge the power supply before going out on Saturday."

"You'll need to pull the equipment as soon as possible after we get my proof."

"No problem. I'll have it back to you by Monday night at the latest."

"That'll work out perfectly. I have to be at Fort Belvoir early Tuesday before I head back to the Pentagon."

Kurt put the equipment back into the box and replaced the cover. He lifted the file box onto his lap and opened the door, stepping out in one fluid motion and shutting the door.

"Give me a call when you've got the stuff set up." Len got a nod in confirmation. He waited for ten minutes after Kurt left before he returned to the Pentagon.

"I'll be back in about an hour...if Martha's plane is on time," Katie said as she picked up her car keys.

Dirk peeked around the door frame. "Did you check her flight information on the computer?"

"Yes, and it shows it's on time, but you know how Reagan can be."

Katie looked at her watch. "If I'm not back by 4 o'clock, would you put the chicken in for me?"

"You got it. By the way, I'm almost finished with the power wash on the main deck. Do you want me to start on the lower decks?"

Katie smiled brightly. "If you've got the time, that would be terrific."

Dirk bowed deeply. "Your wish is my command, my queen."

"Nuh uh. I'm not the queen here." She started to giggle then waved at him, wiggling her fingers merrily.

Katie went to the garage and pressed the garage door opener on her keychain. Getting into her car, she started the ignition and pulled out as soon as the top of the Boxster cleared the door as it lifted. She drove the car down the driveway just as a man exited a truck at the entrance to the cul-de-sac. She read the logo on the side of the truck and waved at the driver, who waved back with a broad smile. She watched him in the rearview mirror as he pulled out a backpack, tripod, sighting rod, and surveying transit. She was surprised he was alone, but maybe that's why it was taking so long to get the work done. Focusing on her driving, she slowed at the main road, looked both ways, and then took a left. She turned on the CD player and started to sing along. She had plenty of time to get to the airport in time to meet Reverend Martha.

Kurt set up the sighting rod at the corner of the property, aiming it along what anyone watching would assume was the east boundary of the property. Then he put on the backpack and grabbed the tripod with the transit and walked down the edge of the property, whistling as he went. Approximately three hundred feet into the property, he stopped and set up the tripod. He took off the backpack and pulled out a clipboard. Kurt adjusted the transit, then jotted some notes on the clipboard. He did this a few more times, then picked up the tripod and moved to another location, edging closer to the back of the house as he went.

Dirk had just finished moving the power washer to the lower level when he noticed the surveyor. The man was just coming down from a tree. "That's weird." He stood and watched as the man reached into his backpack and pulled out an acorn, then looked around the property. When the surveyor stopped and saw Dirk watching him he tossed the acorn to the ground and waved.

"All kinds of stuff falls into my backpack on the job," he said as he picked up the backpack and tripod.

Dirk motioned for the surveyor to come up to the house. "I just made some fresh lemonade and you look like you could use some."

Kurt nodded and backtracked up the ravine. When he got to the top, he set the tripod down, reached into the backpack and removed three small items, which he slipped into his pocket. At the front of the house, Dirk opened the front door and stepped out into the sunshine, two glasses of lemonade in his hands. He offered one to the surveyor and took a seat on the stoop.

Kurt accepted the lemonade and opted to stand, looking the house over carefully. "Nice house you have here," he said as he took a big swig. The lemonade was cold, tart, and refreshing.

"Thanks, but it's not my house. It belongs to a friend."

"Great design. Who was the architect?"

"That would be partly Frank Lloyd Wright and partly my friend."

Kurt turned and memorized every inch of the front, noting the mini cameras. He drained the glass and handed it back to Dirk. "Thanks. That hit the spot."

Dirk stood. "You're welcome. You might want to watch your footing on that slope. The rain we had this morning is sure to make it slick."

"Will do. Thanks." Kurt walked back to where he'd set the tripod. He hesitated and then looked back at Dirk, slightly embarrassed. "Say, would you mind if I used the facilities? I want to get this job done today, and I don't want to have to go back into town looking for a restroom." He looked out at the trees lining the property. "I'd really rather not use the woods."

"Sure. You can use the bathroom in the hall on the next level." Dirk led him into the house and down the stairs.

Kurt considered discreetly placing one of the bugs in his pocket in the kitchen, but knew there would be a good security system and decided against it. He wouldn't be able to get back into the house without raising an alarm, either. He used the bathroom and returned to a waiting Dirk. He looked around with a smile. "Wow, this place is awesome."

"You should see the view from the deck. C'mon, I'll show you." Dirk led him back upstairs and out the slider off the kitchen. When Dirk walked toward the rail, Kurt dropped one of the bugs in the flower planter, knowing he could easily retrieve that one. There were no cameras installed on the back of the house so he knew he wouldn't be observed when he retrieved it. He would have to climb up on the lower deck from the hill below the house. He made a mental note to bring climbing gear. He checked the planter, then joined Dirk at the rail.

Kurt looked out in all directions, checking to see how far out he would have to anchor the boat and not be seen. "I'll bet this is a sight to see in the fall when the leaves are all turning. Well, thanks again. I need to get this job done."

Dirk led him back to the front door where Spice stood staring at the intruder; a guttural growl released from her throat.

"Easy girl," Dirk said as Kurt left. He watched as the man picked up his things, retrieved the sighting rod, and went to the other side of the property. He nearly tripped over Spice who was sitting right by the front door, her tail flipping back and forth in a rhythmic motion. When he reached down and scratched her behind the ears Spice looked up at him, then back at the surveyor who was setting up the sighting rod, and emitted a loud growl.

"Hey, girl," Dirk said as he continued to pet Spice, "it's just the surveyor. Your mommies will be really glad to get his report." Spice looked up at Dirk and flicked her head then moved to the window so she could keep her eyes on the man in the yard.

Katie spotted Martha and waved to get the older woman's attention. Martha saw Katie and smiled, then quickened her pace through the gate area. She pulled Katie to her, hugged her tightly, and placed a light kiss on her cheek.

"Hello, Katie. How are you?"

"Getting better each day, Martha. How about you?"

"I'm glad to be on the ground again. I really don't like flying. My senses go wild on an airplane, picking up all sorts of visions."

Katie frowned and hugged Martha again. "Wow. That must be terrible."

"Yes, but it's better than a train. At least the plane ride is over more quickly." Martha considered for a minute. "Maybe next time

I'll drive. It may take me longer but at least my nerves won't be on overload." She put an arm through Katie's and the two women walked toward the baggage claim area.

"How's Deanna doing?"

Katie smiled at the use of her lover's full name. Martha and Joshua were the only two people that called her Deanna...Joshua, always, and Martha when she was very concerned.

"She's doing okay."

"That doesn't sound too convincing, Katherine."

Uh, oh. I have to remember who I'm talking to here. Katie quickly added, "She's been having a bad summer, Martha. Work has been very troubling and Joshua's passing hasn't been easy on her either."

Martha tipped her head toward Katie and frowned. "There's more to it than that, isn't there?"

Katie shook her head in amazement at Martha's intuition or voyeurism, or whatever it was that let Martha see into people. "Yes, there is." By the time they picked up Martha's luggage, made the trip to the house, and pulled back into the garage, Katie had filled Martha in completely.

When they entered the house, Martha was immediately surrounded by three felines all vying for her attention. Spice, being the leader of the group, was the first to jump into Martha's lap when she sat down on the sofa. The cat immediately curled into a ball and staked out her territory, while Butter and Sugar attached themselves alongside Martha's hips.

"My goodness, I could use the three of you during the winter," Martha said, addressing each cat with gentle petting. Spice looked up at Martha and squeezed her eyes shut in ecstasy, almost smiling, then began to purr loudly.

Katie laughed at the sight. "Yes, they can be quite the winter blanket." Katie picked up Martha's suitcases. "I'll take your things to the guest bedroom and then check on Dirk's progress. Can I get you anything first?"

"No, I'm fine. Just a bit tired from traveling. You go ahead and I'll just relax here with the girls."

Katie watched Dirk turn off the pressure washer and start to roll up the hose. "Wow, you're quick. Remind me to hire you for spring cleaning."

"Ah, you're back already. I figured you'd get caught in rush hour traffic." He coiled the last piece of hose onto the bracket then rolled the equipment to the stairs. "How about giving me a hand up with this?"

"Sure." Katie reached down and picked up the front end of the power washer as Dirk picked up the back. They carried the equipment out to the garage where Dirk had his pickup truck parked.

"Thanks for putting the chicken in the oven. Can I talk you into staying for dinner?"

Dirk shook his head. "Bill and I are going out for all-you-can-eat shrimp tonight. We found this cool place called Jack's that brings bowl after bowl until you tell them to stop."

"It's a wonder you two haven't put Jack's out of business."

"Nah. Not a chance." He laughed. "Now if you and Dean came along some night, we might be able to do some serious damage." Still laughing, Dirk climbed into his truck and backed down the driveway, tossing a wave to Katie before heading down the road.

When he was out of sight, Katie went inside to check on Martha. Finding the reverend sound asleep and surrounded by purring felines, Katie placed a throw over her then quietly went into the kitchen where she pulled out fixings for salad and some side dishes to go with the chicken. She'd just finished cleaning up when she heard Dean's car pull in. Wiping her hands on a towel, Katie went out to meet her.

At the garage door, Katie put a finger to her lips to keep Dean from speaking. In a whisper she said, "Martha is napping," and the two of them silently entered the house and went straight to the master bedroom.

"How was your day?" Katie asked as she took Dean's blouse and started to remove the trappings from her uniform. She placed the bars holding the ribbons, nameplate, and rank epaulets on the dresser. Dean removed her slacks and underclothes and headed to the bathroom. Katie watched Dean as she walked, amazed at how she could project such power and grace, even when she was naked. Katie followed her to the bathroom, resisting the urge to join her in the shower where she could run her hands over that strong body. She was very aware of their guest in the living room and chose discretion over desire...temporarily.

"I'm going to check on dinner. Can I get you something to drink?"

"No, I'll wait 'til dinner. I'll be quick."

"Okay. See you in a bit."

Dean turned and touched Katie's arm, then crooked a finger. "C'mere." Katie did as she was bid and closed her eyes, waiting for Dean's lips to meet hers.

Katie's dinner was splendid, and the three women relished not only the meal but one another's company. They had cleaned up the kitchen and were relaxing in the living room talking about Martha's meeting that would begin tomorrow.

"I'll call for a cab in the morning," Martha said as she set her teacup down.

"You'll do no such thing. I go right by Crystal City on my way to work, so I can drop you off and then pick you up in the evening."

"I don't want to impose. You're already being kind enough to let me stay here with you."

"Martha," Dean said softly, putting a hand on the woman's arm, "it's honestly no imposition. We're family, right?"

Martha smiled broadly. "Yes, we are." She stood and started to gather the teacups. Katie moved to take them from her. "Oh, no you don't," she said. "I'm family, and that means I don't get treated like company. Now, I'm sure you two had a long day, so go," she shooed them with her hand, "and do what you normally do at night. I'll clean up the dessert dishes and the teacups, and then head to bed myself. I'm ready for a good night's sleep."

Katie looked at Dean who grinned and shrugged. "You heard her, she's family. She's entitled to clean up." Dean stood and took Katie by the hand. "C'mon, I want to check the video anyway." They walked hand-in-hand down to the den.

Dean rewound the video and hit the play button. There wasn't much on the tape until a truck stopped at the entry to the cul-de-sac.

"That's the surveyor," Katie said. "I saw him arrive as I was leaving to pick up Martha. Guess that means we'll be able to close on those two pieces of property soon." They watched as he set up the equipment and then went out of range of the cameras when he reached the beginning of the slope. Dean fast forwarded the tape until he reappeared, walking toward the front door.

"That's strange," Dean began and then saw Dirk enter the picture with drinks in hand. "Ah, good old Dirk. Taking pity on the hard working surveyor."

Katie laughed and pointed at the screen. "Yep, that's Dirk, all right. He could give Martha Stewart a run for her money." They watched as the surveyor examined the house and Dirk examined the surveyor as he waited for a comment on the lemonade. They listened to the conversation about the building of the house. Then the surveyor drained his glass and handed it back to Dirk. He asked to use the bathroom and Dirk led him inside. They waited until he reappeared and watched a bit longer as he set up his equipment on the other side of the property and went back to work.

"Does he look familiar to you," Dean asked suddenly.

Katie rewound the video and stopped it on a full view of the man's face. "I don't think so. Why, does he look familiar to you?"

Dean stared at his profile. "Sort of. He looks like someone I've seen before."

"Honey, you've seen a lot of people. Maybe you ran into him at the gas station or the store."

Dean shrugged. "Yeah, I guess you're right."

They finished running through the video and reset the machine. Katie put her arms around Dean and gave her a fierce hug. "Good, now let's get up to bed."

Dean looked at her watch. "You want to go to sleep already? It's only ten."

Katie gave her a sexy smile. "I didn't say I wanted to go to sleep, I said I wanted to go to bed. Martha said to do what we normally do at night, didn't she?"

Kurt picked up the phone and dialed. It rang three times before it was picked up.

"Hello?"

"Good evening, Mrs. Russell. This is Kurt. Is Len available?"

"Yes, he is. Just a minute."

He heard her place her hand over the receiver and call for her husband, then heard an extension pick up.

"You can hang up now, Alice." Len waited until he heard the click of her hang up. "How'd it go? Did you get everything in place?"

"I was able to get one camera and one speaker in place outside."

"That's all? Just one unit?" Len's voice rose and Kurt quickly cut in.

"Easy, Len. I also got another placed on the back deck of the house...where they're planning that ceremony thing."

"How did you do that?"

"The guy that hangs out with that captain of yours was there power washing the decks. He brought me lemonade and I figured, what the hell, so I asked if I could use the bathroom."

"You didn't leave any in the house? You'd never be able to get them out of there."

"Don't worry, Len. I thought of that, so I just planted one right on the deck in a flower pot."

"What about cameras? How many did you get set up?"

"Like I said, I only got one in place. That blond guy was on the deck and almost caught me putting that one in a tree, but I covered it okay."

"Will that be good enough?"

"I checked the reception with the one I set up; it's fine. Not the best situation, I would have preferred two or three, but it'll get you what you want."

"Can't you go back and put up another one?"

"I don't want to raise any suspicions. She's got surveillance cameras mounted on the front of the house."

"What about the back? Maybe they got you placing the camera."

"When I did the other side, I looked. I didn't see any on that side."

Sounding a bit more relaxed, Len asked, "Okay, so you're sure we'll be able to get video and sound?"

"Yeah, we'll be okay." He hesitated, then added, "There is one thing, though. I had to pitch one of the bugs."

"What? Pitch it where?"

"On the ground. I was just getting ready to plant a second bug when that guy that was washing the deck turned and saw me."

"Damn! Can you get it back when you remove the equipment?"

"I'll try, but it was in the acorn cover. It'll be like trying to find a needle in a haystack on that slope. It's loaded with oak trees."

"Well, you'd better. I've got to get those all returned in mint condition. How will I explain one bug missing?"

"If I can't find it, we'll figure out something. Don't worry, Len. I won't let you down."

Katie was sitting at the kitchen table, her arms folded and resting on the table as she stared out the window. She turned when she heard footsteps. "Good morning, Martha," Katie chirped. "Glorious day today, isn't it?"

"Absolutely." She poured herself a cup of coffee and sat at the table with Katie. "And where's your other half?"

"Out getting in a run. Hardly a day goes by that she doesn't run at least five miles." She picked up her coffee cup and peered over the rim at Martha. "You sure seemed to be having a good time last night."

"Oh, I did. Your friends are a hoot, especially that Linna. She had my sides splitting with those stories of hers. Too bad her husband wasn't able to come. I'll bet he's got a few good ones to tell, too."

"We've heard some of those stories a couple of times now, but they still make us laugh," Katie said with a chuckle.

"And the one Tracy told about flying that helicopter in the Bahamas, my word! She and Dean were lucky to get out alive. I can't imagine someone having the nerve to fly such a complicated machine with only computer practice."

"Desperate times call for desperate measures," Katie said. "But then, Dean never gave her a chance to say where she learned to fly or if she had actually flown one for real. They just hopped in and took off."

"Well, they're both very lucky," Martha said with a stern look, then broke out laughing again.

"My favorite story was the one Linna told about her Rambo move in the tunnel under Niagara Falls." Katie shook her head, remembering the sound of gunfire echoing in that underground chamber. Between the roar of Niagara and the automatic weapons fire, she often wondered how she could still hear so well. "If I had been able to actually see that move, I probably would have set off the explosives with my laughing."

Martha shook her head. "That was a really close call for you, wasn't it, dear?"

"Yes, it was. And we have you to thank for getting Dean to me in time."

They sat together silently after that, both thinking about the fragility of life and the gift Martha possessed. Katie shuddered to think what would have happened if Martha had not given Dean insight as to Katie's location.

Martha was thinking about the many lives she had touched through her gift. Sometimes the visions were glorious and her ability to help others was a real blessing. And then sometimes her gift was a curse and brought her pain and sorrow.

"The Lord works in mysterious ways, Katie. I'm certain that His hand helped me to guide Dean to you that day."

"I'm not much into religion, Martha, but I can't help but wonder why He would choose to help someone who is considered an abomination by so many of His self-professed Christians."

"Ah, that's a philosophical debate for another day and time," Martha said with a smile. "Today we concentrate on only good thoughts. It's your wedding day!"

Katie smiled. "You are absolutely right, Martha. No gloomy thoughts today."

"Who's having gloomy thoughts?" Dean asked as she entered the kitchen. She was dripping with perspiration and breathing heavily.

"Ewww," Katie said, looking at her. "You march yourself right into the shower...now! When you're decent, you can come out and play with us."

Dean saluted and started to walk out of the kitchen, but stopped at Katie's chair. She leaned down and whispered in her ear, "Since when are you so averse to a little perspiration? We sure worked up a sweet sweat last night." She kissed a now blushing Katie on the cheek and trotted away to the bathroom.

"She has a point, Katie," Martha said with a knowing smile.

Dean finished dressing and walked out to the kitchen wearing black shorts and a white golf shirt with the Army logo embroidered on the left breast. "Any of that coffee left for me?"

"Sure, love. Want some breakfast to go along with it?"

During the previous two days, Dean's appetite had returned as she relaxed with Katie and Martha and found nothing suspicious on the nightly video checks. She had finally decided that her worries were all in her mind and that, given his inaction after such a long span of time, Russell must be clueless about her infraction at James River Park. She decided that in the future, she would confine her sexual maneuvers to the master bedroom.

"Martha made some awesome waffles and there are enough left to feed an army. Want me to warm them up?"

Dean shook her head. "I'll fix them. You and Martha just relax and enjoy this peace and quiet, because once the rest of the crew gets here..." The doorbell rang. "Forget what I just said. It appears that the crew is here and ready to party."

Dean redirected her path away from the stove and toward the front door. Katie went to the stove and opened the oven, retrieving the plate of waffles. She picked out three of the biggest and put them into the toaster oven. When Dean returned to the kitchen with the crew trailing, the waffles were hot, buttered, and ready for syrup. Dean sat at the table and poured syrup on her waffles and began eating. The run had really felt good and she was ravenous.

Katie stood and welcomed the group, giving each an enthusiastic hug and then introducing them to Martha.

Linna placed a hand on Katie's forehead and shook her head. "You running a fever or something? We met Martha at Christmas and again last night."

Katie blushed and nodded. "Uh, oh, yeah. Must be nerves."

Tracy gave Katie a hug. "I'd be nervous too if I was committing myself to a life with that one." She pointed at Dean and winked, receiving a wink in return.

Regaining her composure, Katie asked, "Anyone want some of Martha's marvelous waffles?" Everyone gave a polite "no" but when Katie persisted, they all relented and took places at the table.

Colleen took a seat next to Martha and whispered, "These gals are so psyched, they hardly slept all night. When the alarm went off at 7 AM, they bounced out of bed and fought over who would shower first."

Martha smiled, understanding their excitement. She was feeling it herself.

"I just stayed in the nice warm bed and waited 'til the dust settled. Then I got up and showered, taking my sweet old time while the two of them," Colleen tilted her head toward Tracy and Linna, "paced like caged tigers. When I asked them if they were going to eat breakfast, they kept saying they were still full from last night's meal." She looked at them wolfing down their waffles. "Yeah, right."

Martha laughed and passed the last plate of waffles from Katie to Colleen, who took her time preparing and eating them. "So, how long have you known these two?"

"Not too long. Almost two years. But Tracy has known Dean for quite a while."

"That's right," Martha said. "She and Dean were stationed together at one point."

"Yes, and then they got re-acquainted when that Catskills operation took place. It's been a hell of a ride since!"

Martha recalled some of the stories she'd heard the others tell about that time. That's where Dean had met Katie and fallen head over heels in love. Martha stole a look over at Dean who now had Katie sitting in her lap. The love shared between them was so obvious she wondered how they could keep their relationship a secret from their colleagues. She was sure it wouldn't have as disastrous an effect on Katie's job, but it would cost Dean dearly if her superiors knew of her love for another woman. Martha understood clearly how the past summer had weighed on Dean. She was glad to see that nothing had come of her slip in public. So far, she hadn't picked up anything that would indicate otherwise... and she was hoping that for once her gift was a blessing and not a curse.

When everyone was done eating, Linna and Tracy loaded the dishwasher and then everyone moved out to the deck where the wedding was going to take place. The deck looked brand new after the power washing, and the planters of flowers that Dirk and Katie had brought in made it look like something out of *House Beautiful*. The only things left to do were to place the candles around the deck and put the tablecloths and center pieces on the tables. The day was warming up nicely and by 1700 the deck would be filled with the aroma of the sun-warmed flowers. They'd planned the ceremony for dusk, when the deck would be cooler and the candlelight would be a perfect accompaniment to the twilight. Martha, Dean, and Katie had already discussed the ceremony and Bill and Tracy were to be the witnesses. Martha brought along a certificate of marriage that was printed on elegant parchment and embossed in gold trim. Only the signatures remained to be filled in.

"The deck looks stunning," Colleen said as she snapped pictures. She had appointed herself the official photographer and had started her picture taking the night before. Years from now, those pictures would conjure up fond memories. She wandered the deck taking pictures of the flowers from every angle possible and many candid shots as the group hammed it up for the camera. Finally, she placed her camera in the bag and sat down with the others. "What's next on today's agenda?" she asked.

Dean replied first, ticking off her list. "I have to pick up the food and drinks, my outfit from the seamstress, ice, and...hmm, there's one more thing." She hesitated deliberately, causing Katie to drum her fingers on the table. Her partner had told her at least ten times already that she would need to pick up their flowers. Katie gave up drumming and gave Dean a light tap on the arm. "Oh, yeah, the flowers...I better not forget those!"

"And what's on your list, Ms. O'Malley?" Tracy asked.

"*I*..." she paused for effect, "just have to transform myself into a princess."

Tracy and Colleen laughed. "That won't take long," they said in unison. "Anything else on your list of to-do?"

"No. Since I took care of everything else already, all I have left to do is set the tables on the deck and put out the candles."

Linna looked at Tracy and Colleen expectantly. Finally, she just couldn't hold it in any longer. "Okay. Tracy, Col, and I have a better idea, so, this is the way the afternoon is going to go: we're going to do the running, fetching, and setting. At precisely 12 noon, you two are going to arrive at the Nirvana Day Spa in town and get pampered — massages, wraps, manicures, pedicures, facials...the works. Tracy will drive you there in the van. At 4:30, Tracy will pick you up and bring you back here. You," she pointed at Katie, "will retreat to the guest bedroom and prepare for the ceremony." She pointed at Dean. "And you will immediately report to the smaller bedroom on the bottom level and get yourself ready. Neither of you will come out of your respective bedrooms until one of us comes for you. Got that?"

Both Dean and Katie cocked an eyebrow at Linna, turned and looked at each other and shrugged. "Sounds like a better plan than ours," Dean said. "What do you think?"

"You bet it's a better plan." Katie turned back to face Linna. "I like the way you gals think!"

At exactly 4:30 PM, Dean and Katie exited the Nirvana Day Spa in downtown Occoquan, giggling like two schoolgirls on holiday. True to Linna's agenda, Tracy was waiting for them at the curb.

"You two look terrific," Tracy said as they got into the van and buckled up. "Okay, let's get this buggy rolling." She put the vehicle in gear and pulled out into the late afternoon traffic.

Dean was sitting in the front seat with Tracy and gave her friend a gentle punch on the arm. "This was a terrific idea."

"Yeah," Katie enthused, "I've been meaning to try that spa but never got around to it. It's definitely a great way to relax."

Ten minutes later they were pulling into the driveway. As they got out, Tracy reminded them they were to go directly to their respective rooms.

"Everything you need is there and the rest of the house is taken care of. Bill and Dirk arrived just before I left and they helped with the finishing touches." Tracy put her hand on the doorknob and waited. "Okay, no wandering around, just straight to your rooms, right?"

"Ma'am, yes, ma'am!" they chorused, and Tracy opened the door. True to their word, each went straight to her appointed room without taking any detours.

When Katie arrived at her assigned bedroom, Martha was waiting at the closed door. "Welcome back. How was your afternoon?"

"Martha, it was heaven on earth."

Martha chuckled at her description as she opened the door to the bedroom. "If there's something missing, just call me on the intercom and I'll fetch it for you, but I think I got everything you need." She waved Katie into the room and then quietly closed the door behind her.

It took Katie's breath away. Her flowers were on the nightstand, her dress was hanging in the open closet, and her underclothes were laid out on the bed. The dressing table held her make-up, ready for her to apply. A small platter of sandwiches and a tall glass of iced tea were on a side table next to the lounge chair in the corner. Soft music was playing in the background. Katie realized she hadn't eaten since their late morning breakfast and immediately went to the plate of sandwiches. She picked up the first quarter sandwich and eagerly devoured it. As she picked up the second quarter, she noticed an envelope propped up by her flowers. It was addressed to her. She put the sandwich down and reached for the envelope. Inside, in careful script was a handwritten note from Martha.

Dear Katie,
I look at you and see kindness and gentle ways in your actions and words. You are the perfect partner for Deanna in every way. You give her balance in life, you guide intuitively, and most of all, you love her completely and unselfishly. Your love for her is total and all consuming, full of passion, courage, and devotion.
The future will present challenges and triumphs, happiness and sorrow, but your love for one another will always see you

through the bad times as well as the good. Joshua was so proud of Deanna and so sad for the loneliness she felt for all those years. He fretted about her when he found out about his terminal cancer, worried that she would be forever lonely. However, when he met you the first time, he told me he could go in peace because he knew Deanna was in good hands. I know this too. And I know if Joshua were here today, he would be filled with joy. Just always remember...you're not alone. Thank you for including me in your family and for giving me the honor of joining your two souls for eternity.

All my love,
Martha

Katie wiped tears from her face and placed the note back into the envelope. "Thank you, Martha," she said softly. She sat there for a moment or two longer, thinking about Martha's words and the evening to come, and realized that no matter what the future held they would face it together. They would never be alone. She smiled. *Besides, we have our own little family with Bill and Dirk, Tracy and Colleen, Linna, and now Martha. What more could we need?*

Dean took the stairs down the two levels to her assigned room and met Bill waiting outside the closed door. He was dressed in a light blue summer sports jacket, white shirt, a blue tie that matched the jacket perfectly, and dark blue slacks.

"Have a good time?" he asked, pleased to see her looking more relaxed than he'd seen her in months.

"Terrific. Better than going three rounds with you." Dean feinted and then punched him lightly in the stomach, eliciting a stifled grunt.

"That's great." He opened the door and led her in. "We brought down everything we thought you would need. If we forgot something, just call on the intercom and we'll bring it to you."

"Ah...never thought I'd be a prisoner in my own home."

"Just trying to keep the suspense going, ma'am," he said with a grin. "Oh, and there's some sandwiches over on the nightstand. We figured they probably didn't feed you at the spa."

"Good move, Bill. I'm starved. All they had at the spa was grapes, pineapple, orange slices, and cheese and crackers with water to wash it down."

His grin broadened. "Sounds like something Katie would like."

"You got that right!"

"I'll be back to get you in about an hour and a half. Relax and take your time." He backed out of the room and closed the door behind him.

Dean walked around the room to make sure that everything she was going to need was there. Satisfied it was, she went over to the night table and sat on the bed. She picked up the plate of small sandwiches and selected one. "This'll hold me 'til later, I guess."

When she finished the last sandwich, she noticed an envelope on the table propped up between the water glass and a bottle of beer. She picked up the beer and twisted off the top, took a swig, and set it down. Next she picked up the envelope and gently pried open the flap. Inside was a neatly scripted note.

Dear Deanna,

Some final instructions from your father are enclosed with this letter. Joshua knew his time was coming, but he hoped he would live long enough to see this day. He really came a long way the past few years...learning to be more accepting, more compassionate, and more willing to forgive and love again. He still had regrets, one very important one that he ran out of time to correct, and that weighed heavily on his heart at the end. Your re-entry into his life aided his spiritual healing process, and his affection and love for you easily grew to include Katie. He knew in his heart that she was the catalyst in your life that not only brought you back to him but back to the light in the world. Although he was proud of what you have done with your life, he was also very aware of the darkness in which you walked. Seeing the light come back to shine on you was very important to him.

For my part, I am grateful to be considered a member of your family. I feel that I have known you from birth, the way Joshua talked about you, so I guess I always hoped to be close to you too. What a surprise it was to have you step into my life with Katie at your side. The two of you are truly meant to be bound together for eternity and I am thankful beyond words that I shall be the one to do the binding. The two of you will face many obstacles and fear will fill your hearts at times, but always remember that whatever the outcome, you are bound for eternity and will never lose one another...ever.

All my love,
Martha

Dean read the letter silently one more time, then folded it and returned it to the envelope. She extracted the other slip of paper and opened it. The unsteady hand told her that it was probably written by her father when he was near to death.

> *My Dearest Daughter,*
>
> *I have done many things wrong in my life and it is a father's duty to instruct his children correctly so they do not make the same mistakes. I was not a part of your life long enough to give you proper guidance, and when you came back, it was too late, for I am dying. So, my dear daughter, please hold these four lessons to your heart.*
>
> *Do not give in to ego — I thought I had mastered that, but I had not and Thad's death was the result. I believed that I was beyond reproach and that God moved through me. He does, my daughter, but I was not listening then; I listened to my ego instead.*
>
> *Be honest in all you do and say — I lied about Thad and it cost me my beloved wife and family, and eventually my own life.*
>
> *Forgive others and you will learn to forgive yourself — It took many years in prison before I understood this. Once I learned to forgive others, I was able to forgive myself. It is hard to forgive yourself, but you will never go forward until you do.*
>
> *But the most important lesson is to let love guide you — I believe that love of all God's creatures is the most important lesson one can learn. From the tiniest ant to the largest elephant, from the most beautiful child to the lost soul sleeping by the curb, we are all God's creatures and must give respect and love to all He created. I made many mistakes when it came to love...thinking some of it vile and disgusting...and I was wrong. Love is pure and lives in the light; hate is sullied and lives in the dark. Never give in to hate or it will devour you.*
>
> *These are my lessons, my daughter. Each time you make a decision, think of these. I wasted my life with punishing instead of forgiving, believing in my ego, spouting dishonesty, and embracing hate. Do not walk in my footsteps. If you are as much in love with Katie as I believe you are, stand up for her love, totally and completely, and never be ashamed or hide in fear of that love. Her love will make you whole and keep you safe.*
>
> *Your father,*
> *Joshua*

It took Dean a few minutes to re-read the note and another few minutes to stop the tears. In her heart she could feel him wrapping his arms around her, offering her comfort and reassurance. She re-

read the last two sentences and knew the truth of those words. Katie had made her whole and kept her safe, and she would never be ashamed of their love or hide it.

Bill knocked on the bedroom door. "Are you ready?" Dean replied by opening the door. She was wearing a dark sapphire blue, single shoulder strap dress that had a handkerchief hem. It was made of silk and shimmered in the indirect lighting of the hall. Around her neck she wore a single strand of diamonds and sapphires, with matching earrings dangling from each ear. Black silk heels finished off the outfit. Her hair was fashioned up, with long curly strands along the sides of her face and behind her ears. Inserted into the hair were white baby's breath flowers that lent an air of subtle elegance to the hairstyle. She was carrying a small bouquet of white roses with the stems wrapped in a deep sapphire ribbon that ended in a bow. Her make-up was subtle, with only a hint of mascara and blue eye shadow to highlight the color of her eyes. She was stunning and, gay or not, Bill was blown away.

"Uh, wow," he stuttered as she stepped into the hallway. "You clean up pretty nice, Colonel." Dean smiled and winked at him. Still stuttering and now a bit embarrassed, he rattled on. "I mean, well, I don't think I've ever seen you dressed like this before. You know, I'm used to uniforms, exercise duds, jeans..."

"Thanks, Bill. If I get a reaction like this from you, imagine what I'll get from Katie."

Laughing, they walked down the hallway to the stairs. As they stepped out onto the deck, all conversation stopped and Colleen had to be nudged to start taking pictures. Martha tucked her arm in Dean's and led her to the back side of the deck.

"Thank you for the note and especially for the note from Dad. I'll treasure them both."

Dean's eyes glistened and Martha gave her a squeeze. "Hey, now...they weren't meant to make you cry."

Dean blinked several times and smiled at her. "I guess I'm just a bit emotional today."

"And well you should be. It's your wedding day, after all. Probably the most emotional day you'll ever have in your life." Martha gave her another squeeze then went over the ceremony one last time.

"Martha, what did you mean about Dad having a regret he didn't have time to correct? We had come to understand each other and love each other again. Was there something he hadn't yet told me?"

Martha sighed and hugged Dean tightly. "Yes, there was something he had not told you, something he was still ashamed about. Something he wanted to do before he died, but it wasn't done." Martha took in Dean's puzzled look. "Your father had a sister that he had cut out of his life early on; when he married, not even your mother knew she existed. From what he told me, she was much like you. She was smart, loving, full of life and enjoying all of it. And he said he could see her in you. In the way you talk, your passion for honesty, and in your eyes. It pained him that he was never able to find her and bring her back into the family."

"Did he say why he closed her out of his life?"

"Yes." Martha nodded. "Because his religious beliefs labeled her an abomination."

"She's a lesbian?"

"Yes. And he could not abide it. He forbade her to ever see him again. She left Kansas when she was nineteen and was never heard from again."

"What was her name? Maybe she's still alive and we can find her." The thought of having an aunt she never knew about was stirring up a desire to find her, to bring her back into the family and tell her about her father and how his life had changed his feelings for her.

"We tried to find her. Her name was...is...Victoria Peterson."

Dean nodded, making a promise to her father that one day she would find his sister and bring the family together again.

"Well, are you ready?" Martha asked.

Dean drew in a deep breath and let it out slowly. "I'm as ready as I can be. Is Katie ready yet?"

"I'm sure she is. Let's get set." Martha led Dean to the other side of the deck where the ceremony was going to take place. She got everyone in place and then sent Tracy to fetch Katie.

Tracy went through the sliding door and across the house to the guest bedroom. She knocked on the door.

"Come in," Katie called.

Tracy opened the door and went in, not prepared for the sight that met her. "Holy Mother of Mercy," she said softly. "You are gorgeous."

"Thank you," Katie said as she slipped her shoes on.

Her dress was a deep coral that had a twisted halter neckline with a keyhole center. It was made from lustrous satin with a gathered fabric detail on her hip. She had matching coral earrings that dangled almost to her shoulders. Her hair was fashioned into a twist with miniature coral roses wound into the tresses. The coral color of the dress reflected on her skin to give Katie's face a warm glowing appearance. She was radiant.

"Dean is one lucky woman," Tracy murmured.

"So am I," Katie replied with a smile. She picked up her bouquet. It was similar to Dean's, but wrapped in a coral ribbon. "C'mon, let's get this show on the road."

Tracy opened the sliding door and went out to her place on the deck. Dean was facing Martha, her back to the sliding door. Katie stepped out and waited.

Facing everyone, Martha was dressed in a purple clerical robe. Around her neck she wore a white wedding stole that was embroidered with a purple wedding monogram. When Martha nodded, Katie began walking forward and Dean turned to see her lover. Her sharp intake of breath could barely be heard. As she watched Katie, everyone else faded into the background. All of her senses were focused on the woman she loved and she wanted to run to her and sweep her up in her arms, but her feet stayed rooted to the deck. Her heart rate seemed to increase with each step Katie took, and it seemed she was walking in slow motion. Their eyes met and their hearts beat as one.

Katie smiled at her lover and reached out to hold Dean's hand. "Hello, love," she said in a soft whisper.

Dean's smile broadened. "Hello, gorgeous."

They turned together to face Martha.

Kurt was watching the ceremony on the small monitor that came with the bugging equipment. He was surprised at how clear the mini camera's reception was, even in the dim lighting of the evening. The candles helped some, but the resolution was amazing. When the colonel came out, he was amazed at how stunning she looked out of uniform. When the blonde came out, he was really beginning to question how the two beautiful women could be lesbians.

He adjusted the sound and listened in as the ceremony started. The sound from the two microphones he planted was also quite an improvement from the top of the line ones available commercially. He was thinking that if he ever found the lost acorn mic, he might just decide to keep it. He was getting everything Len would need to put the colonel out of the military...and more. Len might even decide to go after that captain on his staff and his civilian boy friend. Heck, he might go after everyone at the ceremony, although he didn't know who the other women were.

When Len had first come to him with this project, he wasn't sure he wanted to get involved. Colonel Peterson had quite a reputation as a tough and demanding officer, but she was also known for fairness. Her excellence in field work was evidenced by the ribbons she wore on her chest, and she was extremely intelligent and could grasp the big picture faster than anyone he knew. She had made many friends in high places with her heroics, including the former president. She also made a lot of enemies with her rapid rise through the ranks. But, she was obviously a lesbian, and Kurt couldn't tolerate homosexuality in the military. It led to poor unit morale and cohesion and was a severe liability for potential compromise in intelligence work. She had to be reported and face a court martial.

Kurt's attention was drawn back to the screen as the ceremony drew to a close. He wanted to get a good close-up of their kiss.

"In the eyes of God and through His word, I bless this union. Ladies, you may now...kiss," Martha said with a big grin. Dean leaned down and Katie stretched up slightly until their lips met. Dean felt awkward at first. Kissing Katie before her friends was not something she was in the habit of doing, but as their lips met, she remembered the words in her father's letter, "...never be ashamed or hide in fear of that love. Her love will make you whole and keep you safe." She tossed her bouquet over her shoulder toward Martha and wrapped Katie in her arms, kissing her passionately albeit briefly, then gently released Katie from her embrace. When they broke apart, Katie's eyes were wide and a huge grin formed on her lips. They turned and faced their friends, who applauded, cheered, and wiped tears from their eyes. Walking forward to meet their friends, they were greeted with hugs, kisses, and well wishes.

Martha, clutching the bouquet, walked toward the group. "Well now," she said as she placed the flowers on the table, "I think it's time to celebrate. Dirk, will you pop the cork on that champagne?" Dirk eagerly removed the bottle from the wine bucket, peeled off the foil and wire holder, then manipulated the cork until it popped into the air and sailed away into the dark.

"Time to party!" he announced as he began filling the champagne flutes.

Chapter Twenty-six
September 2

The post-wedding celebration finally broke up in the wee hours of the morning of September second. Colleen, who was not much of a drinker, was the designated driver for her crew. She was glad they'd brought the van as a very tipsy trio loaded themselves into the back. Martha joined her in the front seat.

"Thanks for arranging a room for me at your hotel. I think Dean and Katie need a bit of privacy tonight," Martha said as she buckled her seat belt. "But I hate to inconvenience anyone."

"Actually, we made the reservation last week. We knew you wouldn't want to stay at the house tonight. Besides, we're all going on that picnic tomorrow...um, make that today...so, it's not an imposition. We'll all come back together."

Dean and Katie stood at the door, arm-in-arm, and waved at their friends as they pulled away.

"Good thing they brought a van."

"Colleen is always thinking ahead, like getting the room for Martha." She led Katie inside. "C'mon, love. Let's take advantage of the quiet. They'll all be back at 1300 and ready to party again."

Dean closed and locked the front door, set the security code, and followed Katie to the master bedroom. When they opened the door, they understood why neither of them had been sent to dress in that room. It was gorgeous...and ostentatious at the same time. There was a chilled bottle of wine next to the night table along with a bowl of grapes, a basket of chocolates, and other delectable treats. And there were flowers...lots of flowers, bouquets of flowers everywhere. All kinds of flowers and all were white. The room had the overwhelming aroma of a florist shop.

"Phew," Katie said, wrinkling her nose. "It's a bit over-powering, isn't it?"

"I can fix that. I'll be right back." Dean went down to the den where the main control for the security system was located and reset the system to allow the master bedroom windows and sliding glass door to be off-line. She returned to the bedroom and opened the windows, allowing a fresh breeze to enter the room. She also slid back the glass door on the patio, but left the screen door closed.

"Is that better?"

"Hmm, yes, but there's one other thing…" Katie smiled wickedly as she moved to stand behind Dean. She took hold of the zipper and slowly pulled it down, enjoying the sight of each bit of skin as it was exposed. Peeling off the shoulder strap, she let the silk dress fall to the floor. Her hands moved to the bra strap and released that garment to float downward to lie on top of the dress. Her fingertips danced over smooth skin and around to Deans breasts. Teasing and fondling, she played until the nipples were hard. She knew she was nearing Dean's breaking point and wasn't ready to go there quite yet, so she dallied a bit longer. Finally her hands slipped inside Dean's bikinis and slid around to the front, letting her fingers explore the wetness that was pooling between her legs. Again, just to the brink, then she stopped.

"You are such a tease," Dean said in a throaty whisper.

"And you love every minute." Katie slowly slipped the bikinis down the length of the long legs, then moved around to stand in front of Dean, indicating her own zipper. Dean stepped forward and readily accepted the invitation.

Out on the reservoir, Kurt was about to pack up, but just as he put the camera monitor in its case, he heard voices coming in over the audio receiver. He put the headphones on and fine tuned the incoming sounds. A broad smile creased his face. "Oh, yeah. Len is gonna love this!" He quickly pulled the camera monitor out and reconnected it to the power supply and turned it on. "Crap, the camera angle is all wrong," he grinned wider, "but the audio is perfect!" He flicked on the recorder. "Oh, yeah. Len will be able to nail the lid shut on her with this audio alone!"

The newlyweds stood face to face for the longest time, each gazing at the other, hands lightly tracing outlines of face, shoulders, breasts, lips. Then their bodies melded together, feeling the warmth of skin on skin.

"I love you," Dean whispered softly.

"And I love you." Katie slipped a hand behind Dean's head and tugged her down. When their lips met, the conflagration was ignited. As the heat consumed them, they moved to the bed and slipped between the satin sheets.

Their exploration began tentatively, almost as though it were their first time. Lips caressed skin, hands touched breasts, kisses were exchanged, and love was both spoken and unspoken. As their passion rose, their lovemaking became more intense, their bodies moving against each other and eliciting moans of desire. They reached out for each other and they reached into each other. Tongues dueled as bodies strove for that one last movement that would bring them to a climatic union of body and soul. Sounds of loving filled the night air, and when the last gasp of passion soared on the wind, they slept, entwined as one.

When the action was over, Kurt flipped off the recorder. The audio was a real gold mine for Len. Kurt packed up, started the motor, and headed back to the marina. He planned to return to the house via the reservoir to retrieve the camera and microphones when the group left for their picnic later that day. When he eventually returned to his office, he would review the material and pull out the best pieces, then make a tape, put together some photos, and wrap the package with a bow for Len.

Back at the house, three felines stood guard by the sliding screen door. Spice was unusually watchful as she glared into the night then back up at her mistresses, occasionally emitting a low, sorrowful growl.

Waiting in his car at the same parking area in Rock Creek Park where he'd previously met with Kurt, Len impatiently looked at his watch. It was nearly 1700 hours and the park would be closing shortly. He was starting to get concerned when his cell phone rang.

"Russell," he answered tersely.

"Len, it's Kurt. I'm stuck in traffic and I know the park is going to close before I can get there. Can you get to Reagan airport? I can get on the Metro from here and meet you there, in the bar at Legal Seafood."

Russell checked his watch and estimated his travel time. "Okay. I'll meet you there."

"Great. I'll find a spot to park and jump on the Metro. I should be able to get there in about half an hour. See you there."

Len started his car and pulled out just as a National Park Service ranger pulled into the lot. Len waved at the ranger, receiving a salute in return. Forty minutes later he was parking in the short term parking lot at the airport. Inside Legal Seafood, he found a table at the end of the bar where he could stay out of sight and still see everyone who came in. He checked his watch. Kurt should have been there already and he started to worry again. Maybe Kurt had been in an accident. What if all the evidence he'd gathered was destroyed? There wasn't time to have it all done over again. He broke out in a sweat.

"Sir," the waitress asked for a second time but a bit louder. "May I help you?"

Len started, then nodded. "Yes, a beer, draft."

"We have—"

"Any draft is fine."

"Yes, sir," she said, and went to place the order.

The beer and Kurt arrived at the same time. "Bring me one of those too," he said to the waitress as he took a seat. He placed a folder on the table and pushed it toward Len.

"Those are the pictures." He waited as Len pulled them out and went through them. He'd put the shot of the final kiss during the ceremony at the bottom.

Len grinned. "Terrific," he said. "This one alone will end her career."

"I can guarantee that this," Kurt held up a tape, "will slam the lid shut for sure." He pulled out a tape player and mini headphones. "There's a lot of audio, but I pulled out the best of the best."

Len put the tape in the player and the headphones in his ears and pressed "play". Kurt watched as he closed his eyes, intermittently shaking his head and nodding. He could tell when Len got to the bedroom portion because he actually started to turn red. Finally, Len pulled out the headphones and turned off the player.

"Hot, huh?"

"This is great stuff, Kurt. You really came through for me."

"When are you going to drop the axe?"

"She's 'on leave' this week. I'll give her the ultimatum on Monday when she comes back. If she doesn't resign, I'll take the proof to the general."

"She's in pretty tight with the general, Len. Maybe you should send it up the line past her."

Len considered for a moment. "I'll have to think about that one. If I bypass the general, it could do me some harm. Why didn't I come to her first... Might get the general thinking twice about a promotion recommendation. By next Monday, I'll figure it out."

"Your call," Kurt said. "I'll have a second set for you by Friday, one for her viewing and listening pleasure."

The waitress came back with Kurt's beer and a menu. "Are you gentlemen going to be ordering something to eat?" They both shook their heads and she left the bar bill on the table.

"I've got it," Len said as Kurt reached into his pocket. Len pulled out his wallet and threw a twenty dollar bill on the tab. "Did you get the equipment picked up?"

"Yes, I went back out on Sunday. That whole bunch went off on a picnic or something. I've got your stuff in my car. You just have to take me over to where I parked it."

Len nodded in agreement. "Did you find the missing microphone?"

"No. I went over the area several times and couldn't come up with it. Some squirrel was probably really disappointed when he got that back to his nest. Just tell them one of the non-coms stepped on it and crushed it into oblivion. Or hell, tell them the acorn was so realistic a squirrel ran off with it."

"Shit," Len muttered. "Do you realize how many damn forms I'm going to have to fill out for missing equipment?"

"Look on the bright side, Len. At least you will have done the Army a service by getting rid of a potential security risk. That lezzie could have been compromised anytime, maybe already has! Besides, what's a few measly forms in comparison with the big picture?" He took his glass and drained the contents. "C'mon, take me back to my car and I'll give you your precious stuff."

Dirk pulled over to the curb and put the car in park. He got out from behind the wheel and went to the trunk, while Bill opened the back door for Martha. He gave her a hand stepping out and then wrapped her in a hug.

"Have a safe trip home, Martha," Bill whispered.

"As safe as the Lord sees fit," she said as she hugged him back. "Thanks for bringing me to the airport. It was nice of you to offer to drop me off."

"No sense in the girls coming this way and having to turn around and go back. The airport is right on our way home." He gave her another hug, a bit tighter this time. "We happen to love you too, Martha."

Dirk gave the bag to the skycap, then waited for Bill and Martha to release each other.

"Bill, watch out for her, okay? I have a feeling she's in for some bad times," Martha said with glistening eyes.

Bill cocked his head, a look of confusion on his face, followed by acceptance. "I always do, Martha. Always do. We watch out for each other."

"Okay, you two, break it up." Dirk moved in to get his hug from Martha. "It was sure good to see you again. It's been a long time since Christmas. Speaking of which, are you coming back this year?"

Martha smiled. "That depends on whether I'm invited."

"Consider yourself invited. If the newlyweds are still acting like newlyweds, you can come and stay with us."

"Hah! Like they'll ever stop that!" Bill crowed.

The three of them laughed, hugs were shared one more time, and then Martha turned to the skycap and got out her plane ticket so he could process the bag.

Bill stepped forward. "Martha, are you sure you don't want us to come in and wait with you?"

"Oh my, no. I'll be just fine. You two go and relax. You have to work tomorrow. As they got into the car, she waved. "See you around, boys!"

Bill and Dirk waved back and pulled away from the curb. As they passed the far entrance, Dirk noticed an Army officer and another man exiting the terminal. "Hey, isn't that your boss?"

Bill got a quick glimpse in the rearview mirror as Major Russell and another man jogged across the road toward the short term parking lot. "Sure looks like Russell."

"The other guy looks real familiar, but I can't place him. Do you know who he is?"

Bill looked again but could no longer see the twosome. "No clue. I never saw him before."

Dean pulled her black Boxster into a parking place and turned off the ignition. Reaching over into the passenger seat, she picked up her hat and set it on her head, adjusting it in the rearview mirror. She grabbed her briefcase and a shopping bag and stepped out of the car, bumping the door shut with her hip. She punched the lock button on the car remote and slipped it into her pocket. Whistling softly and with a noticeable bounce in her step, she walked toward the Pentagon.

Sergeant Rowland watched from just inside the entrance as Colonel Peterson approached. He opened the door with his left hand and saluted with his right.

"Good morning, Sergeant. Thanks for getting the door."

"You're welcome, Colonel." He released the door and walked to the security table with her. "How was your leave?"

"Terrific!" she replied. "By the way, this is for your little girl. We found it at the beach and thought it would be perfect for her next year." She handed him the shopping bag.

"Thank you, ma'am, but you didn't—"

"Nope, didn't have to, but wanted to. Let's see, Jenny is just over three months now, isn't she?"

"Yes, ma'am. And she's the apple of my eye."

"I bet she is, Sergeant, and I bet you have a recent picture of her, too."

Sergeant Rowland pulled out his wallet and took out three pictures. "Here's one we took at Sears two weeks ago. We just got them last night." The picture was of Jenny surrounded by her brothers, who all seemed to be smitten by their little sister.

"What a cutie pie. She certainly takes after Ginny with all those beautiful blond curls, and the dimples, too."

He held out another with Jenny in Ginny's lap, and the third one was a candid shot of the youngster and the family dog.

"You have a lot to be proud of, Sergeant." Dean handed back the pictures. "Have a great day!" she said as she turned toward the elevators.

"Thank you, ma'am. You, too. And thanks again for the gift."

"You're welcome," she said over her shoulder as she stepped into the elevator.

Sergeant Rowland and the other guards watched as the elevator door closed. "I'd willingly follow her into hell if she ordered it," he said to the others sitting at the table.

"She really is in a great mood today," the female corporal observed. "She must have had a great time on leave last week."

"What'd she get the kid?" the other soldier asked.

Sergeant Rowland looked into the bag and pulled out a beach outfit that consisted of a two piece outfit, matching hat, sandals, and sunglasses. The outfit was a sea blue background with all varieties of colorful fish printed on it. The sunglasses had tiny dolphins on each side, and the sandals were sea blue with yellow straps. He looked at the size tag and smiled, noting the outfit should fit perfectly by next summer.

"Awww, those are really cute," the corporal cooed.

"Ginny's gonna love it." He put the items back in the bag and set it behind the table. As he resumed his post, a smile spread across his face.

The morning was hectic, like most mornings on the first day back from a vacation. Dean had piles of reports to go through and several memos to send, meetings with staff, and a two hour meeting scheduled with General Carlton at 1400. At 1100 she decided to take a break. She needed to move and stretch. She went to her closet and pulled out a set of work-out clothes, and then proceeded to the IOC to see if Bill could slip away for thirty minutes of sparring.

She went straight to Bill's office. As she walked past the windows, she saw him on the phone so she walked in quietly and sat in the visitor chair across from his desk, waiting for him to finish his call.

Bill hung up and said cheerfully, "Welcome back, Colonel. How was the vacation?"

Dean grinned. "It was wonderful. Katie flew us down to the Keys and we had a terrific time. We did some snorkeling, some deep sea fishing, and a lot of relaxing in the sun."

"Catch any fish?"

"Not anything to brag about. Katie caught a nice grouper that we shared with the crew. By the way, that B & B that Dirk told us about was superb. The owners treated us like royalty."

"They're old college buds of Dirk's. When he told them why you were coming down, they promised to go overboard for you two."

"Well, they certainly did. Tell Dirk thanks." She noted the stacks of papers on his desk and pointed. "Same old same old, or something new?"

"Actually, it's been quiet, but then today the NSA started to intercept multiple communications. I just got off the phone with Rodney over there. Seems a couple of them are referring to zero hour and something about a match beginning. They're still sorting out the translations."

"Anything else? How about that guy the FBI arrested? Did they get anything on him?"

"They're labeling him a fanatic, the type to do anything for the cause. The FBI notified the CIA about him."

"Anyone clue in the White House?"

"Not yet." Bill frowned. "I can't figure out why not, either. If the guy is a zealot, who knows what he was up to?"

"What about the FAA?"

"No new warnings there, either."

"Anything up with Russell? He's requested a meeting with me at 1630."

Bill shook his head. "No. Actually he's been in a pretty good mood lately. Today when he came in, he was smiling."

"Well, at least he's not on your case." Dean patted her gym bag. "Do you have time for thirty minutes of sparring? I'm really in need of a diversion right now and a short session would do us both good."

Bill checked his watch. He wasn't expecting Major Russell back until 1300 and he'd just finished his last report, so he agreed. "I'll get my stuff." He went to the credenza and opened it, pulling out a small gym bag. He opened the door and held it for Dean.

"Lieutenant," Bill called to the floor officer, "I'll be back in an hour. If you need me, call my cell."

"C'mon, Bill. You're getting slow in your old age!" Dean bounced and danced around him, grinning and teasing.

"Where on earth do you get all your energy?" he panted, as he stopped trying to follow her. Dropping his hands to his sides, he conceded. "I give."

"Aww, we were just getting started." Dean threw an arm around his shoulder. "Maybe you just need a vacation. It's amazing what that can do for you. I feel terrific. Back to my old self!" She shot a gloved fist into the air.

Bill looked at her critically. The gaunt features had vanished, her weight was back up and maybe even a pound or two over her normal weight, her eyes were bright, and she was definitely back to her old devilish self. "Maybe you're right. You are, without a doubt, back to normal."

"Seriously, Bill, you need a vacation. In fact, I'm ordering you to take one, and soon. How's next week sound to you? Do you think Dirk can get off that quickly?"

"I'll ask him tonight."

"Good. Now let's get cleaned up and stop by the cafeteria before we get mired down in reports and memos and meetings."

Dean checked her watch as she and several of her staff members walked out of the general's office following their meeting. It was nearly 1630 and time for her appointment with Major Russell. As she was moving toward the door, she saw Sergeant Major Tibbitts approaching. *Let Russell wait.*

"Colonel, do you have a minute?"

"Sure, Sergeant Major." They stepped over to the corner sitting area and waited until the rest of the staff cleared the office. "What's up?"

"The general's birthday is in a few weeks and I was wondering...well, hoping, actually, that you wouldn't mind hosting a surprise party for her at your house. She's been a bit depressed about turning fifty and I thought a good party might cheer her up."

"That's a terrific idea, Tibbitts. Let me talk to Katie tonight and I'll let you know tomorrow. I don't think it will be a problem, though. You know how Katie loves to throw parties. She sees them as a great excuse to try out new recipes on unsuspecting souls."

"Thanks, Colonel. I think this will really help lift the general's mood."

Major Russell was waiting for Dean outside her office. When he saw her approaching, he opened the door for her and followed her in.

Dean tossed her file folders onto her desk and went to the credenza and poured herself a glass of water. "Water, Major?"

"No thank you, ma'am."

"Have a seat, Major." She walked back to her desk and sat down. "What's on your mind?"

He slid a manila envelope across the desk to her.

"What's this?"

"Your ticket out of this man's Army." Russell smiled broadly.

Dean felt her heart skip a beat. She looked him in the eye, then reached for the envelope and pulled out the stack of photos, flipping through them quickly. The bile rose in her stomach and her head began to spin. Dean sat back as she fought a wave of nausea. The treachery of his actions sullied the uniform he wore and she was filled with revulsion. Not only were there incriminating shots of her and Katie kissing, but several also included Dirk and Bill and Tracy and Colleen in similar shots. Some were even of her and Katie during their trip to Provincetown, where the photographer caught them wrestling on the sand and running naked from the hose at the side of the house to the hot tub. *My God, he's been following us all summer and I had no clue.*

"I'm not vindictive; I'll allow you to resign. You have until noon tomorrow to turn in a letter of resignation to General Carlton, effective immediately. You can use any justification you want, I don't care. I just want you out of here."

"And, what makes you think I give a good goddamn about your request? These photos could have been doctored."

"I have sworn affidavits from the photographers and even an affidavit from a Jeremiah Jones, who will testify to seeing you two kissing in his limo. You have no shame, Colonel, making out with your...girlfriend on the way to bury your father!" He shook his head in disgust.

Dean's anger rose, but before she could speak, Russell played his trump card.

"And, then there's this." He tossed the tape player on the desk. "Go ahead and listen."

Dean turned it on and heard the sounds of their lovemaking on their wedding night. She snapped off the player and pinned him with a deadly look, the muscles of her jaw rigid and her hands clenched. She knew she could not contest the audio tape. A voice analysis would come back a one hundred percent match for their voices.

"Maybe you and your blond slut can get a job doing porn films," Russell said with a sneer. "Too bad we couldn't get video of that!"

Dean stood abruptly and surged around the desk to stand beside him. Her heart was racing and adrenaline coursed through her body. Her hands were opening and closing, finally remaining closed in tight fists. Her whole body was taut; she was ready to explode. Enraged and on the brink, she towered over him. Russell stood quickly, knocking the chair backward. "Russell, you were a slimy piece of shit back in Fort Huachuca," Dean said through clenched teeth as she moved closer to him, "and you're still a slimy piece of shit." She stepped into his personal space. "I should have taken care of your sorry ass back then." She stood nose to nose with him and her voice was a steely promise. "If you ever again call Katie a slut, I'll personally crush you with my bare hands."

"Go ahead, Colonel. I'd love to add that to my UCMJ charges." He backed away and Dean held her ground. "If that resignation isn't on the general's desk by noon tomorrow, I'll add your little fag captain to the charges. Right now, I'm just interested in you, but push me and I'll drag his ass and his lover boy's ass into the mix. I'll dig up so much crap on the rest of your homo friends, it'll make your head spin." Russell backed toward the door and pointed at her. "Noon, Colonel. It's not a request; it's an order. Oh, and you can keep the tape and pictures. Maybe you can add them to your queer wedding memorabilia!" He turned and opened the door, slamming it behind him as he left.

Dean didn't know how long she stood there, heart pounding and head throbbing, but she became conscious of time having passed when there was a knock on the door.

When she didn't answer, Bill opened the door and peeked in. As soon as he saw her, he rushed in, closing the door behind him. "Colonel?" She didn't respond, but turned and went back to her desk, dropping heavily into her chair. Bill followed her to the desk, looking at her with concern. "Colonel...Dean," he said urgently, "are you all right? You look...look..."

"Pissed off is how I look!" she nearly shouted. In a quieter voice she added, "That goddamn prick. That fucking goddamn prick."

Bill saw the photos on her desk and the one on top was a shot of her and Katie sealing their vows with a kiss. "Shit!" He picked up the stack and went through them.

"You'd better get Dirk up here." Dean stood and went to the window as Bill dialed Dirk's extension and told him to hurry up to Dean's office. When Dirk arrived, she took a seat behind her desk.

"Evidently Major Russell has been following Katie and me most of the summer. He's been collecting photos and recordings and has sworn affidavits as to the authenticity of these items." She tossed the photos to Dirk, who went through them.

"How on earth..." He slammed the photos down on the desk. "The surveyor," he said softly. "That's the guy we saw Russell with at the airport." He turned to Bill. "The night we dropped Reverend Martha off. Remember, I thought he looked familiar? Well, that guy was the surveyor." He looked at Dean. "Oh, my God, Dean. If only I had placed him that night, maybe we could have done something about these. He must have planted a camera in that tree. And I gave the son of a bitch lemonade!"

"It's not your fault, Dirk, it's mine. All mine. And all because of that one fucking lapse at James River Park!" Dean took a drink from her untouched glass of water. "I'm the one to blame for all of this."

Bill looked at the damning pictures lying on the desk. "So, what does Russell want? Is he blackmailing you for a promotion?"

"He's demanding my resignation by noon tomorrow."

"That's crap, Dean!" Dirk shouted.

Dean held up a hand. "It may be crap, but he's going to file UCMJ charges against me, Bill, and you, if I *don't* resign by tomorrow. And then he'll drag Katie, Tracy, and Colleen into it." She reached into her drawer and brought out a bottle of Advil, tapped three tablets into her hand and popped them into her mouth, washing them down with the rest of the water in her glass. She refilled her glass and leaned against the credenza.

"Dean, the general...she'll stand behind you. I think you should fight this. We'll fight it with you." Bill looked at Dirk for confirmation and got an affirmative nod.

"Please, don't give in to him. I'm sure we can find something to counter this. He's got to have some dirt in his background," Dirk added.

"No, the bastard is too slick. He did a good surveillance job on me. I never saw this coming. Too bad he doesn't put this kind of effort into his job."

She gathered her briefcase, stuffed the photos and the tape into it, and snapped it shut. "I just wanted you to know. I won't let him drag you or anyone else into my mess. I made it, and I'll take care of it. And you two should talk over the possibility that he will make Bill's life hell from here on out." She looked at Bill and softened her tone. "I'm sorry, Bill. You should think about putting in for a transfer and do it quickly. I wouldn't trust him to keep his word about leaving you and Dirk out of his plan to destroy me." She snatched her hat off the coat rack and strode out of the office.

When the door clicked shut, Dirk turned to Bill. "Isn't there something we can do?"

"I don't know, but let's see if we can find something... anything. C'mon, we'll go to my office." It was a slim hope that they would find anything at all, and very unlikely that they could do so before noon the next day.

Dean managed to make her way out of the Pentagon without drawing attention to herself. Years of fieldwork kicking in, she assumed an air of confidence. As she was driving the Boxster down the highway toward home, her fury broke. She slammed her fist on the steering wheel, causing the car to jerk to the right. "Shit," she yelled as she corrected the steering. "Shit, shit, shit!" Each word was louder and louder. She wiped the tears from her eyes and concentrated on getting home...home to Katie. Katie was her soulmate, her confidante, her lover, and she needed her more now than ever before.

The emotional drain of the past hour was taking its toll and she was suddenly exhausted. The tears returned and she blinked hard to keep her vision from blurring, but they continued to streak down her face until, at last, there were no tears left to fall.

As she made the final turn to her house, the voice of her father came to her: "*Stand up for her love, totally and completely and never be ashamed or hide in fear of that love.*" Inside the garage, she turned off the car and sat there for a few moments, thinking of her father's words. There was no other course of action. Nodding calmly, she said softly, "I will, Dad. I will."

Dean walked into the house and went directly to the kitchen, putting her briefcase down on the table. Katie was working at the sink, washing lettuce and vegetables for a salad she was preparing. Dean could smell the chicken grilling outside.

"Hey, love, how was your day?" Katie asked without looking up from her chore.

"You don't want to know." Dean went to the liquor cabinet and pulled out a bottle of Makers Mark and a tumbler. She poured herself two fingers of whiskey and downed it, then refilled the glass half full.

"So, it was a typical Monday after a vacation, huh?" Katie said brightly.

"Not exactly." Dean leaned against the counter beside Katie.

Katie finished washing the last tomato and wiped her hands on the towel, then looked up at Dean. Dean's eyes were bloodshot, tracks from the tears were still visible on her face, and her blouse bore the vestiges of the wetness from her tears.

"Oh, my God, Dean, what's wrong? What happened today?" She searched her lover's eyes, seeing the pain and sadness. "What on earth happened?"

She raised a hand to stroke Dean's face, but Dean pushed away from the counter, sidestepping Katie and pointing at her briefcase on the table. "It's in there, in the manila envelope," she said in a whisper. "I'm going to soak in the hot tub." She took her glass of whiskey with her as she left the room.

In the master bedroom, she emptied her pockets, putting the items on the dresser. She caught sight of the tattered fortune cookie slip. She held it in her hand. She knew the words by heart: *Your destiny lies before you. Choose wisely.* She tossed the fortune into the trash basket, then stripped off all of her clothes and stepped out onto the deck and into the hot tub.

When Dean was out of sight, Katie went to the briefcase and opened it. The envelope was on top. She took it out and shook the contents onto the table. A sharp intake of breath punctuated her first sight of the pictures. She spread them over the table and started to shake. Then she picked up the tape player and listened. At first she was confused by the moans and sounds of movement, then she realized she was listening to a tape of their lovemaking. She looked toward the bedroom and back down at the pictures, then shut off the tape.

"Son of a bitch!" She picked up the snapshot from Provincetown. "The son of a bitch has been stalking her all summer!" She tossed the photo on the pile and went out to the patio and turned off the grill. Then she went into the master bedroom.

Dean was already in the hot tub on the deck and had the Jacuzzi jets going. Her glass was on the tub ledge and half empty. When Katie walked out, Dean was stretched out and staring at her toes. She looked up and raised her glass, draining the last of the whiskey. "There are some really good shots of us kissing," Dean said with an ironic grin. "And the tape...now, that's the kicker. One hundred percent voice match."

Katie stood next to the tub, tears glistening in her eyes. "That son of a bitch was stalking you all summer."

"Yep, he sure was, and I didn't catch a clue."

"So, what does Russell want?"

"Nothing much, just my resignation on General Carlton's desk before noon tomorrow or he'll file UCMJ charges against me...and Bill. Then he'll drag in you and Tracy and Colleen..."

"Oh, Dean! What are we going to do?"

"Do? Well, the first thing you're going to do is strip off those clothes and come join me. Then we'll talk."

Katie looked at their surroundings. The hot tub was on the deck off the master bedroom, but it was still outside and in the open. Normally they didn't get in it naked during daylight hours, so she was hesitant.

"Love, there's nothing to worry about. I'm sure he's picked up the camera already, and if he hasn't, what's a couple more shots to add to his arsenal?"

Katie took off her shorts and tank top, then slipped out of her underclothes. She stepped into the tub and slid next to Dean. "So, what's the plan? How do we stop Russell?"

Dean put her arm around Katie and pulled her close. "It's going to be a nice night." She looked into Katie's eyes and knew that she was making the right decision. Smiling, she pulled Katie closer and kissed her softly. "Have I told you today that I love you?"

"Dean, are you drunk?" She looked deeply into Dean's eyes, but they were alert and the bloodshot lines were beginning to fade.

"No. Not a chance. And I have no intention of getting drunk. I just needed to unwind. The tension from the confrontation with Russell and the ride home had my muscles in a knot." She laughed. "It was all I could do not to pound that prick into next week. I really, really wanted to hurt him right then."

Katie shook her head in confusion. "But now you're not upset?"

"Oh, I'm upset all right...pissed off royally. But on the way up our road, I remembered the words my father wrote in his note." She smiled. "You know, the one Martha gave me on our wedding day." Katie nodded. "He said I was to stand up for your love and never be ashamed or hide in fear. Katie, I've been hiding in fear all summer, and you know what? I'm glad it's over. I'm tired of hiding my feelings for you because of the Army's archaic policy. 'Don't ask, don't tell' is a crock, and I'm ashamed to have served in silence. There's nothing wrong with our love. Like Dad said, 'love is pure and lives in the light'. I'm not going to live in darkness anymore." She pulled Katie close and kissed her again. It was a deeper, more passionate kiss, and they were both breathless when their lips parted. "I'm not ashamed of loving you, and I don't give a crap who knows it. I'm sorry that I haven't accepted that sooner. You don't deserve to live in shadows. You're the love of my life and I promised to love and honor you until death."

"But what about the Army, love? It's been your life for twenty years."

Dean put two fingers on Katie's lips. "No, Katherine O'Malley-Peterson is my life. The Army was a job, and I can find a job anywhere. You are more important to me than anything else in this world; you're all I care about." Tears formed in Katie's eyes, and one spilled over and ran down her cheek. Dean reached up and wiped it away. "Tomorrow, I'll turn in my resignation, and then we can begin our future together — openly and unafraid."

"Are you sure?"

"I have never been more sure about anything in my life!" Dean grinned and her smile was infectious. "Look, I'll have to take care of a few things before I turn in the letter. Can you take me in tomorrow and then pick me up mid-morning?"

"Sure. But, we need to agree on one thing first. If you're going to resign, I'm going to resign, too. That way we will truly begin a new life together. Agreed?"

Dean nodded and put out her hand. Katie grabbed it and they shook. "Okay, I'll drop you off, and then run by the DEA office in Arlington and come back to pick you up at, say, 10 o'clock."

"Perfect. I shouldn't need to be at the Pentagon any longer than that."

They stayed in the hot tub until the jets timed off and then they finished preparing dinner. Afterwards, they walked down to the flagstone patio and sat watching geese and ducks and listening to the joyful sound of crickets. They didn't talk much, but sat with arms around each other, snuggling close and enjoying touching and kissing without having to cast a watchful eye. When sunset settled into darkness, they went back up to the house and made sweet, incredible love well into the night. At last, bodies spent, they slept.

Chapter Twenty-nine
September 11

Katie hurried out of the DEA office. The news reports about the double air strikes on the Twin Towers had everyone in rapid response mode and she needed to get to Dean. All hell was breaking loose and she knew Dean would be able to fill her in better than the inadequate suppositions of the media. She tried calling, but the lines were busy and Dean's cell phone was going unanswered. She looked at her watch; it was 0920. She pulled out her key fob and unlocked the doors to the Boxster as she ran to her car, then slid behind the wheel and fumbled the key into the ignition. The car roared to life and she sped out of the lot, hoping traffic wouldn't be too heavy since most offices opened for business at 0900. Turning onto U.S. Highway 1, she headed for the Pentagon exit, slipping in and out of traffic as she raced ahead. She pulled off onto the highway that led to the main entrance of the Pentagon. The loop would take her around the south side of the building, past the Metro entrance, then past the west side to the main parking lot. As she slowed to make the curve, she saw a low flying plane in the distance. She watched in horror as it dipped out of sight. There was a thunderous explosion and a fireball erupted from the far side of the Pentagon. Katie knew exactly what services were on that side — part Navy and part Army. Her scream was lost in the accelerating whine as she floored the Boxster toward the main entrance parking lot, hoping that the plane had fallen short and crashed into Arlington Cemetery. Her head was telling her otherwise. Her heart was racing as the west side of the complex came into view. When she saw the flames and smoke, she slammed on the brakes and sat in stunned collapse as her world spun off its axis. Tears rolling down her face, she choked out, "Dean, please...be safe."

Amazingly, emergency response vehicles were already in the area and teams were heading into the building. Katie forced herself into action, inching forward to find a place to park. People were rushing out of the building, most of them looking untouched. Many were helping others who apparently were in, or close to, the impact zone. Sirens were screaming in the background and an Army helicopter swung in over Arlington and descended toward an open area. Katie pulled off the roadway onto a grassy slope. She got out of the car and studied the people running away from the building, looking for anyone she might know, but her tears were blurring the figures and making it hard to discern their features. She climbed over the guardrail to make her way closer and search for her lover.

The building stopped shaking and the fireman that had reached out to Dean as she fell couldn't believe the eerie scene before him. The colonel was buried from the chest down in plaster, chunks of concrete, electrical conduit, and a large section of steel beam that had broken loose from the ceiling. The back of her head was bleeding, and when he looked closer, he could see that a piece of her scalp had been scraped loose, exposing her skull beneath.

"Chet!" the fireman shouted. "Get some men back here, and make it fast." He quickly analyzed the situation and wasn't happy with his assessment. The floor was buckled and the integrity of the remaining supports was deteriorating with every passing second. The smoke was returning, thicker and deadlier than before. He could feel the heat increasing, too, and was afraid there would be another explosion. If that happened, they'd all be watching the aftermath from heaven. He checked the colonel for a pulse. It was there, though erratic and weak. He slipped his secondary tank off his shoulder and placed it next to the colonel, affixing the mask gently over her face. He ran back to where they'd dropped the emergency kit and pulled out gauze and some large pads. Returning to the colonel, he placed the pads over the open wound on the back of her head and carefully wrapped the gauze around as best he could without moving her head. Hearing Chet and some others returning, he shouted, "Bring a 'C' collar, backboard, splints, and pry bars!" then he carefully started removing the lighter rubble that was entombing the colonel.

"What do we have here, John?" the lead fire officer asked.

"Sir, we've got a colonel under all that and a captain buried somewhere in what's left of that office over there." He pointed at the tangle of beams and concrete wreckage. "They pulled a soldier out of what was left of that office over there, just before that last explosion. The colonel was coming toward me when the explosion hit and the walls and ceiling came in on her. The captain went back into that office to get the dog tags from a dead soldier buried in the rubble from the first impact."

"Is she still alive?" John nodded. "Okay, let's get her out of here before the rest of this section goes. I'll call for some more men to get to the captain."

Five firemen worked together to move the obstructions covering Dean. One by one, starting with the lighter pieces, they cleared those off quickly, then came the more difficult, trickier parts. Moving the large concrete chunks and the beam were going to test their skill to the maximum. With extreme caution, so they did not cause any further injury, they attacked the remaining pieces as if they were deconstructing a giant game of jackstraws. Each piece had to be evaluated before they chose the next piece to remove. They moved as quickly as they dared, constantly aware that the next explosion could bury them all.

Another group of rescue workers arrived and started to remove the remains of the entrance to the office. They moved several pieces of concrete chunks and had a small hole opened up near the top of the ceiling.

"Josh, crawl up there and take a look."

The smallest of the three rescue workers carefully climbed up the debris. At the top he took out his flashlight and shone it into the room, slipping his head and shoulder in after it. The interior of the room, or what was left of it, looked like a bomb had gone off in it.

"What do you see?"

Josh fanned the flashlight around the room, settling the beam on a man's arm protruding from under the pile on which he was standing. Blood streams were glistening along the exposed arm ending in a pool of dark fluid below it. Josh crawled back out of the hole and deftly climbed down.

"He's under this pile of concrete, Larry," Josh said. "I don't think he could be alive under all that."

"Well, let's get this stuff off him. C'mon men, move it!"

As the other five firemen worked to release the colonel, John, the medic with them kept an eye on the colonel's blood pressure. When they finally moved the last pieces off of her legs, he gave them a thumbs-up. Her pressure stayed steady, so he proceeded with the collar and the splints. With the help of the other firemen, they got the collar secured and her legs splinted, then gently rolled her onto the backboard and strapped her down.

"Okay, let's move it, men! I don't trust this section to hold much longer."

"What about the captain?" Larry called back to their squad leader. "We're just about to reach him."

Josh reached his arm through a hole in the pile and felt for the captain's carotid. "He's gone," he said as he withdrew his arm.

"Okay," their leader shouted, "let's get going. We'll come back for him if this section holds and they get the fires under control."

The men had carried the backboard with Dean about fifty feet when they heard the next rumble as it rippled through the building. "Double time it, men!" They increased their pace and didn't look back as the section from which they had rescued the colonel fell into an abyss of smoke and flame.

Dirk was pacing outside the Pentagon where they'd set up triage for the injured. He was waiting for word on the survivors. He knew the section that sustained the impact was close to where Bill and Dean worked, and he became worried when Bill didn't answer his cell phone.

The EMTs set a stretcher down on the ground for the doctor to check the injured woman, and when the examination was completed and the doctor moved on to the next victim, Dirk moved closer.

Dirk knelt down next to the stretcher. "Were you in the C Ring when the plane hit?"

"Yes. I was lucky. Colonel Peterson and Captain Jarvis came in and got me out," Hawadi replied.

Dirk looked up trying to locate the colonel. "I don't see her. Didn't she come out with you?"

"No. Some firemen came and they took me out to the EMTs and then went back in."

"Did they go back for someone else?"

"I don't think so. The only other person in the waiting room with me was dead. I heard Colonel Peterson tell the firemen she was right behind them, then there was a rumble and another blast and the guys rushed me out." She looked up at the man's worried face. "You don't suppose..."

Dirk shook his head. "No. I'm sure she's fine. She'll be out soon. I know she will. They both will."

What the man was saying and the look on his face didn't match up. As his eyes searched the crowd, Hawadi sent up a prayer for their safe exit.

Dirk was becoming more worried with each minute that passed. He went to search the stretchers that were now coming out. On many of them, the bodies were covered with blankets. Few were hurried over to triage. He stopped dead when he heard his name called.

"Dirk," Katie shouted again and again as she ran toward him. He caught her in his arms and pulled her close. "Where's Dean?" she asked, pulling away from him.

"I'm not sure. She went back in to save a soldier...a Private Hawadi. She's here; she said Dean and Bill were coming out right behind her, but I haven't seen them yet."

The worried look on his face told Katie more than he was saying and she started to shake. "She's got to be okay, Dirk. She's got to be. Today is supposed to be a new beginning for us." She looked at the wreckage of the Pentagon, smoke billowing from the jagged opening. "Is this going to be our future?"

"They'll be out soon, Katie. They're both tough and smart. They'll be fine." Dirk's voice sounded encouraging but inside he was falling apart.

Four firemen transporting a stretcher came running into the triage area, shouting for a doctor. Dirk and Katie turned to watch and their search for Dean came to an abrupt end. She was the badly injured occupant of the stretcher. Her eyes were closed; a bloody bandage was wrapped around her head. She had a collar around her neck to immobilize her and her legs were splinted together.

"Oh, my God!" Katie cried, running toward the stretcher. Dirk grabbed her and pulled her into his arms, wanting to give the doctors the chance to get to Dean first. He looked around for Bill or another stretcher, but didn't see either.

"She's strong, Katie. She'll be okay. They have to immobilize her to prevent further injury, just to be safe. Let the doctors look her over and then we'll see what they say."

They listened as the medic filled in the doctor on the patient's injuries. "...head trauma, possible broken legs and spinal injury. She's been out cold since the beam hit her fifteen minutes ago. Her pulse is weak and erratic. Pupils are reactive." A paramedic started an IV and the doctor called for an immediate medical evacuation to Walter Reed. With their focus on their patient, they didn't see Katie faint into Dirk's arms.

Dirk took the ammonia inhalant capsule from the medic, broke it, and waved it under Katie's nose. It brought her around immediately. She shook her head and moved Dirk's hand away from her face.

"Where's your car?" he asked as she sat up slowly.

Katie looked around and spotted it on the side of the road. She pointed to it. "There."

"Okay. Are you all right now?" he asked, searching her eyes.

"Yeah, I'm okay...I just..."

"Fainted, yeah." Dirk gave her an encouraging hug. "It's okay."

Katie looked over to where Dean had been lying. "Where's Dean?"

"They med evac'd her out of here to Walter Reed. Do you think you can drive over there by yourself?" Katie nodded. "Okay, I'm going to stay here until I find Bill. We'll come by the hospital as soon as we can." He looked at Katie again, searching her eyes. "Are you sure you're okay?"

"Yes, I'll be okay. How about you?"

"I'll be fine once Bill shows up. You need to go and be there for Dean. Don't worry about us right now."

Dirk helped Katie to her feet and walked her back to her car. He gave her a hug then jogged back to the triage area to find Hawadi.

"We found the colonel," he said bending down by Hawadi's stretcher. "She's hurt bad, but she's a survivor. You two will probably be causing trouble at Walter Reed by tomorrow night."

"Thank you. She means a lot to me."

"And to me, too, Hawadi. I'll check in on you at the hospital later." He turned away and resumed his search for Bill. Looking around the devastation, he spotted one of the EMTs that had brought Dean out. He jogged over to the man, steeling himself for a worst-case scenario. He knew that Bill would have been right with Dean if he were alive.

Katie skillfully wove the Boxster in and out of the traffic and around various emergency vehicles that were crowding the access road to the Pentagon. When she finally got on the road to Walter Reed, she picked up speed as best she could. It was amazing how much traffic was on the roads, and she had to pull over several times to let ambulances pass. Katie blinked back tears as she drove.

"Go ahead and cry," she told herself. "You'll feel better if you do and you need to get it out of your system before you get to the hospital. Dean will need me to be strong and I will be strong for her. She needs me now." By the time she reached Walter Reed Army Medical Center, Katie was back in control of her emotions.

As she pulled into the visitor's parking area, another ambulance arrived and a medical evacuation helicopter took off from the helipad heading back toward the Pentagon. She got out of the Boxster and hurried directly to the Emergency Room. The place looked chaotic, but it was operating quickly and efficiently with corpsmen, nurses, and doctors all focusing on expertly treating the injured. She followed the signs to the registration desk.

The corpsman behind the desk looked up from his computer monitor. He was obviously prepared to assist relatives of the injured. "Patient's name?"

"Colonel Deanna Peterson," Katie supplied.

He typed the name into the computer and then looked up at the blonde making the inquiry. "She's being prepped for surgery. Are you family?"

"Well, no, not by blood," Katie began. "I'm technically the only family she has. Her father passed away this summer and the rest of her family is deceased." Katie paused then added, "I do have her power of attorney. I can go home and get it if you need to see it."

The corpsman looked at Katie and typed in a few keystrokes. "May I have your name?"

"Katie...Katherine O'Malley."

"Her records have you listed as having her power of attorney. Take these elevators," he pointed to the bank of silver doors behind the desk, "to the third floor, take a right and go to the waiting lounge. The surgeon will come out and speak to you when she's out of surgery." He waited to be sure she had gotten all the directions. He typed in Katie's name and sent it up to the corpsman in the waiting room.

"Okay, you're all set. When you get there, you'll need to check in with the corpsman on duty. The cafeteria is on the ground floor off the B elevators."

Katie slipped around the desk and went to the elevators, punching the up button several times. "C'mon, c'mon," she pleaded impatiently.

The elevator arrived and she rode it up to the third floor, where she followed the signage to the surgical waiting room. When she opened the door, she saw that the room was already filled with families of injured soldiers.

"Looks like it might be a while," she said under her breath. "I'll bet the surgical suites are probably backed up." She walked over to the corpsman to check in. "I'm here for Colonel Peterson."

The corpsman checked his list and nodded. "She just went into surgery. If you want to get something to eat..."

"I know where the cafeteria is," Katie interrupted. "Can you tell me what they're doing?"

"No. Sorry, ma'am. We only know when they go in and come out, not what they're in for."

"Oh, okay. Thank you," Katie's disappointment was clear in her voice. She looked around the room, spotting a seat by the window. She sat and waited, not saying anything for a long time, just clasping her hands and staring at her wedding ring.

"Can I get you some coffee or tea or something?"

Katie looked up into the concerned face of the corpsman. "No, I'm fine, thanks." She leaned back resting her head on the back of the chair and closed her eyes. "Dean's tough; she's been through worse. She'll be okay."

A surgeon still in scrubs entered the waiting room. "Katherine O'Malley?" he called and looked at the expectant faces in the room. Katie stood and hurried over to the doctor. He led her into the hall.

"Colonel Peterson is in the recovery room. She suffered massive trauma to the right side of her body. The field notes indicate that a steel ceiling beam broke loose and swung down, clipping her entire right side before it crashed down and pinned her lower legs. Pieces of concrete and other debris fell on top of that. Her legs were hit hard by the beam and she has compound fractures of both tibias in the lower leg. She also has a fracture of the right patella. We've set the breaks and had to put a pin in the right leg. At some future date, we might need to do surgery to repair the kneecap, but not right now. She also has a fractured pelvis on the right side and we had to remove her right kidney. It was crushed by the beam. Her head, right scapula, and back side of her ribcage received a violent blow from the ceiling beam. Her right shoulder took most of the force. Her scapula is fractured, as are several ribs near where they meet the spine." He reached around his side and indicated the area he was describing. "The most immediate problem is her traumatic head injury. The beam caught her head a glancing blow, but in a contest between steel and bone, it's the bone that will always come out the loser. Luckily, the fracture to the skull isn't as bad as it could have been. As I said, it was a glancing blow, but it will remain to be seen if the resulting concussion will have any long term effects."

Katie inhaled sharply. "Brain injury is a possibility?"

The surgeon's face remained noncommittal, but he confirmed, "That's always a possibility in a traumatic head injury. Time will tell. We'll know more when she regains consciousness. There was also a small part of the scalp that was torn away from the bone with significant bleeding. She was very lucky the beam hit that portion of the skull. The bone density is thickest in that area. The corpsman on the scene put a pressure bandage on it and most of the bleeding was controlled before she arrived here. We cleaned out the wound and stitched up the scalp. Hopefully it will heal without any complications."

"Was she conscious when she came in?" Katie asked.

"She started to come around while we were prepping her. The CAT scan was negative for internal bleeding, but swelling of the brain could be a danger. We'll be checking her regularly in the recovery room, but there's always that chance of brain injury. All-in-all, she's a very lucky woman. If the beam had come down an inch more toward the center of her head, she wouldn't have survived the blow."

"When can I see her?" Katie asked.

"As soon as she's cleared in the recovery room, she'll be in ICU for a few days until we can determine the extent of the head injury. We'll need to monitor her intracranial pressure and the blood flow to the brain. If necessary, we will take her back into surgery to relieve pressure from the swelling. We'll be doing more tests once she's awake."

Katie just listened, not knowing what else to ask.

The surgeon smiled, trying to project a positive prognosis. "She looks to be in terrific physical shape. If all goes well with the recovery of the head injury, the rest will just be a lot of rehabilitation. ICU is in the other wing on this floor. Just follow the signs to the waiting room. Once she's out of recovery, they'll notify you."

"Thank you, doctor."

"You're welcome. If you will excuse me, I'm sorry to say I have another patient that needs my attention. Today is going to be a very busy day."

She watched him walk briskly back through the doors to the surgical suite before turning to find the signs to lead her to the ICU waiting room. As she walked down the hall, she saw Dirk coming toward her.

"Dean's out of surgery. She's banged up pretty good, but she's going to be all right," she said with a grin. When Dirk got closer, she noticed his tear-streaked face and red eyes. "Oh, my God... what's happened? Where's Bill?"

"He...they tried, but..." Dirk's eyes welled up again and Katie rushed to him and hugged him tightly. Dirk sobbed deeply his chest heaving with every tear that fell. They clung to each other for several minutes until Dirk was cried out.

Katie pulled out a wad of tissues from her purse and handed them to her friend. "C'mon, let's find someplace to talk." She led

Dirk to the elevators and rode down to the main floor. Exiting the elevator, Katie and Dirk went out the main doors and walked to a series of benches set under a stand of trees. "Let's sit here." Katie indicated one of the empty benches. They sat there quietly for nearly a quarter of an hour.

"He's gone, Katie. He was buried under a pile of concrete when the area they were in gave way. Then the last explosion...when the impact area collapsed...he went with it."

"Oh, Dirk," Katie whispered, "I'm so sorry. I can't imagine how you must be hurting."

Dirk turned to face her. "I don't know what I'm going to do. I can't even think of being without him. We've been together almost ten years, and now he's gone. Why? Who the hell is responsible for this?" He stood and started to pace, anger replacing agony. He bent down and picked up an acorn that had dropped from one of the surrounding oak trees and tossed it back and forth in his hands and then threw it as hard as he could at the nearest tree trunk. "Damn it, Katie! What is going on? Why Bill?"

Katie stood and took his hand, gently stroking it with her thumb. "Why did any of the people that died today have to die? It's insane."

They walked hand-in-hand around the grounds, each lost in thoughts of the devastation and death that had dropped from the sky. As they rounded the building, Dirk stopped and looked at Katie. "I'm glad Dean is going to be all right." He sighed. "I need to go. I need some time...I have to figure things out."

Katie hugged him. "I understand. But, please, if you need something...or just want someone to talk to...let me know. You know Dean and I consider you family so..."

"Yes, we are family."

"And that means we don't have to handle things alone. We need each other more now than ever, Dirk. We have no one else to lean on."

Dirk hugged her again. "You're right."

"Are you going to be okay?"

He stepped back. "Honestly? I don't know. I need some time to work things through. Keep me posted on Dean, okay?"

"I will." Tears filled Katie's eyes as she watched him walk away.

Chapter Thirty
September 12

The room was typical of most ICUs. There was a bank of monitors above and to the side of the bed, a plethora of vital connections on the wall mounts for oxygen, suction, and monitoring inputs, and a glass wall that allowed the nurses to keep a visual check on their patients from the nursing station. There were two IV poles alongside the bed with several bags of fluid that provided nourishment and medications through an IV line inserted in Dean's hand. A track in the ceiling allowed a curtain to be pulled around for privacy. In the corner close to Dean's bed, Katie slept in a makeshift bed of two chairs and wrapped in a spare blanket.

Katie woke when the morning shift nurse came in to check on Dean. Most of her vital signs were monitored electronically, but the nurses still came in periodically to do a physical check.

"Good morning," the nurse said as she opened the vertical blinds.

"Morning." Katie removed the light blanket from around her body and pulled her feet down off of the extra chair. She stood and stretched her hands upward and twisted a few times, did some neck rolls and some back stretches.

"I'll get a hospital recliner in here for you later. It's a lot more comfortable for sleeping in than a couple of chairs." The nurse pointed at the chairs Katie had put together. "There's fresh coffee in the waiting room and a local bakery sent up a batch of rolls for the staff. Most of us have been working twenty-four hours since yesterday and I guess they wanted to help in some way. There's way more than our staff can eat. I'll bring you a nice croissant with that coffee, okay?"

"Thanks," Katie looked at the nurse's nametag, "Captain Raez. That'd be terrific. Oh, Captain, is there any way to lift the family-only restriction? All her relatives are deceased and there's just me and a few friends. We're all like family."

"They're usually pretty strict about the visiting list until she's off the critical list, but these are unusual times. I'll see what I can do."

"Thanks, that's all I can ask."

Raez left and Katie stood at the bedside and looked down at her lover. Dean's head was swathed in bandages; she had black eyes, a tube down her throat, and she was still wearing a neck brace. Her right shoulder was also wrapped in bandages, and her right arm was cinched against her chest to keep her from moving that side. Judging by the bumps under the covers, there were also bandages in the pelvic area. Both legs were set in casts and Dean had multiple lacerations on her face and arms. There were wires from the monitors, a catheter snaked its way from under the sheet to empty into a waiting bag hung on the bed frame. An oxygen mask covered her mouth and an automatic blood pressure cuff on her arm monitored her pressure at regular intervals. The monitors above her head registered heart readings, temperature, oxygen levels, and respiration rate.

"Wow," Katie whispered, "you look awful, sweetheart. But to me, you're still absolutely beautiful." She gently picked up the uninjured left hand and stroked her knuckles. Her wedding ring was covered with surgical tape. Carefully, she removed the tape and smiled when she saw the ring had made it through the chaos without a scratch. It would need to be cleaned, there was concrete dust and other grime in the crevices, but she could easily remedy that.

"I'll be right back," she whispered. She left the room and headed to the restroom, wishing for a toothbrush and toothpaste. On the way, she passed Captain Raez carrying a cup of coffee with a croissant balanced on top in one hand and toiletry items in the other.

"Katherine," she called, "thought you might like these." She handed her a hospital toothbrush wrapped in clear cellophane, a small tube of toothpaste, and a washcloth and towel.

"Thanks." Katie accepted the items gratefully. "You're a mind reader, Captain."

"Nah, just been an ICU nurse for a long time. I'll leave your coffee and croissant in the room. You can use the staff lounge if you want." She led Katie to the staff lounge door. "There's a shower in the back on the right."

"Thanks. A shower sounds pretty good."

When Katie got back to the room, a corpsman was rearranging Dean on her bed after changing her sheets. He smiled at Katie. "She's all cleaned up for the day. I'm Lorenzo. If you need anything, just ask for me."

"Thank you, Sergeant. Has she woken up yet?"

"No, ma'am." He picked up the dirty linen and towels. "The doctor should be around in an hour or two; he'll give you an update. You have plenty of time to run down to the cafeteria if you're hungry."

Katie picked up the coffee and croissant. "I'm set. Thanks." She took a big bite out of the pastry.

"Go ahead and talk to her. We don't know for sure that they can hear us, but it never hurts." He was whistling as he walked out with the soiled laundry.

Katie set down her coffee and half eaten croissant and pulled her chair over to the bed. "Hey, love. So, you think you can get by just lying around and doing nothing, eh? Well, let me tell you..."

A middle-aged woman approached the patient information desk. Tall, she gave the impression of being a former athlete from the way she carried her fit physique with confidence and poise. Her hair was dark with a healthy smattering of gray, and her eyes were clear and bright, an unusual shade of blue. Although she walked with two canes, she was surprisingly agile as she made her way to the desk.

"Good afternoon," she said with a broad smile. "I'm here to see my niece. Her name is Deanna Peterson."

The clerk checked the patient list. "Yes, ma'am." He paused a moment to check the visitor information for the patient. "Ma'am, you're not on the visitor list and I don't see you listed as a relative. The only relative she had listed is deceased."

"That, unfortunately, is something I mean to correct, starting today." Victoria pulled out a copy of her birth certificate and a copy of Joshua's birth certificate and handed them to the clerk.

Looking at the certificates, the corpsman smiled and nodded. "Twins, eh?"

"Yes, and I'm sorry to say that we weren't very close." A sadness crossed Victoria's face. "I want to remedy that with my niece. May I go up and see her?"

The clerk handed the papers back. "Yes, ma'am. She's in ICU. Third floor, west wing." The clerk gave her directions to the elevators and the ICU.

"Thank you." With a genuine smile, Victoria placed the papers back in her purse and moved toward the bank of elevators.

"Her vital signs are looking good, and so far the pressure in her skull is within a safe range. After consultation with my colleagues, I decided that it would be prudent to keep her in a medically induced coma. This will reduce the chances of a secondary injury to the brain because she won't be moving around and aggravating her injuries. That will help control swelling, thereby reducing the chance of restricted blood flow. The coma will also help keep her pain in check; she won't be awake to feel it."

"How long will you keep her under?" Katie asked.

"Only as long as necessary, Ms. O'Malley. Perhaps for a week, but I'd definitely like to bring her out within ten days. She's a strong woman. I'm amazed by how quickly she's healing already."

"Is there anything I can do for her?"

"I noticed you were talking to her when I came in. That's a good thing to keep up. There's not a lot of research on it, but we in the medical profession encourage family to talk to their loved ones. Patients seem to pick up on the positive talk, though we can't prove it."

Katie nodded. "I can do that."

"I'll be checking in on her every day, and the nurses will let me know if there are any changes I need to be aware of at any time." He looked Katie over with a practiced eye. "You might want to take some time for yourself. She's going to need a lot of support, emotional and physical support, when she leaves the hospital."

"Thank you, Colonel. I'll do my best."

"I've had Colonel Peterson as a patient before. It was a long time ago. I know she'll be chomping at the bit to get out of here. Your toughest job will be getting her to take it easy. Life can be short. Yesterday was a perfect example of that. She'll need to slow down and take care of herself for optimum recovery."

"You really have her pegged, Colonel. Don't worry, I'll make sure she takes it slow and easy."

When she arrived at Dean's room, Victoria stepped in as quietly as possible. Katie was in the chair by Dean's bed, head resting on her arms. One hand was holding Dean's. Victoria silently moved to the remaining chair and waited.

"Mmpf," Katie mumbled as she lifted her head. "Sorry, love, must have dozed off there. Now, where were we?" She sat up and stretched. When she opened her eyes, she saw a woman sitting in the chair at the foot of the bed, smiling broadly, eyes twinkling...very familiar eyes twinkling at her.

"Who... Wait, I know you. You're the woman we met on the rental car bus in Kansas City, Victoria something." She thought a minute. "Delanore, right?" She cocked her head, taking in the piercing blue eyes. "Oh, my God, it's really Victoria Peterson, isn't it? You were at the funeral home, at the church, and on the hill at the cemetery."

"You're very observant, Katie. I wasn't expecting anyone to see me there. Tell me, how did you put two and two together so quickly?"

"Besides the dead give-away eyes your family shares?" Katie laughed. "Your brother...I'm assuming Joshua was your brother?"

"That's correct. We were twins."

"Well, your brother left Dean a letter he wrote just before he died. He alluded to a regret he didn't have time to correct. Dean asked Reverend Martha if she knew what that was and she told us Joshua had a sister. That he had cut you out of his life because—"

"I am an abomination?" Victoria supplied.

"Well, at that earlier time in his life, I guess that was how he felt, but he changed. They tried to find you, but it had been too long. And, obviously you had changed your name."

"Yes, but not to hide from Joshua. I took my lover's name," Victoria said with a sad smile. "She died four years ago in a car accident. That's where I picked up these." She tapped her crutches. Diverting attention from herself, Victoria looked at her niece. "She looks like she was run over by a truck."

A crooked smile appeared on Katie's face. "That's exactly my take, too."

"She sure is a sound sleeper. Either that, or she's on heavy duty drugs!"

"Neither," Katie said sadly. "She hasn't woken up yet. The surgeon said they are going to keep her in an induced coma for a few days. He said it would help reduce intracranial pressure and lessen the chance of brain injury. I've been talking to her all morning. A corpsman and Colonel Mathers, the surgeon, suggested that might help."

"Well then, let's keep talking. Supposing I tell you two about my life..."

Dean was sitting up, sipping water through a straw in a glass held by Sergeant Lorenzo. The head bandage had been removed and Dean's hair was showing a stubble of growth.

"Looks like you've got company, Colonel," the corpsman said as he placed the glass down on the adjustable bed table. "I'll be back in a bit to see if you're hungry." As Katie entered, he said, "You can give her some ice chips. It'll help her throat to recover. Oh, and they'll be moving her to an orthopedic floor later today."

Dean gave him a weak smile and let her head fall back to the pillow, wincing as it landed harder than she intended.

"Yeah, bet that hurts." Katie peeked around the area, making sure no one was looking, then gave Dean a quick kiss on the cheek. She set the flowers she'd brought on the windowsill and stood next to the bed. "They were talking about bringing you out of the coma yesterday; I just didn't think it would be so quick."

"Sergeant Lorenzo said I've been under for longer than a week." Dean's voice was a soft rasp, and it was obvious it pained her to speak. Katie got the cup of ice and spooned a few chips into Dean's mouth.

"Nine days," Katie told her as she spooned in a few more chips. Katie ran her fingers lightly over Dean's stubble of hair. "How long do you think it will take to get it to grow all the way back?"

"Who cares, as long as it grows," Dean rasped. "Stitches are out. Looks good, too," she croaked. "Sergeant Lorenzo gave me mirrors to check it out. What do you think?"

Katie peered at the surgeon's handiwork for the first time, amazed at how fine the repair was. She figured by the time it healed, the scar would be just a fine line in Dean's scalp. "I give the colonel two thumbs-up. The scar should be almost invisible by the time it heals."

Dean swallowed and winced. "More ice, please." Katie reached for the ice cup and spooned some chips into Dean's mouth. When she had swallowed them, she said, "Everything is fuzzy on the inside of my head, too. What happened?"

The doctor had warned Katie that Dean's short term memory might be affected; she might not remember what happened immediately prior to her injury. Katie filled her in on the 9/11 attacks, their rescue of the general and Major Russell, and how she and Bill saved Hawadi then wound up at the bottom of a pile of building parts. She knew she was going to have to tell her lover about Bill. Certain the news would devastate Dean, Katie had decided to wait until she was stronger and better able to handle the news. She hoped she could move on to other subjects before Dean asked how Bill was.

"You were pretty badly injured, love, but they put you back together in ICU." She reviewed Dean's injuries and the prognosis. "The flowers are from all the people who care about you." She pointed to all the bouquets around the room that were from friends and fellow soldiers. There was a huge spray of mixed flowers from General Carlton and an even bigger one from the ex-President, along with a card wishing her a speedy recovery.

"And this one," she pointed at a vase holding nine white roses in various stages of blooming, "has a flower for every day you've been in here. And it's from—"

"Me." Dean turned to look at the voice coming from the doorway. She was holding a new white rosebud. "Hello, Deanna. I'm your Aunt Victoria."

Katie rose and gave Victoria a hug and whispered in her ear, "She's asking about Bill. I don't think she's ready to hear about his death quite yet. She just woke up."

Victoria nodded and walked over to the bedside. "Well, young lady, I think it's about time we met formally."

Dean watched the woman amble expertly into the room on her crutches as she mentally tried to place the familiar face. When Victoria sat next to the bed and looked up at Dean with her piercing sapphire eyes, Dean inhaled sharply as she saw the distinct resemblance to her father.

"Look a little familiar, do I?" Victoria said with a crooked smile. "I guess I should. Your father and I are...were...twins. And, we have met before."

Dean eased back into her pillow as faint memories began to stir. "Yes," she said softly, "at the car rental office?"

"Exactly!" Victoria nodded, visually glad to see that Dean's memory was intact.

"But why now?" Dean asked a bit miffed by Victoria's years of nonexistence. "Why did you wait until now to introduce yourself as my family?"

"I...well, your father and I had a nasty parting...and I was forbidden to have any contact with our family."

"Forbidden?" Dean asked a bit mockingly.

"Let me start at the beginning."

Katie moved her chair along side the bed and Victoria's chair so she would be able to gage Dean's reaction to the story she already heard. She reached over and took Dean's hand and gave it a gentle squeeze of reassurance.

Victoria began her tale. "Your father and I were very close when we were young. Inseparable rascals we were, as twins tend to be. Even when we were teens you could rarely see us apart. We loved each other very much and had such great fun together... until..." She hesitated as a memory crossed her mind and she sighed sadly. "Until we both fell in love with the same girl."

Dean's eyebrows rose in understanding as she imagined the rift this tryst would have triggered and how it could develop into an abyss so deep it would be impossible to cross.

Victoria nodded slightly and then continued with her story. "We were unaware at first that our affections were directed at the same person and we often fell into conversation discussing our feelings for the person we were in love with. Joshua and I shared all our feelings and always told each other our deepest thoughts...with one exception. I always hid my sexual orientation from him knowing that our strict upbringing would put a wedge between us quickly. Anyway, we shared our feelings freely and also our hopes and desires that we had found our one true love. I certainly thought I had and so did Joshua."

"And neither of you had a clue it was the same girl?" Dean asked softly as Victoria's story had her completely absorbed. "Dad never revealed the name of the girl he was dating?"

"No, neither of us had a clue she was the same person. It was kind of like a game with us. It was a secret that we were keeping to ourselves until we were ready for the family to know. I was never going to tell my family for obvious reasons. In fact, I had been making elaborate plans to ask Sarah to move away with me after we turned eighteen. I never got to ask her," Victoria said sadly, "but after we found out it was the same person, I realized she had been playing Joshua for a fool. I was devastated when the truth came out and Joshua...well, Joshua changed after that day." Victoria picked up a plastic cup still wrapped in cellophane and slowly took off the wrapping. She poured herself a small sip of water from Dean's pitcher then held the cup in her hands in her lap.

Dean observed Victoria as she went through the motions for her drink, intently watching the wave of emotion that crossed her aunt's face in the brief silence. Dean was overwhelmed with compassion for her aunt and knew that her banishment from the family was a crushing blow.

Victoria looked up shaking the thoughts of the past away as though they were sticky cobwebs blocking her path. "Oh, now where was I? Yes, that's right, the summer we turned eighteen. That summer was going to be the best summer ever. We had both graduated from our little high school and Joshua was going to the seminary in the fall. I was set to go to a school in August a couple of towns away that prepared nannies for private service. Mother and father had arranged for a one room flat for me for the six month course and even had a position lined up as soon as I finished. My nanny position had private quarters over the garage. Sarah's family was very wealthy and well respected and they were sending Sarah to a college for women in the town where my position was set. Oh, my plans were wonderful and my expectations were high. Everything was working out as I had hoped. Sarah and I planned to meet on Saturday by a small waterfall in a glen that Joshua and I had discovered on old Mr. Miller's farm. I prepared an elaborate picnic and had a few other ideas in mind for that day. The glen was in a very rocky and hilly area that Mr. Miller never used and we never saw any tracks other than small animals around the pool at the base of the falls. It was secluded and romantic. A perfect setting for what I had planned. Sarah and I had been there before to go swimming, so we planned to meet there at 1 o'clock. I had gotten there early and had the blanket spread out and the picnic basket emptied as I waited with jittery nerves for her to arrive. We were so in love, or so I thought." Victoria smiled sadly once more before she continued.

"At precisely 1 o'clock Sarah promptly entered the small glen. I was so excited I ran to meet her and we embraced and kissed passionately before walking over to the blanket. The solitude of the glen made us feel safe and soon our passion was taking precedence over the picnic I had packed. We never heard Joshua approach and stand over our naked bodies until we felt the sting of the willow branch he began hitting us with. Sarah shouted at him to stop and he did stop hitting her, but then focused his rage at me accusing me of turning his Sarah to the ways of the devil. Sarah managed to move away first and dress while Joshua continued hitting me with the branch and shout accusations at me. I never saw her leave and I never saw her again. My wits finally returned and I managed to wrestle the branch away from Joshua. He fell to the ground sobbing and still accusing me of turning his girlfriend into a scion of the devil. That's when it hit me that Sarah had been his 'true love' too. I dressed quickly while he sobbed and then went to console him. He pushed me away, stood, and ran from the glen. When I got back home...well...it was no longer my home. Father had thrown all my things out of the house and locked the doors. I could hear mother weeping inside, but he and Joshua shouted at me to leave and forbade me to ever come back. I was no longer his daughter and no longer Joshua's sister. I didn't know what to do or where to go. I grabbed a few of my clothes and put them in a sack that was also tossed out and walked into town. After the initial shock wore off, I went to Sarah's house. That encounter went even worse with her parents threatening to have me arrested. It seemed like I wandered for days on end but in actuality it was only two days before I was befriended by a woman that taught at our school...Adrianna Wilson. She had heard through rumors about what had happened and she took me in."

Dean raised one eyebrow in wariness of what was to come. Victoria smiled at the response. "No it's not what you imagine. Adrianna was a kind woman and she had a parallel situation in her life. Her daughter was a lesbian and her husband had thrown her out in similar fashion. Their daughter did not fare well after that and soon turned to prostitution to survive. In those days, prostitutes repeatedly contracted sexually transmitted diseases and had very little in the way of knowledge of prevention or even access to medical care. Adrianna's daughter died of syphilis within the year, then her marriage fell apart and she vowed never to let that happen to another child...hers or someone else's. She helped me get into college and earn a degree in law. When I got my license I went to work for a lesbian law firm in New York City. That's where I met Cassandra Delanore. We became fast friends at first, then lovers and lived a very happy life together. At least until four years ago when she died in an automobile accident and I wound up with these." She tapped her crutches and sighed.

"And that's pretty much it," Victoria said as she finished the brief recounting of her life.

"It sounds somewhat familiar for some reason," Dean croaked. Victoria and Katie looked at one another and smiled. "But it doesn't answer my question. Why did you decide to come into my life now?"

"Fair question," Victoria replied. "I tried to remain in contact with Joshua throughout his life, well, not personal contact, but through inquiries with friends. When Thad's death occurred I was devastated. I wanted to come back and help, but when I tried to call, he would hang up on me. Then I heard that you had left and sent a friend in search of you in case you needed support. When I heard you joined the Army I assumed you would be okay. I didn't know if Joshua or his family knew anything about me at all, or if they did what they were told. My belief was that I would still not be accepted, especially after he hung up repeatedly after Thad's death. I also believed that if you were in the Army, you would not want anything to do with me either since the Army is not accepting of gays and lesbians and assumed you may be the same way." Dean nodded at the latter comment.

"So, when I ran into the two of you in Kansas City I immediately saw that I had been wrong to stay away. You two are obviously very much in love and my heart soared at the possibilities of finally reconnecting with family. Although, I was still hesitant because I did not want to jeopardize your career...my life's been an open book and especially my sexuality...that's why I continued to stay at arms length. I had been following your career as best as I could all these years and knew you were in a very important and classified position where any hint of family impropriety could affect you. Then after I met you and believed what I did about your relationship with Katie, I even feared more that if it were exposed it would lead to a discharge. Then when I heard about the attack on the Pentagon and found you had been injured I just couldn't stay away any longer. Life is too short and family is too important. I wasted too much time for fear of non-acceptance and hoped I could still become a part of it."

"Dean and I know how very important family is," Katie interjected, "and I'm glad that you have come into our lives now." She looked over at Dean who seemed to be evaluating her Aunt's explanation. "I'm especially glad to have you in my life right now and I don't know how I would have managed the last few days without your support and love."

Dean looked at Katie and saw the sincerity in her eyes as well as the worry and fear she must have felt since the attack. She realized that it took courage for her aunt to come to her, even now. Rejection is an awful feeling and she knew repeated rejection can leave a person numb with feelings of depression. Turning to her aunt, Dean reached out her good hand and said, "Victoria, or should I say, Aunt Victoria...welcome back to the family!"

Tears welled up in Victoria's eyes as she reached for Dean's extended hand and gently squeezed it. "Thank you Deanna. I've been waiting to hear those words for a very long time."

Sergeant Lorenzo tapped on the door way and immediately became concerned when he saw the tears flowing from everyone's eyes. "Everything okay in here?" he asked cautiously.

"Yes," was a combined response from the three women.

"Everything is perfect," Katie said as she wiped her eyes.

"Uh, okay." He walked in and stood by the bed to address Dean. "I just wanted to let you know that we'll be moving you down to the Ortho unit in a few minutes, Colonel."

"Thank you, Sergeant. I'll be ready." She watched him leave and then turned to Katie. "How's Hawadi doing? And Bill?" Dean asked. "Where is he? I half expected to see him perched on the chair next to you."

Katie looked at Victoria and shrugged knowing that this was going to come up sooner or later. She had just hoped that it would have been later. Deciding to start with the good news, she took Dean's hand and said, "Private Hawadi is doing pretty well. She's in a cast up to her hip, but her prognosis is good. She'll be running laps around you in no time." Katie chuckled, but stopped abruptly as Dean turned and looked out the window.

"She sure picked the wrong day to start work at the Pentagon." The sadness in Dean's eyes was evidence of the thoughts in her head.

"Hey, love. I'm sure she'll be back to 100 percent in no time. She's young and fit and should bounce back easier than most." Dean looked back at Katie, sadness still in her eyes. "I'm sorry, I shouldn't upset you with this."

"No, it's all right. It's just a lot to take in at once." She took a deep breath and flinched at the pain. "Forgot about the ribs." She exhaled slowly. "Damn, this is a heck of a way to start our new life." She closed her eyes and Katie squeezed her hand.

"At least we have a life to start together."

Dean opened her eyes and looked at Katie for a very long moment. "Always the optimist," she said quietly. "I love you, Katie."

"I love you, too," Katie whispered back as they gazed at one another.

"So, where's Bill? Is he trying to put the unit back together by himself?"

"Dean," Katie began, knowing that Dean would continue to ask about Bill until she knew the truth, "about Bill...there's something you need to know."

The seriousness of Katie's tone alerted Dean and she opened her eyes, concern on her face. "What's happened? He got out of there okay didn't he?"

"Bill," Katie began quietly. "He—"

"He's all right, right?" Dean hoped that the itching at the nape of her neck was from the healing incisions.

Katie shook her head slightly. "No, love. He's not. He was killed in the collapse that partially buried you. The rescue crew tried to dig him out, but when they got close enough to check his pulse, he was already gone. The final explosion buried him in tons of rubble. They just recovered his body yesterday."

Dean turned away from her two visitors. Her shoulders sagged and her body shuddered as she wept. Katie held her good hand and squeezed it gently.

"How's Dirk?" Dean asked after a short while, still looking out the window.

"He's doing better. Each day has been a struggle, but he's taking them one at a time. His parents are here staying with him." Katie smiled. "They're really sweet people and they're really helping him cope. They loved Bill, too."

"Yeah." Dean turned back to face them. "I met them once a couple of years ago. It was so nice to see Dirk's family be so accepting of their relationship."

"Bill's parents will be coming in tomorrow for the memorial. He'll be buried in Arlington on the 23rd."

Dean reached out for Katie's hand. "You need to go and be there for Dirk. Bill's parents never accepted their relationship and they're bound to make trouble, even if Dirk's parents are there. I don't want Bill's memorial to be sullied by them."

"I'll be there." Katie gave Dean's hand a gentle squeeze. "And Tracy and the others will be there too."

Sergeant Lorenzo rapped on the doorframe and entered the room. "It's time to move you down to the orthopedic floor, Colonel."

He slipped behind her bed and removed the call button and set it on the nightstand. Katie moved the adjustable tray over to the window, while the corpsman unplugged the bed from the electric socket and released the brakes on the wheels. He wheeled the bed toward the door.

"She'll be in 5A. It's a private corner unit with lots of room for all the flowers. And, there's a nice couch in it for all the guests she'll be able to receive *legally*, now that she'll be out of ICU.

There's a cart outside the door for the flowers and her personal items. I'll bring the flowers down after we get her settled."

"We can do that." Katie waited for him to clear the door and then retrieved the cart.

Victoria looked at the cart and then at all the flowers. "Looks like it might take two trips," she said as she started to place the vases on the cart.

The staff had bent the rules as far as they could to let Dirk visit the ICU on occasion for a few minutes at a time. Now that she would be in a regular room, Katie would be calling the New York crew to tell them the visitation restrictions had been lifted.

It took three trips to get all the flowers moved, but they were finally settled in the new room.

"Well, I am going to head back to my hotel for a bit. I'll be back later to see you." Victoria stood.

"Why don't you check out of that hotel and come stay at the house?" Katie said as she reached for Victoria's arm. "Dean will be stuck here for a while longer and there's no sense in you living in a hotel room...especially now that you're officially back in the family. Besides, you have to meet our family."

"Your family?"

"Yes. There's Sugar, Butter, and Spice for now and then eventually you'll meet the rest of our extended crew. So, what do you think? Hotel or house?"

"House of course!"

"Great, I'll pick you up around six. Get your bags packed."

Victoria smiled and turned toward the doorway. "See you in a few."

"Hey, this is nice," Katie said as she walked around the large room. "And, there's no glass wall looking out to the nurse's station," she added with a wicked smile. "You know what that means, don't you?" She walked over to the door and closed it.

"Yes, I do," Dean replied solemnly. "But go easy on me, will ya?"

Katie laughed hard. Dean managed a controlled laugh, but had to stop when her ribs began to ache. When Katie's mirth subsided, she went to the bed and leaned over, face to face with a grinning Dean. "I love you, Deanna." She leaned in close and kissed her partner firmly.

There was a soft knock on the door and it swung open slowly. Katie and Dean broke their kiss, a bit of a blush on their cheeks.

They turned toward the doorway and were surprised to see Major Len Russell standing there, manila file folder in hand.

"I can come back if this is a bad time," Russell said, turning away.

Katie looked at Dean who shook her head, indicating he should come in. "No," Katie said. "Come in."

Len Russell walked in and handed the folder to Katie. "I brought this from your office, Colonel."

Katie opened the folder; it held Dean's letter of resignation. A flush of anger rose on her cheeks. "And you want her to sign it to make it official?" she said sarcastically.

"No. No. I..." He paused, obviously searching for his next words. "I wanted to return it to her," he said quickly. He turned to Dean and began hesitantly, "Colonel, I came here because I owe you my life. I'm not saying that I accept you and your..." he turned away then quickly looked back at her, "your homosexuality. I cannot abide that, and I still believe you have no right to be in the military...but, I owe you my life. I destroyed all the evidence I collected and I'm returning this letter to you." He glanced at Katie and then his gaze dropped to the floor. Finally he squared his shoulders and looked Dean in the eye. "I honestly don't know how I would have reacted if I had been in your shoes that Tuesday. You not only saved my life, but you and Captain Jarvis saved Private Hawadi's life and put your own at risk." He paused. "I am sorry that Jarvis died; I hope you can believe that." He took a deep breath. "Why did you do it? Why did you pull me out of the Pentagon? You could have put an end to my coercion by letting me die there. No one would have known and you could have saved yourself."

Dean's voice was strong and clear. "Because, Major, I believe in honor and duty. I believe in the integrity and character of officers. And, I believe in always doing the right thing...no matter what the consequences. I knew saving a fallen soldier was what I needed to do, no matter who that soldier was. I don't judge someone by the color of their skin, their religion, their politics, or their sexual orientation. In the end, everyone is judged by their deeds and actions."

Major Russell nodded. "I knew that would be your answer; I'm not sure it would have been mine. That's why I resigned today. I'm ashamed of my actions and my motives." He pointed at the folder Katie was still gripping tightly. "I'm the only one in the chain of command who knows about that. As I said, I destroyed all the evidence I collected and I wanted you to have the letter back before it fell into other hands." He moved toward the door, then stopped and turned back. "Thank you, Colonel. You taught me more about myself through that one act than I could have learned in a lifetime. I hope it's not too late to turn myself around." His exit left a stunned silence behind him.

Katie looked at Dean and grinned. "Dean, this is terrific. You can stay in the Army!"

Dean looked thoughtfully at the empty doorway, unsure whether she felt the same elation as Katie did. It was a relief to know that Bill's record would remain unblemished and his sexuality would remain secret. Her thoughts turned to her father and she knew his words were going to guide her.

Chapter Thirty-two
October 20

Katie walked down the hall of the rehab unit carrying a small overnight bag. She hoped she was going to be early enough to see the doctor before he released Dean from the hospital. She knew Dean would pooh-pooh the doctor's orders if she didn't hear them for herself and Katie wanted to make sure that her lover followed those orders to a "t". She didn't want to have any complications popping up while they were planning the rest of their lives together.

Dean had already taken the biggest step, deciding she would resign from the Army. She was going to wait until her rehab was complete and then return to active duty for one last day to turn in her letter of resignation. The days since the attack were filled with speculation as to who was behind the carnage, but the President was convinced that Osama Bin Laden was the instigator of the terror attack and he had declared a war on terrorism, vowing to bring the members of al Qaeda to justice. Dean could see the writing on the wall: the U.S. would eventually go after Saddam Hussein as a party to the events of 9/11 and she wanted no part of it.

Katie turned the corner and entered Dean's room. Her lover was sitting in the corner with a frown on her face. "Hey, what's with the frown? You should be in a great mood today...you're going home!"

"I am if the doctor ever shows up! I've been waiting since 0500."

Katie closed the door behind her and quickly stole a kiss. "Hmmm. Did that perk up your spirits?"

Dean grinned up at Katie. "You always make my bad moods evaporate. How about another?"

Katie obliged eagerly and then stepped back to take a good look at her lover. "You really look amazing, you know? I mean, it's only a little over two months and you're the picture of health! I don't know how you do it."

"Just a quick healer, I guess. But I'm getting damn tired of all the doctors coming in to examine me. I can hear them in the hall talking about me like I'm some kind of space alien with super healing powers. They've taken enough blood samples to study to last for eons!"

Katie patted Dean's shoulder and smiled brightly. "Well, I for one am glad that you have healed so quickly."

A knock at the door interrupted their conversation and Captain O'Brien entered. "Hey, good lookin', are you ready to go home?"

"Figures they'd send you down to release me," Dean said with a smirk. Dean had met Pete O'Brien while undercover and once General Carlson found out he was a top notch medical resident, she talked him into going Army green for the rest of his residency. His application was processed quickly and he was in uniform in time for the end of that undercover operation to patch up the bullet wound Tracy received.

"Exactly," Captain O'Brien said with a grin. "They knew that you'd bite the head off anyone else that showed up so I got the short straw." He moved to stand in front of Dean. "You're one remarkable woman, you know that? We're all bashing our heads on the wall trying to figure out what makes you heal so fast."

"Well, I certainly heal faster than the service around this place," Dean said grinning and elicited a good chuckle from everyone in the room. "Honestly, Pete, I have no clue how, I'm just glad that I did."

"Well, you certainly have me scratching my head. Even when I first met you in that warehouse and had to patch you up, that wound took some time to heal and it was a minor injury, not like what you've just gone through. Have you been doing anything different lately? Eaten new foods or tried new a combo of vitamins?"

Dean laughed. "Katie is always trying to get me to eat new things but I doubt they have that kind of affect! They're mainly regular vegetables."

"Well, you are an enigma that's for sure." He flipped through her chart and then took out the discharge papers. "So...are you ready to leave this place?"

Katie moved to the bed and let Captain O'Brien sit in the other chair. "She's champing at the bit."

"Well, let's get this paperwork done so you can get out of here." He handed her the release forms to sign while he went over her rehab orders for home, pointing out each one as she read the papers. "And lastly, just take it easy for a while, Colonel. You've been through a lot the last couple of months and you deserve the time off. I'm recommending two more months at home before you return to active duty."

"Two months?" Dean asked in astonishment. "Why so long? I feel great."

"Yes, two months. And don't ask me to shorten it because I won't. I don't know how you managed to heal so quickly and I'd love to put you under a microscope to find out how your body works like that, but right now I'm not taking any chances." He pointed a finger at her. "Two months, and that's an order, Colonel. I may only be a captain, but I outrank you in this arena. You're only human and I don't want to see you back here again." He smiled and took Dean's hand. "Like I said, I knew you were an amazing woman the first time I saw you in that warehouse, and you kept proving it to me these last few months. Go home, relax, enjoy the time with Katie. Life's too short, you know."

Dean nodded, thinking about the short life Bill had had. "Yes, I know. Thanks, Pete. If you're ever in our neighborhood, stop by for a visit, okay?"

"You bet. Now, just wait for the corpsman with the wheelchair and you'll be on your way home." Captain O'Brien looked over at Katie. "Take good care of her, Katie."

"I will. Thanks, Pete."

The ride to their home in Occoquan took longer than usual. Military vehicles were on the roads everywhere in and around Washington, D.C. and their slower pace clogged many of the roadways. Life after 9/11 was proving to be more restrictive. Already new rules were being put in place concerning travel. Security was an issue in all venues, and the country was being whipped into a patriotic frenzy. Everywhere they looked American flags were flying, like it was the Fourth of July every day. Dean was glad to see the people uniting in a cause but hoped that the patriotic fervor wouldn't turn sour in the months to come.

"How's Dirk doing?"

"He called last night. He seems to be doing better. Spending time with his parents was a good decision. He's planning on staying there through the holidays."

"That sounds like a wise decision. The holidays will be especially hard for him."

"He said he's working on some ideas that he wants us to look at."

"What's he got in mind?"

"He hasn't gone into it, but it sounds like a business plan of some kind. He said he'd fill us in when he has everything worked out."

As Katie turned into the lane that eventually led to their cul de sac, she said, "Hey, I forgot to tell you. Aunt Victoria sold her Manhattan apartment and is closing on the condo she found on Swan Point Road next week."

"That was fast. What's the condo like?"

"It's lovely and perfect for her. There are no stairs which will be a blessing for her after all the one's she's had to climb at our place and it has a gorgeous river view. She can tell you all about it when we get home."

Dean sat silently for the last few miles lost in thoughts of how lucky they were to have family and friends in their lives and even more so that she survived that terrible day. Her heart still ached at thoughts of Bill, but she trained her focus on the good memories of their short time together. Her life was now going in a new direction but with Katie at her side she knew it would be a wonderful life. Every minute, hour, and day would be cherished and she was never going take life for granted. Life was truly too short and she intended to make the most of theirs.

"Here you go, love. Door to door service." She beeped the horn and the front door opened. Tracey, Colleen, Linna, and Reverend Martha hurried out to greet Dean.

"Welcome home!" they all shouted, and in the window Dean could see three felines watching and meowing their welcome along with a grinning waiving Aunt Victoria who was holding the door open.

Dean leaned over toward Katie and gave her a quick kiss. "C'mon," she said as their lips parted. "We've got a lot of living to do!"

Trish Kocialski brings many of her life experiences to her writing. She has worked in the fields of education and recreation for over thirty years, served in the U.S. Army Reserves, and likes to travel as much as possible. She lives in Albany, New York with her partner Carol and three feline companions. The original inspirations for the felines featured in her stories have all gone over the Rainbow Bridge, but the new crew of felines: Spookit, Libby, and Shasha have accepted the legacy of Whitley (Butter), Shug (Sugar), and Jasmine (Spice) by providing a seamless continuity of matching personalities that will keep the lives of Butter, Sugar, and Spice active in future writings. As an educator for over thirty years, Trish tries to impart bits and pieces of knowledge in every story; information about a hobby, locations detailed in story, or a life lesson to be learned, there's usually something to be gleamed from each story. She welcomes comments from readers and can be contacted at trish.kocialski@gmail.com

Other works by Trish Kocialski:

Forces of Evil

ISBN: 978 - 1 - 933720 - 06 - 7 (1-933720-06-9)

A chance meeting in a Catskill Mountain town brings two agents, Lieutenant Colonel Deanna "Dean" Peterson and Katie O'Malley, together as they unknowingly work undercover on the same case in an exciting tangle of politics, secrecy, and danger of not only national, but global proportions.

Blue Holes to Terror

ISBN: 978 - 1 - 933720 - 28 - 9 (1-933720-28-X)

The sequel to *Forces of Evil* picks up the adventures of Lieutenant Colonel Deanna Peterson and Special Agent Katherine O'Malley, beginning in Washington, D.C. and culminating on Grand Bahama Island as the two find themselves unraveling a terrorist/mercenary initiative designed to sabotage a multi-national military exercise.

Deadly Challenge

ISBN: 978 - 1 - 933720 - 44 - 9 (1-933720-44-1)

The breathtaking third installment of the adventures of Colonel Deanna Pererson and Special Agent Katherine O'Malley: the euphoria after completing another successful operation to thwart a terrorist attack is short lived as it becomes apparent that someone has an axe to grind and it's being weilded at Deanna's friends.

The Visitors

ISBN: 978 - 1 - 933720 - 51 - 7 (1-933720-51-4)

The exciting adventures of Dean and Katie continue in *The Visitors* as our heroines are back from a quick vacation to St. John in the U.S. Virgin Islands and settling back into their routines they find their lives turned upside down after a series of bizarre incidents plunge them into a sea of death and destruction.

Available at your favorite bookstore.

Printed in the United States
219326BV00002B/7/P

9 781933 720609